John S. C. Abbott

Davy Crockett: His Life and Adventures

John S. C. Abbott

Davy Crockett: His Life and Adventures

Davy Crockett: His Life and Adventures

By

John S. C. Abbott

Contents

CHAPTER I.

Parentage and Childhood.

The Emigrant.—Crossing the Alleghanies.—The boundless Wilderness.—The Hut on the Holston.—Life's Necessaries.—The Massacre.—Birth of David Crockett.—Peril of the Boys.—Anecdote.—Removal to Greenville; to Cove Creek.—Increased Emigration.—Loss of the Mill.—The Tavern.—Engagement with the Drover.—Adventures in the Wilderness.—Virtual Captivity.—The Escape.—The Return.—The Runaway.—New Adventures.

A little more than a hundred years ago, a poor man, by the name of Crockett, embarked on board an emigrant-ship, in Ireland, for the New World. He was in the humblest station in life. But very little is known respecting his uneventful career excepting its tragical close. His family consisted of a wife and three or four children. Just before he sailed, or on the Atlantic passage, a son was born, to whom he gave the name of John. The family probably landed in Philadelphia, and dwelt somewhere in Pennsylvania, for a year or two, in one of those slab shanties, with which all are familiar as the abodes of the poorest class of Irish emigrants.

After a year or two, Crockett, with his little family, crossed the almost pathless Alleghanies. Father, mother, and children trudged along through the rugged defiles and over the rocky cliffs, on foot. Probably a single pack-horse conveyed their few household goods. The hatchet and the rifle were the only means of obtaining food, shelter, and even clothing. With the hatchet, in an hour or two, a comfortable camp could be constructed, which would protect them from wind and rain. The camp-fire, cheering the darkness of the night, drying their often wet garments, and warming their chilled limbs with its genial glow, enabled them to enjoy that almost greatest of earthly luxuries, peaceful sleep.

The rifle supplied them with food. The fattest of turkeys and the most tender steaks of venison, roasted upon forked sticks, which they held in their hands over the coals, feasted their voracious appetites. This, to them, was almost sumptuous food. The skin of the deer, by a rapid and simple process of tanning, supplied them with moccasons, and afforded material for the repair of their tattered garments.

We can scarcely comprehend the motive which led this solitary family to push on, league after league, farther and farther from civilization, through the trackless forests. At length they reached the Holston River. This stream takes its rise among the western ravines of the Alleghanies, in Southwestern Virginia. Flowing hundreds of miles through one of the most solitary and romantic regions upon the globe, it finally unites with the Clinch River, thus forming the majestic Tennessee.

One hundred years ago, this whole region, west of the Alleghanies, was an unexplored and an unknown wilderness. Its silent rivers, its forests, and its prairies were crowded with game. Countless Indian tribes, whose names even had never been heard east of the Alleghanies, ranged this vast expanse, pursuing, in the chase, wild beasts scarcely more savage than themselves.

The origin of these Indian tribes and their past history are lost in oblivion. Centuries have come and gone, during which joys and griefs, of which we now can know nothing, visited their humble lodges. Providence seems to have raised up a peculiar class of men, among the descendants of the emigrants from the Old

World, who, weary of the restraints of civilization, were ever ready to plunge into the wildest depths of the wilderness, and to rear their lonely huts in the midst of all its perils, privations, and hardships.

This solitary family of the Crocketts followed down the northwestern banks of the Hawkins River for many a weary mile, until they came to a spot which struck their fancy as a suitable place to build their Cabin. In subsequent years a small village called Rogersville was gradually reared upon this spot, and the territory immediately around was organized into what is now known as Hawkins County. But then, for leagues in every direction, the solemn forest stood in all its grandeur. Here Mr. Crockett, alone and unaided save by his wife and children, constructed a little shanty, which could have been but little more than a hunter's camp. He could not lift solid logs to build a substantial house. The hard-trodden ground was the only floor of the single room which he enclosed. It was roofed with bark of trees piled heavily on, which afforded quite effectual protection from the rain. A hole cut through the slender logs was the only window. A fire was built in one corner, and the smoke eddied through a hole left in the roof. The skins of bears, buffaloes, and wolves provided couches, all sufficient for weary ones, who needed no artificial opiate to promote sleep. Such, in general, were the primitive homes of many of those bold emigrants who abandoned the comforts of civilized life for the solitudes of the wilderness.

They did not want for most of what are called the necessaries of life. The river and the forest furnished a great variety of fish and game. Their hut, humble as it was, effectually protected them from the deluging tempest and the inclement cold. The climate was genial in a very high degree, and the soil, in its wonderful fertility, abundantly supplied them with corn and other simple vegetables. But the silence and solitude which reigned are represented, by those who experienced them, as at times something dreadful.

One principal motive which led these people to cross the mountains, was the prospect of an ultimate fortune in the rise of land. Every man who built a cabin and raised a crop of grain, however small, was entitled to four hundred acres of land, and a preemption right to one thousand more adjoining, to be secured by a land-office warrant.

In this lonely home, Mr. Crockett, with his wife and children, dwelt for some months, perhaps years—we know not how long. One night, the awful yell of the savage was heard, and a band of human demons came rushing upon the defenceless family. Imagination cannot paint the tragedy which ensued. Though this lost world, ever since the fall of Adam, has been filled to repletion with these scenes of woe, it causes one's blood to curdle in his veins as he contemplates this one deed of cruelty and blood.

The howling fiends were expeditious in their work. The father and mother were pierced by arrows, mangled with the tomahawk, and scalped. One son, severely wounded, escaped into the forest. Another little boy, who was deaf and dumb, was taken captive and carried by the Indians to their distant tribe, where he remained, adopted into the tribe, for about eighteen years. He was then discovered by some of his relatives, and was purchased back at a considerable ransom. The torch was applied to the cabin, and the bodies of the dead were consumed in the crackling flames.

What became of the remainder of the children, if there were any others present in this midnight scene of conflagration and blood, we know not. There was no reporter to give us the details. We simply know that in some way John Crockett, who subsequently became the father of that David whose history we now write, was not involved in the general massacre. It is probable that he was not then with the family, but that he was a hired boy of all work in some farmer's family in Pennsylvania.

As a day-laborer he grew up to manhood, and married a woman in his own sphere of life, by the name of Mary Hawkins. He enlisted as a common soldier in the Revolutionary War, and took part in the battle of King's Mountain. At the close of the war he reared a humble cabin in the frontier wilds of North Carolina. There he lived for a few years, at but one remove, in point of civilization, from the savages around him. It is not probable that either he or his wife could read or write. It is not probable that they had any religious thoughts; that their minds ever wandered into the regions of that mysterious immortality which reaches out beyond the grave. Theirs was apparently purely an animal existence, like that of the Indian, almost like that of the wild animals they pursued in the chase.

At length, John Crockett, with his wife and three or four children, unintimidated by the awful fate of his father's family, wandered from North Carolina, through the long and dreary defiles of the mountains, to the sunny valleys and the transparent skies of East Tennessee. It was about the year 1783. Here he came to a rivulet of crystal water, winding through majestic forests and plains of luxuriant verdure. Upon a green mound, with this stream flowing near his door, John Crockett built his rude and floorless hut. Punching holes in the soil with a stick, he dropped in kernels of corn, and obtained a far richer harvest than it would be supposed such culture could produce. As we have mentioned, the building of this hut and the planting of this crop made poor John Crockett the proprietor of four hundred acres of land of almost inexhaustible fertility.

In this lonely cabin, far away in the wilderness, David Crockett was born, on the 17th of August, 1786. He had then four brothers. Subsequently four other children were added to the family.

His childhood's home was more humble than the majority of the readers of this volume can imagine. It was destitute of everything which, in a higher state of civilization, is deemed essential to comfort. The wigwam of the Indian afforded as much protection from the weather, and was as well furnished, as the cabin of logs and bark which sheltered his father's family. It would seem, from David Crockett's autobiography, that in his childhood he went mainly without any clothing, like the pappooses of an Indian squaw. These facts of his early life must be known, that we may understand the circumstances by which his peculiar character was formed.

He had no instruction whatever in religion, morals, manners, or mental culture. It cannot be supposed that his illiterate parents were very gentle in their domestic discipline, or that their example could have been of any essential advantage in preparing him for the arduous struggle of life. It would be difficult to find any human being, in a civilized land, who can have enjoyed less opportunities for moral culture than David Crockett enjoyed in his early years.

There was quite a fall on thc Nolachucky River, a little below the cabin of John Crockett. Here the water rushed foaming over the rocks, with fury which would at once swamp any canoe. When David was four or five years old, and several other emigrants had come and reared their cabins in that vicinity, he was one morning out playing with his brothers on the bank of the river. There was a canoe tied to the shore. The boys got into it, and, to amuse themselves, pushed out into the stream, leaving little David, greatly to his indignation, on the shore.

But the boys did not know how to manage the canoe, and though they plied the paddies with all vigor, they soon found themselves caught in the current, and floating rapidly down toward the falls, where, should they be swept over, the death of all was inevitable.

A man chanced to be working in a field not far distant. He heard the cries of the boys and saw their danger. There was not a moment to be lost. He started upon the full run, throwing off coat and waistcoat and shoes, in his almost frantic speed, till he reached the water. He then plunged in, and, by swimming and wading, seized the canoe when it was within but about twenty feet of the roaring falls. With almost superhuman exertions he succeeded in dragging it to the shore.

This event David Crockett has mentioned as the first which left any lasting imprint upon his memory. Not long after this, another occurrence took place characteristic of frontier life. Joseph Hawkins, a brother of David's mother, crossed the mountains and joined the Crockett family in their forest home. One morning he went out to shoot a deer, repairing to a portion of the forest much frequented by this animal. As he passed a very dense thicket, he saw the boughs swaying to and fro, where a deer was apparently browsing. Very cautiously he crept within rifle-shot, occasionally catching a glimpse, through the thick foliage, of the ear of the animal,—as he supposed.

Taking deliberate aim he fired, and immediately heard a loud outcry. Rushing to the spot, he found that he had shot a neighbor, who was there gathering grapes. The ball passed through his side, inflicting a very serious though not a fatal wound, as it chanced not to strike any vital part. The wounded man was carried home; and the rude surgery which was practised upon him was to insert a silk handkerchief with a ramrod in at the bullet-hole, and draw it through his body. He recovered from the wound.

Such a man as John Crockett forms no local attachments, and never remains long in one place. Probably some one came to his region and offered him a few dollars for his improvements. He abandoned his cabin, with its growing neighborhood, and packing his few household goods upon one or two horses, pushed back fifty miles farther southwest, into the trackless wilderness. Here he found, about ten miles above the present site of Greenville, a fertile and beautiful region. Upon the banks of a little brook, which furnished him with an abundant supply of pure water, he reared another shanty, and took possession of another four hundred acres of forest land. Some of his boys were now old enough to furnish efficient help in the field and in the chase.

How long John Crockett remained here we know not. Neither do we know what induced him to make another move. But we soon find him pushing still farther back into the wilderness, with his hapless family of sons and daughters, dooming them, in all their ignorance, to the society only of bears and wolves. He now established himself upon a considerable stream, unknown to geography, called Cue Creek.

David Crockett was now about eight years old. During these years emigration had been rapidly flowing from the Atlantic States into this vast and beautiful valley south of the Ohio. With the increasing emigration came an increasing demand for the comforts of civilization. Framed houses began to rise here and there, and lumber, in its various forms, was needed.

John Crockett, with another man by the name of Thomas Galbraith, undertook to build a mill upon Cove Creek. They had nearly completed it, having expended all their slender means in its construction, when there came a terrible freshet, and all their works were swept away. The flood even inundated Crockett's cabin, and the family was compelled to fly to a neighboring eminence for safety.

Disheartened by this calamity, John Crockett made another move. Knoxville, on the Holston River, had by this time become quite a thriving little settlement of log huts. The main route of emigration was across the mountains to Abingdon, in Southwestern Virginia, and then by an extremely rough forest-road across the country to the valley of the Holston, and down that valley to Knoxville. This route was mainly traversed by pack-horses and emigrants on foot. But stout wagons, with great labor, could be driven through.

John Crockett moved still westward to this Holston valley, where he reared a pretty large log house on this forest road; and opened what he called a tavern for the entertainment of teamsters and other emigrants. It was indeed a rude resting-place. But in a fierce storm the exhausted animals could find a partial shelter beneath a shed of logs, with corn to eat; and the hardy pioneers could sleep on bear-skins, with their feet perhaps soaked with rain, feeling the warmth of the cabin fire. The rifle of John Crockett supplied his guests with the choicest venison steaks, and his wife baked in the ashes the "journey cake," since called johnny cake, made of meal from corn pounded in a mortar or ground in a hand-mill. The brilliant flame of the pitch-pine knot illumined the cabin; and around the fire these hardy men often kept wakeful until midnight, smoking their pipes, telling their stories, and singing their songs.

This house stood alone in the forest. Often the silence of the night was disturbed by the cry of the grizzly bear and the howling of wolves. Here David remained four years, aiding his father in all the laborious work of clearing the land and tending the cattle. There was of course no school here, and the boy grew up in entire ignorance of all book learning. But in these early years he often went into the woods with his gun in pursuit of game, and, young as he was, acquired considerable reputation as a marksman.

One day, a Dutchman by the name of Jacob Siler came to the cabin, driving a large herd of cattle. He had gathered them farther west, from the luxuriant pastures in the vicinity of Knoxville, where cattle multiplied with marvellous rapidity, and was taking them back to market in Virginia. The drover found some difficulty in managing so many half wild cattle, as he pressed them forward through the wilderness, and he bargained with John Crockett to let his son David, who, as we have said, was then twelve years of age, go with him as his hired help. Whatever wages he gave was paid to the father.

The boy was to go on foot with this Dutchman four hundred miles, driving the cattle. This transaction shows very clearly the hard and unfeeling character of David's parents. When he reached the end of his journey, so many weary leagues from home, the only way by which he could return was to attach himself to some emigrant party or some company of teamsters, and walk back, paying for such food as he might consume, by the assistance he could render on the way. There are few parents who could thus have treated a child of twelve years.

The little fellow, whose affections had never been more cultivated than those of the whelp of the wolf or the cub of the bear, still left home, as he tells us, with a heavy heart. The Dutchman was an entire stranger to him, and he knew not what treatment he was to expect at his hands. He had already experienced enough of forest travel to know its hardships. A journey of four hundred miles seemed to him like going to the uttermost parts of the earth. As the pioneers had smoked their pipes at his father's cabin fire, he had heard many appalling accounts of bloody conflicts with the Indians, of massacres, scalpings, tortures, and captivity.

David's father had taught him, very sternly, one lesson, and that was implicit and prompt obedience to his demands. The boy knew full well that it would be of no avail for him to make any remonstrance. Silently, and trying to conceal his tears, he set out on the perilous enterprise. The cattle could be driven but about fifteen or twenty miles a day. Between twenty and thirty days were occupied in the toilsome and perilous journey. The route led them often through marshy ground, where the mire was trampled knee-deep. All the streams had to be forded. At times, swollen by the rains, they were very deep. There were frequent days of storm, when, through the long hours, the poor boy trudged onward, drenched with rain and shivering with cold. Their fare was most meagre, consisting almost entirely of such game as they chanced to shoot, which they roasted on forked sticks before the fire.

When night came, often dark and stormy, the cattle were generally too much fatigued by their long tramp to stray away. Some instinct also induced them to cluster together. A rude shanty was thrown up. Often everything was so soaked with rain that it was impossible to build a fire. The poor boy, weary and supperless, spattered with mud and drenched with rain, threw himself upon the wet ground for that blessed sleep in which the weary forget their woes. Happy was he if he could induce one of the shaggy dogs to lie down by his side, that he might hug the faithful animal in his arms, and thus obtain a little warmth.

Great was the luxury when, at the close of a toilsome day, a few pieces of bark could be so piled as to protect from wind and rain, and a roaring fire could blaze and crackle before the little camp. Then the appetite which hunger gives would enable him to feast upon the tender cuts of venison broiled upon the coals, with more satisfaction than the gourmand takes in the choicest viands of the restaurant. Having feasted to satiety, he would stretch himself upon the ground, with his feet to the fire, and soon be lost to all earth's cares, in sweet oblivion.

The journey was safely accomplished. The Dutchman had a father-in-law, by the name of Hartley, who lived in Virginia, having reared his cabin within about three miles of the Natural Bridge. Here the boy's contract came to an end. It would seem that the Dutchman was a good sort of man, as the world goes, and that he treated the boy kindly. He was so well pleased with David's energy and fidelity, that he was inclined to retain him in his service. Seeing the boy's anxiety to return home, he was disposed to throw around him invisible chains, and to hold him a captive. He thus threw every possible hindrance in the way of his return, offered to hire him as his boy of all work, and made him a present of five or six dollars, which perhaps he considered payment in advance, which bound the boy to remain with him until he had worked it out.

David soon perceived that his movements were watched, and that he was not his own master to go or stay as he pleased. This increased his restlessness. Four or five weeks thus passed away, when, one morning, three wagons laden with merchandise came along, bound to Knoxville. They were driven by an old man by the name of Dugan, and his two stalwart sons. They had traversed the road before, and David had seen the old man at his father's tavern. Secretly the shrewd boy revealed to him his situation, and his desire to get back to his home. The father and sons conferred together upon the subject. They were moved with sympathy for the boy, and, after due deliberation, told him that they should stop for the night about seven miles from that place, and should set out again on their journey with the earliest light of the morning; and that if he could get to them before daylight, he might follow their wagons.

It was Sunday morning, and it so happened that the Dutchman and the family had gone away on a visit. David collected his clothes and the little money he had, and hid them in a bundle under his bed. A very small bundle held them all. The family returned, and, suspecting nothing, all retired to sleep.

David had naturally a very affectionate heart. He never had been from home before. His lonely situation roused all the slumbering emotions of his childhood. In describing this event, he writes:

"I went to bed early that night, but sleep seemed to be a stranger to me. For though I was a wild boy, yet I dearly loved my father and mother; and their images appeared to be so deeply fixed in my mind that I could not sleep for thinking of them. And then the fear that when I should attempt to go out I should be discovered and called to a halt, filled me with anxiety."

A little after midnight, when the family were in profoundest sleep, David cautiously rose, and taking his little bundle, crept out doors. To his disappointment he found that it was snowing fast, eight inches having already fallen; and the wintry gale moaned dismally through the treetops. It was a dark, moonless night. The cabin was in the fields, half a mile from the road along which the wagons had passed. This boy of twelve years, alone in the darkness, was to breast the gale and wade through the snow, amid forest glooms, a distance of seven miles, before he could reach the appointed rendezvous.

For a moment his heart sank within him. Then recovering his resolution, he pushed out boldly into the storm. For three hours he toiled along, the snow rapidly increasing in depth until it reached up to his knees. Just before the dawn of the morning he reached the wagons. The men were up, harnessing their teams. The Dunns were astounded at the appearance of the little boy amid the darkness and the tempest. They took him into the house, warmed him by the fire, and gave him a good breakfast, speaking to him words of sympathy and encouragement. The affectionate heart of David was deeply moved by this tenderness, to which he was quite unaccustomed.

And then, though exhausted by the toil of a three hours' wading through the drifts, he commenced, in the midst of a mountain storm, a long day's journey upon foot. It was as much as the horses could do to drag the heavily laden wagons over the encumbered road. However weary, he could not ride. However exhausted, the wagons could not wait for him; neither was there any place in the smothering snow for rest.

Day after day they toiled along, in the endurance of hardships now with difficulty comprehended. Sometimes they were gladdened with sunny skies and smooth paths. Again the clouds would gather, and the rain, the sleet, and the snow would envelop them in glooms truly dismal. Under these circumstances the progress of the wagons was very slow. David was impatient. As he watched the sluggish turns of the wheels, he thought that he could travel very much faster if he should push forward alone, leaving the wagons behind him.

At length he became so impatient, thoughts of home having obtained entire possession of his mind, that he informed Mr. Dunn of his intention to press forward as fast as he could. His elder companions deemed it very imprudent for such a mere child, thus alone, to attempt to traverse the wilderness, and they said all they could to dissuade him, but in vain. He therefore, early the next morning, bade them farewell, and with light footsteps and a light heart tripped forward, leaving them behind, and accomplishing nearly as much in one day as the wagons could in two. We are not furnished with any of the details of this wonderful journey of a solitary child through a wilderness of one or two hundred miles. We know not how he slept at night, or how he obtained food by day. He informs us that he was at length overtaken by a drover, who had been to Virginia with a herd of cattle, and was returning to Knoxville riding one horse and leading another.

The man was amazed in meeting a mere child in such lonely wilds, and upon hearing his story, his kind heart was touched. David was a frail little fellow, whose weight would be no burden for a horse, and the good man directed him to mount the animal which he led. The boy had begun to be very tired. He was just approaching a turbid stream, whose icy waters, reaching almost to his neck, he would have had to wade but for this Providential assistance.

Travellers in the wilderness seldom trot their horses. On such a journey, an animal who naturally walks fast is of much more value than one which has attained high speed upon the race-course. Thus pleasantly mounted, David and his kind protector rode along together until they came within about fifteen miles of John Crockett's tavern, where their roads diverged. Here David dismounted, and bidding adieu to his benefactor, almost ran the remaining distance, reaching home that evening.

"The name of this kind gentleman," he writes, "I have forgotten; for it deserves a high place in my little book. A remembrance of his kindness to a little straggling boy has, however, a resting-place in my heart, and there it will remain as long as I live."

It was the spring of the year when David reached his father's cabin. He spent a part of the summer there. The picture which David gives of his home is revolting in the extreme. John Crockett, the tavern-keeper, had become intemperate, and he was profane and brutal. But his son, never having seen any home much better, does not seem to have been aware that there were any different abodes upon earth. Of David's mother we know nothing. She was probably a mere household drudge, crushed by an unfeeling husband, without sufficient sensibilities to have been aware of her degraded condition.

Several other cabins had risen in the vicinity of John Crockett's. A man came along, by the name of Kitchen, who undertook to open a school to teach the boys to read. David went to school four days, but found it very difficult to master his letters. He was a wiry little fellow, very athletic, and his nerves seemed made of steel. When roused by anger, he was as fierce and reckless as a catamount. A boy, much larger than himself, had offended him. David decided not to attack him near the school-house, lest the master might separate them.

He therefore slipped out of school, just before it was dismissed, and running along the road, hid in a thicket, near which his victim would have to pass on his way home. As the boy came unsuspectingly along, young Crockett, with the leap of a panther, sprang upon his back. With tooth and nail he assailed him, biting, scratching, pounding, until the boy cried for mercy.

The next morning, David was afraid to go to school, apprehending the severe punishment he might get from the master. He therefore left home as usual, but played truant, hiding himself in the woods all day. He did the same the next morning, and so continued for several days. At last the master sent word to John

Crockett, inquiring why his son David no longer came to school. The boy was called to an account, and the whole affair came out.

John Crockett had been drinking. His eyes flashed fire. He cut a stout hickory stick, and with oaths declared that he would give his boy an "eternal sight" worse whipping than the master would give him, unless he went directly back to school. As the drunken father approached brandishing his stick, the boy ran, and in a direction opposite from that of the school-house. The enraged father pursued, and the unnatural race continued for nearly a mile. A slight turn in the road concealed the boy for a moment from the view of his pursuer, and he plunged into the forest and hid. The father, with staggering gait, rushed along, but having lost sight of the boy, soon gave up the chase, and returned home.

This revolting spectacle, of such a father and such a son, over which one would think that angels might weep, only excited the derision of this strange boy. It was what he had been accustomed to all his life. He describes it in ludicrous terms, with the slang phrases which were ever dropping from his lips. David knew that a terrible whipping awaited him should he go back to the cabin.

He therefore pushed on several miles, to the hut of a settler whom he knew. He was, by this time, too much accustomed to the rough and tumble of life to feel any anxiety about the future. Arriving at the cabin, it so chanced that he found a man, by the name of Jesse Cheek, who was just starting with a drove of cattle for Virginia. Very readily, David, who had experience in that business, engaged to accompany him. An elder brother also, either weary of his wretched home or anxious to see more of the world, entered into the same service.

The incidents of this journey were essentially the same with those of the preceding one, though the route led two hundred miles farther into the heart of Virginia. The road they took passed through Abingdon, Witheville, Lynchburg, Charlottesville, Orange Court House, to Front Royal in Warren County. Though these frontier regions then, seventy-five years ago, were in a very primitive condition, still young Crockett caught glimpses of a somewhat higher civilization than he had ever encountered before in his almost savage life.

Here the drove was sold, and David found himself with a few dollars in his pocket. His brother decided to look for work in that region. David, then thirteen years of age, hoping tremblingly that time enough had elapsed to save him from a whipping, turned his thoughts homeward. A brother of the drover was about to return on horseback. David decided to accompany him, thinking that the man would permit him to ride a part of the way.

Much to his disgust, the man preferred to ride himself. The horse was his own. David had no claim to it whatever. He was therefore left to trudge along on foot. Thus he journeyed for three days. He then made an excuse for stopping a little while, leaving his companion to go on alone. He was very careful not again to overtake him. The boy had then, with four dollars in his pocket, a foot journey before him of between three and four hundred miles. And this was to be taken through desolate regions of morass and forest, where, not unfrequently, the lurking Indian had tomahawked, or gangs of half-famished wolves had devoured the passing traveller. He was also liable, at any time, to be caught by night and storm, without any shelter.

9

As he was sauntering along slowly, that he might be sure and not overtake his undesirable companion, he met a wagoner coming from Greenville, in Tennessee, and bound for Gerardstown, Berkeley County, in the extreme northerly part of Virginia. His route lay directly over the road which David had traversed. The man's name was Adam Myers. He was a jovial fellow, and at once won the heart of the vagrant boy. David soon entered into a bargain with Myers, and turned back with him. The state of mind in which the boy was may be inferred from the following extract taken from his autobiography. I omit the profanity, which was ever sprinkled through all his utterances:

"I often thought of home, and, indeed, wished bad enough to be there. But when I thought of the school-house, and of Kitchen, my master, and of the race with my father, and of the big hickory stick he carried, and of the fierceness of the storm of wrath I had left him in, I was afraid to venture back. I knew my father's nature so well, that I was certain his anger would hang on to him like a turtle does to a fisherman's toe. The promised whipping came slap down upon every thought of home."

Travelling back with the wagon, after two days' journey, he met his brother again, who had then decided to return himself to the parental cabin in Tennessee. He pleaded hard with David to accompany him reminding him of the love of his mother and his sisters. The boy, though all unused to weeping, was moved to tears. But the thought of the hickory stick, and of his father's brawny arm, decided the question. With his friend Myers he pressed on, farther and farther from home, to Gerardstown.

CHAPTER II.

Youthful Adventures.

David at Gerardstown.—Trip to Baltimore.—Anecdotes.—He ships for London.—Disappointment.—Defrauded of his Wages.—Escapes.—New Adventures.—Crossing the River.—Returns Home.—His Reception.—A Farm Laborer.—Generosity to his Father.—Love Adventure.—The Wreck of his Hopes.—His School Education.—Second Love Adventure.—Bitter Disappointment.—Life in the Backwoods.—Third Love Adventure.

The wagoner whom David had accompanied to Gerardstown was disappointed in his endeavors to find a load to take back to Tennessee. He therefore took a load to Alexandria, on the Potomac. David decided to remain at Gerardstown until Myers should return. He therefore engaged to work for a man by the name of John Gray, for twenty-five cents a day. It was light farm-work in which he was employed, and he was so faithful in the performance of his duties that he pleased the farmer, who was an old man, very much.

Myers continued for the winter in teaming backward and forward between Gerardstown and Baltimore, while David found a comfortable home of easy industry with the farmer. He was very careful in the expenditure of his money, and in the spring found that he had saved enough from his small wages to purchase him a suit of coarse but substantial clothes. He then, wishing to see a little more of the world, decided to make a trip with the wagoner to Baltimore.

David had then seven dollars in his pocket, the careful savings of the labors of half a year. He deposited the treasure with the wagoner for safe keeping. They started on their journey, with a wagon heavily laden with barrels of flour. As they were approaching a small settlement called Ellicott's Mills, David, a little ashamed to approach the houses in the ragged and mud-bespattered clothes which he wore on the way, crept into the wagon to put on his better garments.

While there in the midst of the flour barrels piled up all around him, the horses took fright at some strange sight which they encountered, and in a terrible scare rushed down a steep hill, turned a sharp corner, broke the tongue of the wagon and both of the axle-trees, and whirled the heavy barrels about in every direction. The escape of David from very serious injuries seemed almost miraculous. But our little barbarian leaped from the ruins unscathed. It does not appear that he had ever cherished any conception whatever of an overruling Providence. Probably, a religious thought had never entered his mind. A colt running by the side of the horses could not have been more insensible to every idea of death, and responsibility at God's bar, than was David Crockett. And he can be hardly blamed for this. The savages had some idea of the Great Spirit and of a future world. David was as uninstructed in those thoughts as are the wolves and the bears. Many years afterward, in writing of this occurrence, he says, with characteristic flippancy, interlarded with coarse phrases:

"This proved to me, if a fellow is born to be hung he will never be drowned; and further, that if he is born for a seat in Congress, even flour barrels can't make a mash of him. I didn't know how soon I should be knocked into a cocked hat, and get my walking-papers for another country."

The wagon was quite demolished by the disaster. Another was obtained, the flour reloaded, and they proceeded to Baltimore, dragging the wreck behind them, to be repaired there. Here young Crockett was amazed at the aspect of civilization which was opened before him. He wandered along the wharves gazing bewildered upon the majestic ships, with their towering masts, cordage, and sails, which he saw floating there He had never conceived of such fabrics before. The mansions, the churches, the long lines of brick stores excited his amazement. It seemed to him that he had been suddenly introduced into a sort of fairy-land. All thoughts of home now vanished from his mind. The great world was expanding before him, and the curiosity of his intensely active mind was roused to explore more of its wonders.

One morning he ventured on board one of the ships at a wharf, and was curiously and cautiously peering about, when the captain caught sight of him. It so happened that he was in need of a sailor-boy, and being pleased with the appearance of the lad, asked David if he would not like to enter into his service to take a voyage to London. The boy had no more idea of where London was, or what it was, than of a place in the moon. But eagerly he responded, "Yes," for he cared little where he went or what became of him, he was so glad of an opportunity to see more of the wonders of this unknown world.

The captain made a few inquiries respecting his friends, his home, and his past modes of life, and then engaged him for the cruise. David, in a state of high, joyous excitement, hurried back to the wagoner, to get his seven dollars of money and some clothes he had left with him. But Myers put a very prompt veto upon the lad's procedure, assuming that he was the boy's master, he declared that he should not go to sea. He refused to let him have either his clothes or his money, asserting that it was his duty to take him back to his parents in Tennessee. David would gladly have fled from him, and embarked without money and without clothes; but the wagoner watched him so closely that escape was impossible.

David was greatly down-hearted at this disappointment, and watched eagerly for an opportunity to obtain deliverance from his bondage. But Myers was a burly teamster who swung a very heavy wagon-whip, threatening the boy with a heavy punishment if he should make any attempt to run away.

After a few days, Myers loaded his team for Tennessee, and with his reluctant boy set out on his long journey. David was exceedingly restless. He now hated the man who was so tyranically domineering over him. He had no desire to return to his home, and he dreaded the hickory stick with which he feared his brutal father would assail him. One dark night, an hour or two before the morning, David carefully took his little bundle of clothes, and creeping noiselessly from the cabin, rushed forward as rapidly as his nimble feet could carry him. He soon felt quite easy in reference to his escape. He knew that the wagoner slept soundly, and that two hours at least must elapse before he would open his eyes. He then would not know with certainty in what direction the boy had fled. He could not safely leave his horses and wagon alone in the wilderness, to pursue him; and even should he unharness one of the horses and gallop forward in search of the fugitive, David, by keeping a vigilant watch, would see him in the distance and could easily plunge into the thickets of the forest, and thus elude pursuit.

He had run along five or six miles, when just as the sun was rising he overtook another wagon. He had already begun to feel very lonely and disconsolate. He had naturally an affectionate heart and a strong mind; traits of character which gleamed through all the dark clouds that obscured his life. He was alone in the wilderness, without a penny; and he knew not what to do, or which way to turn. The moment he caught sight of the teamster his heart yearned for sympathy. Tears moistened his eyes, and hastening to the stranger, the friendless boy of but thirteen years frankly told his whole story. The wagoner was a rough, profane, burly man, of generous feelings. There was an air of sincerity in the boy, which convinced him of the entire truth of his statements. His indignation was aroused, and he gave expression to that indignation in unmeasured terms. Cracking his whip in his anger, he declared that Myers was a scoundrel, thus to rob a friendless boy, and that he would lash the money out of him.

This man, whose name also chanced to be Myers, was of the tiger breed, fearing nothing, ever ready for a fight, and almost invariably coming off conqueror. In his generous rage he halted his team, grasped his wagon-whip, and, accompanied by the trembling boy, turned back, breathing vengeance. David was much alarmed, and told his protector that he was afraid to meet the wagoner, who had so often threatened him with his whip. But his new friend said, "Have no fear. The man shall give you back your money, or I will thrash it out of him."

They had proceeded but about two miles when they met the approaching team of Adam Myers. Henry Myers, David's new friend, leading him by the hand, advanced menacingly upon the other teamster, and greeted him with the words:

"You accursed scoundrel, what do you mean by robbing this friendless boy of his money?" Adam Myers confessed that he had received seven dollars of the boy's money. He said, however, that he had no money with him; that he had invested all he had in articles in his wagon, and that he intended to repay the boy as soon as they got back to Tennessee. This settled the question, and David returned with Henry Myers to his wagon, and accompanied him for several days on his slow and toilsome journey westward.

The impatient boy, as once before, soon got weary of the loitering pace of the heavily laden team, and concluded to leave his friend and press forward more rapidly alone. It chanced, one evening, that several wagons met, and the teamsters encamped for the night together. Henry Myers told them the story of the friendless boy, and that he was now about to set out alone for the long journey, most of it through an entire wilderness, and through a land of strangers wherever there might chance to be a few scattered cabins. They took up a collection for David, and presented him with three dollars.

The little fellow pressed along, about one hundred and twenty-five miles, down the valley between the Alleghany and the Blue ridges, until he reached Montgomery Court House. The region then, nearly three quarters of a century ago, presented only here and there a spot where the light of civilization had entered. Occasionally the log cabin of some poor emigrant was found in the vast expanse. David, too proud to beg, when he had any money with which to pay, found his purse empty when he had accomplished this small portion of his journey.

In this emergence, he hired out to work for a man a month for five dollars, which was at the rate of about one shilling a day. Faithfully he fulfilled his contract, and then, rather dreading to return home, entered into an engagement with a hatter, Elijah Griffith, to work in his shop for four years. Here he worked diligently eighteen months without receiving any pay. His employer then failed, broke up, and left the country. Again this poor boy, thus the sport of fortune, found himself without a penny, with but few clothes, and those much worn.

But it was not his nature to lay anything very deeply to heart. He laughed at misfortune, and pressed on singing and whistling through all storms. He had a stout pair of hands, good nature, and adaptation to any kind of work. There was no danger of his starving; and exposures, which many would deem hardships, were no hardships for him. Undismayed he ran here and there, catching at such employment as he could find, until he had supplied himself with some comfortable clothing, and had a few dollars of ready money in his purse. Again he set out alone and on foot for his far-distant home. He had been absent over two years, and was new fifteen years of age.

He trudged along, day after day, through rain and sunshine, until he reached a broad stream called New River. It was wintry weather. The stream was swollen by recent rains, and a gale then blowing was ploughing the surface into angry waves. Teams forded the stream many miles above. There was a log hut here, and the owner had a frail canoe in which he could paddle an occasional traveller across the river. But nothing would induce him to risk his life in an attempt to cross in such a storm.

The impetuous boy, in his ignorance of the effect of wind upon waves, resolved to attempt to cross, at every hazard, and notwithstanding all remonstrances. He obtained a leaky canoe, which was half stranded upon the shore, and pushed out on his perilous voyage. He tied his little bundle of clothes to the bows of the boat, that they might not be washed or blown away, and soon found himself exposed to the full force of the wind, and tossed by billows such as he had never dreamed of before. He was greatly frightened, and would have given all he had in the world, to have been safely back again upon the shore. But he was sure to be swamped if he should attempt to turn the boat broadside to the waves in such a gale. The only possible salvation for him was to cut the approaching billows with the bows of the boat. Thus he might possibly ride over them, though at the imminent peril, every moment, of shipping a sea which would engulf him and his frail boat in a watery grave.

In this way he reached the shore, two miles above the proper landing-place. The canoe was then half full of water. He was drenched with spray, which was frozen into almost a coat of mail upon his garments. Shivering with cold, he had to walk three miles through the forest before he found a cabin at whose fire he could warm and dry himself. Without any unnecessary delay he pushed on until he crossed the extreme western frontier line of Virginia, and entered Sullivan County, Tennessee.

An able-bodied young man like David Crockett, strong, athletic, willing to work, and knowing how to turn his hand to anything, could, in the humblest cabin, find employment which would provide him with board and lodging. He was in no danger of starving. There was, at that time, but one main path of travel from the East into the regions of the boundless West.

As David was pressing along this path he came to a little hamlet of log huts, where he found the brother whom he had left when he started from home eighteen months before with the drove of cattle. He remained with him for two or three weeks, probably paying his expenses by farm labor and hunting. Again he set out for home. The evening twilight was darkening into night when he caught sight of his father's humble cabin. Several wagons were standing around, showing that there must be considerable company in the house.

With not a little embarrassment, he ventured in. It was rather dark. His mother and sisters were preparing supper at the immense fireside. Quite a group of teamsters were scattered around the room, smoking their pipes, and telling their marvellous stories. David, during his absence of two years, had grown, and changed considerably in personal appearance. None of the family recognized him. They generally supposed, as he had been absent so long, that he was dead.

David inquired if he could remain all night. Being answered in the affirmative, he took a seat in a corner and remained perfectly silent, gazing upon the familiar scene, and watching the movements of his father, mother, and sisters. At length supper was ready, and all took seats at the table. As David came more into the light, one of his sisters, observing him, was struck with his resemblance to her lost brother. Fixing her eyes upon him, she, in a moment, rushed forward and threw her arms around his neck, exclaiming, "Here is my brother David."

Quite a scene ensued. The returning prodigal was received with as much affection as could be expected in a family with such uncultivated hearts and such unrefined habits as were found in the cabin of John Crockett. Even the stern old man forgot his hickory switch, and David, much to his relief, found that he should escape the long-dreaded whipping. Many years after this, when David Crockett, to his own surprise, and that of the whole nation, found himself elevated to the position of one of our national legislators, he wrote:

"But it will be a source of astonishment to many, who reflect that I am now a member of the American Congress, the most enlightened body of men in the world, that, at so advanced an age, the age of fifteen, I did not know the first letter in the book."

By the laws and customs of our land, David was bound to obey his father and work for him until he was twenty-one years of age. Until that time, whatever wages he might earn belonged to his father. It is often an act of great generosity for a hard-working farmer to release a stout lad of eighteen or nineteen from this obligation, and "to give him," as it is phrased, "his time."

John Crockett owed a neighbor, Abraham Wilson, thirty-six dollars. He told David that if he would work for Mr. Wilson until his wages paid that sum, he would then release him from all his obligations to his father, and his son might go free. It was a shrewd bargain for the old man, for he had already learned that David was abundantly capable of taking care of himself, and that he would come and go when and where he pleased.

The boy, weary of his wanderings, consented to the arrangement, and engaged to work for Mr. Wilson for six months, in payment for which, the note was to be delivered up to his father. It was characteristic of David that whatever he undertook he engaged in with all his might. He was a rude, coarse boy. It was scarcely possible, with his past training, that he should be otherwise. But he was very faithful in fulfilling his obligations. Though his sense of right and wrong was very obtuse, he was still disposed to do the right so far as his uncultivated conscience revealed it to him.

For six months, David worked for Mr. Wilson with the utmost fidelity and zeal. He then received the note, presented it to his father, and, before he was sixteen years of age, stood up proudly his own man. His father had no longer the right to whip him. His father had no longer the right to call upon him for any service without paying him for it. And on the other hand, he could no longer look to his father for food or clothing. This thought gave him no trouble. He had already taken care of himself for two years, and he felt no more solicitude in regard to the future than did the buffalo's calf or the wolf's whelp.

Wilson was a bad man, dissipated and unprincipled. But he had found David to be so valuable a laborer that he offered him high wages if he would remain and work for him. It shows a latent, underlying principle of goodness in David, that he should have refused the offer. He writes:

"The reason was, it was a place where a heap of bad company met to drink and gamble; and I wanted to get away from them, for I know'd very well, if I staid there, I should get a bad name, as nobody could be respectable that would live there."

About this time a Quaker, somewhat advanced in years, a good, honest man, by the name of John Kennedy, emigrated from North Carolina, and selecting his four hundred acres of land about fifteen miles from John Crockett's, reared a log hut and commenced a clearing. In some transaction with Crockett he took his neighbor's note for forty dollars. He chanced to see David, a stout lad of prepossessing appearance, and proposed that he should work for him for two shillings a day taking him one week upon trial. At the close of the week the Quaker expressed himself as highly satisfied with his work, and offered to pay him with his father's note of forty dollars for six months' labor on his farm.

David knew full well how ready his father was to give his note, and how slow he was to pay it. He was fully aware that the note was not worth, to him, the paper upon which it was written. But he reflected that the note was an obligation upon his father, that he was very poor, and his lot in life was hard. It certainly indicated much innate nobility of nature that this boy, under these circumstances, should have accepted the offer of the Quaker. But David did this. For six months he labored assiduously, without the slightest hope of reward, excepting that he would thus relieve his father, whom he had no great cause either to respect or love, from the embarrassment of the debt.

For a whole half-year David toiled upon the farm of the Quaker, never once during that time visiting his home. At the end of the term he received his pay for those long months of labor, in a little piece of rumpled paper, upon which his father had probably made his mark. It was Saturday evening. The next morning he borrowed a horse of his employer and set out for a visit home. He was kindly welcomed. His father knew nothing of the agreement which his son had made with Mr. Kennedy. As the family were talking together around the cabin fire, David drew the note from his pocket and presented it to his father. The old man seemed much troubled. He supposed Mr. Kennedy had sent it for collection. As usual, he began to make excuses. He said that he was very sorry that he could not pay it, that he had met with many misfortunes, that he had no money, and that he did not know what to do.

David then told his father that he did not hand him the bill for collection, but that it was a present from him—that he had paid it in full. It is easy for old and broken-down men to weep. John Crockett seemed much affected by this generosity of his son, and David says "he shed a heap of tears." He, however, avowed his inability to pay anything whatever, upon the note.

David had now worked a year without getting any money for himself. His clothes were worn out, and altogether he was in a very dilapidated condition. He went back to the Quaker's, and again engaged in his service, desiring to earn some money to purchase clothes. Two months thus passed away. Every ardent, impetuous boy must have a love adventure. David had his. A very pretty young Quakeress, of about David's age, came from North Carolina to visit Mr. Kennedy, who was her uncle. David fell desperately in love with her. We cannot better describe this adventure than in the unpolished diction of this illiterate boy. If one would understand this extraordinary character, it is necessary thus to catch such glimpses as we can of his inner life. Let this necessity atone for the unpleasant rudeness of speech. Be it remembered that this reminiscence was written after David Crockett was a member of Congress.

"I soon found myself head over heels in love with this girl. I thought that if all the hills about there were pure chink, and all belonged to me, I would give them if I could just talk to her as I wanted to. But I was afraid to begin; for when I would think of saying anything to her, my heart would begin to flutter like a duck in a puddle. And if I tried to outdo it and speak, it would get right smack up in my throat, and choke me like a cold potato. It bore on my mind in this way, till at last I concluded I must die if I didn't broach the subject. So I determined to begin and hang on a-trying to speak, till my heart would get out of my throat one way or t'other.

"And so one day at it I went, and after several trials I could say a little. I told her how I loved her; that she was the darling object of my soul and body, and I must have her, or else I should pine down to nothing, and just die away with consumption.

"I found my talk was not disagreeable to her. But she was an honest girl, and didn't want to deceive nobody. She told me she was engaged to her cousin, a son of the old Quaker. This news was worse to me than war, pestilence, or famine. But still I know'd I could not help myself. I saw quick enough my cake was dough; and I tried to cool off as fast as possible. But I had hardly safety pipes enough, as my love was so hot as mighty nigh to burst my boilers. But I didn't press my claims any more, seeing there was no chance to do anything."

David's grief was very sincere, and continued as long as is usually the case with disappointed lovers.

David soon began to cherish some slight idea of the deficiency in his education. He had never been to school but four days; and in that time he had learned absolutely nothing. A young man, a Quaker, had opened a school about a mile and a half from Mr. Kennedy's. David made an arrangement with his employer by which he was to go to school four days in the week, and work the other two days for his board. He continued in this way for six months. But it was very evident that David was not born for a scholar. At the end of that time he could read a little in the first primer. With difficulty he could make certain hieroglyphics which looked like his name. He could also perform simple sums in addition, subtraction, and multiplication. The mysteries of division he never surmounted.

This was the extent of his education. He left school, and in the laborious life upon which he entered, never after improved any opportunity for mental culture. The disappointment which David had encountered in his love affair, only made him more eager to seek a new object upon which he might fix his affections. Not far from Mr. Kennedy's there was the cabin of a settler, where there were two or three girls. David had occasionally met them. Boy as he was, for he was not yet eighteen, he suddenly and impetuously set out to see if he could not pick, from them, one for a wife.

Without delay he made his choice, and made his offer, and was as promptly accepted as a lover. Though they were both very young, and neither of them had a dollar, still as those considerations would not have influenced David in the slightest degree, we know not why they where not immediately married. Several months of very desperate and satisfactory courtship passed away, when the time came for the nuptials of the little Quaker girl, which ceremony was to take place at the cabin of her uncle David and his "girl" were invited to the wedding. The scene only inflamed the desires of David to hasten his marriage-day. He was very importunate in pressing his claims. She seemed quite reluctant to fix the day, but at last consented;

and says David, "I thought if that day come, I should be the happiest man in the created world, or in the moon, or anywhere else."

In the mean time David had become very fond of his rifle, and had raised enough money to buy him one. He was still living with the Quaker. Game was abundant, and the young hunter often brought in valuable supplies of animal food. There were frequent shooting-matches in that region. David, proud of his skill, was fond of attending them. But his Quaker employer considered them a species of gambling, which drew together all the idlers and vagrants of the region, and he could not approve of them.

There was another boy living at that time with the Quaker. They practised all sorts of deceptions to steal away to the shooting-matches under pretence that they were engaged in other things. This boy was quite in love with a sister of David's intended wife. The staid member of the Society of Friends did not approve of the rude courting frolics of those times, which frequently occupied nearly the whole night.

The two boys slept in a garret, in what was called the gable end of the house. There was a small window in their rough apartment. One Sunday, when the Quaker and his wife were absent attending a meeting, the boys cut a long pole, and leaned it up against the side of the house, as high as the window, but so that it would not attract any attention. They were as nimble as catamounts, and could run up and down the pole without the slightest difficulty. They would go to bed at the usual early hour. As soon as all were quiet, they would creep from the house, dressed in their best apparel, and taking the two farm-horses, would mount their backs and ride, as fast as possible, ten miles through the forest road to where the girls lived. They were generally expected. After spending all the hours of the middle of the night in the varied frolics of country courtship, they would again mount their horses and gallop home, being especially careful to creep in at their window before the dawn of day The course of true love seemed for once to be running smoothly. Saturday came, and the next week, on Thursday, David was to be married.

It so happened that there was to be a shooting match on Saturday, at one of the cabins not far from the home of his intended bride. David made some excuse as to the necessity of going home to prepare for his wedding, and in the morning set out early, and directed his steps straight to the shooting-match. Here he was very successful in his shots, and won about five dollars. In great elation of spirits, and fully convinced that he was one of the greatest and happiest men in the world, he pressed on toward the home of his intended bride.

He had walked but a couple of miles, when he reached the cabin of the girl's uncle. Considering the members of the family already as his relatives, he stepped in, very patronizingly, to greet them. He doubted not that they were very proud of the approaching alliance of their niece with so distinguished a man as himself—a man who had actually five dollars, in silver, in his pocket. Entering the cabin, he found a sister of his betrothed there. Instead of greeting him with the cordiality he expected, she seemed greatly embarrassed. David had penetration enough to see that something was wrong. The reception she gave him was not such as he thought a brother-in-law ought to receive. He made more particular inquiries. The result we will give in David's language.

"She then burst into tears, and told me that her sister was going to deceive me; and that she was to be married to another man the next day. This was as sudden to me as a clap of thunder of a bright sunshiny day. It was the capstone of all the afflictions I had ever met with; and it seemed to me that it was more than any human creature could endure. It struck me perfectly speechless for some time, and made me feel so weak that I thought I should sink down. I however recovered from the shock after a little, and rose and started without any ceremony, or even bidding anybody good-bye. The young woman followed me out to the gate, and entreated me to go on to her father's, and said she would go with me.

"She said the young man who was going to marry her sister had got his license and asked for her. But she assured me that her father and mother both preferred me to him; and that she had no doubt that if I would go on I could break off the match. But I found that I could go no farther. My heart was bruised, and my spirits were broken down. So I bid her farewell, and turned my lonesome and miserable steps back again homeward, concluding that I was only born for hardship, misery, and disappointment. I now began to think that in making me it was entirely forgotten to make my mate; that I was born odd, and should always remain so, and that nobody would have me.

"But all these reflections did not satisfy my mind, for I had no peace, day nor night, for several weeks. My appetite failed me, and I grew daily worse and worse. They all thought I was sick; and so I was. And it was the worst kind of sickness, a sickness of the heart, and all the tender parts, produced by disappointed love."

For some time David continued in a state of great dejection, a lovelorn swain of seventeen years. Thus disconsolate, he loved to roam the forest alone, with his rifle as his only companion, brooding over his sorrows. The gloom of the forest was congenial to him, and the excitement of pursuing the game afforded some slight relief to his agitated spirit. One day, when he had wandered far from home, he came upon the cabin of a Dutchman with whom he had formed some previous acquaintance. He had a daughter, who was exceedingly plain in her personal appearance, but who had a very active mind, and was a bright, talkative girl.

She had heard of David's misadventure, and rather unfeelingly rallied him upon his loss. She however endeavored to comfort him by the assurance that there were as good fish in the sea as had ever been caught out of it. David did not believe in this doctrine at all, as applied to his own case, He thought his loss utterly irretrievable. And in his still high appreciation of himself, notwithstanding his deep mortification, he thought that the lively Dutch girl was endeavoring to catch him for her lover. In this, however, he soon found himself mistaken.

She told him that there was to be a reaping frolic in their neighborhood in a few days, and that if he would attend it, she would show him one of the prettiest girls upon whom he ever fixed his eyes. Difficult as he found it to shut out from his mind his lost love, upon whom his thoughts were dwelling by day and by night, he very wisely decided that his best remedy would be found in what Dr. Chalmers calls "the expulsive power of a new affection;" that is, that he would try and fall in love with some other girl as soon as possible. His own language, in describing his feelings at that time, is certainly very different from that which the philosopher or the modern novelist would have used, but it is quite characteristic of the man. The Dutch maiden assured him that the girl who had deceived him was not to be compared in beauty with the one she would show to him. He writes:

"I didn't believe a word of all this, for I had thought that such a piece of flesh and blood as she had never been manufactured, and never would again. I agreed with her that the little varmint had treated me so bad that I ought to forget her, and yet I couldn't do it. I concluded that the best way to accomplish it was to cut out again, and see if I could find any other that would answer me; and so I told the Dutch girl that I would be at the reaping, and would bring as many as I could with me."

David seems at this time to have abandoned all constant industry, and to be loafing about with his rifle, thus supporting himself with the game he took. He traversed the still but slightly broken forest in all directions, carrying to many scattered farm-houses intelligence of the approaching reaping frolic. He informed the good Quaker with whom he had worked of his intention to be there. Mr. Kennedy endeavored to dissuade him. He said that there would be much bad company there; that there would be drinking and carousing, and that David had been so good a boy that he should be very sorry to have him get a bad name.

The curiosity of the impetuous young man was, however, by this time, too much aroused for any persuasions to hold him back. Shouldering his rifle, he hastened to the reaping at the appointed day. Upon his arrival at the place he found a large company already assembled. He looked around for the pretty girl, but she was nowhere to be seen. She chanced to be in a shed frolicking with some others of the young people.

But as David, with his rifle on his shoulder, sauntered around, an aged Irish woman, full of nerve and volubility, caught sight of him. She was the mother of the girl, and had been told of the object of David's visit. He must have appeared very boyish, for he had not yet entered his eighteenth year, and though very wiry and athletic, he was of slender frame, and rather small in stature.

The Irish woman hastened to David; lavished upon him compliments respecting his rosy cheeks, and assured him that she had exactly such a sweet heart for him as he needed. She did not allow, David to have any doubt that she would gladly welcome him as the husband of her daughter.

Pretty soon the young, fresh, blooming, mirthful girl came along; and David fell in love with her at first sight. Not much formality of introduction was necessary: each was looking for the other. Both of the previous loves of the young man were forgotten in an instant. He devoted himself with the utmost assiduity, to the little Irish girl. He was soon dancing with her. After a very vigorous "double shuffle," as they were seated side by side on a bench intensely talking, for David Crockett was never at a loss for words, the mother came up, and, in her wonderfully frank mode of match-making, jocosely addressed him as her son-in-law.

Even David's imperturbable self-possession was disturbed by this assailment. Still he was much pleased to find both mother and daughter so favorably disposed toward him. The rustic frolicking continued nearly all night. In the morning, David, in a very happy frame of mind, returned to the Quaker's, and in anticipation of soon setting up farming for himself, engaged to work for him for six months for a low-priced horse.

CHAPTER III.

Marriage and Settlement.

Rustic Courtship.—The Rival Lover.—Romantic Incident.—The Purchase of a Horse.—The Wedding.— Singular Ceremonies.—The Termagant.—Bridal Days.—They commence Housekeeping.—The Bridal Mansion and Outfit.—Family Possessions.—The Removal to Central Tennessee.—Mode of Transportation.—The New Home and its Surroundings.—Busy Idleness.—The Third Move.—The Massacre at Fort Mimms.

David took possession of his horse, and began to work very diligently to pay for it. He felt that now he was a man of property. After the lapse of a few weeks he mounted his horse and rode over to the Irishman's cabin to see his girl, and to find out how she lived, and what sort of people composed the family. Arriving at the log hut, he found the father to be a silent, staid old man, and the mother as voluble and nervous a little woman as ever lived. Much to his disappointment, the girl was away. After an hour or two she returned, having been absent at some meeting or merry-making, and, much to his chagrin, she brought back with her a stout young fellow who was evidently her lover.

The new-comer was not at all disposed to relinquish his claims in favor of David Crockett. He stuck close to the maiden, and kept up such an incessant chatter that David could scarcely edge in a word. In characteristic figure of speech he says, "I began to think I was barking up the wrong tree again. But I determined to stand up to my rack, fodder or no fodder." He thought he was sure of the favor of her parents, and he was not certain that the girl herself had not given him sundry glances indicative of her preference. Dark night was now coming on, and David had a rough road of fifteen miles to traverse through the forest before he could reach home. He thought that if the Irishman's daughter cherished any tender feelings toward him, she would be reluctant to have him set out at that late hour on such a journey. He therefore rose to take leave.

His stratagem proved successful. The girl immediately came, leaving her other companion, and in earnest tones entreated him not to go that evening. The lover was easily persuaded. His heart grew lighter and his spirit bolder. She soon made it so manifest in what direction her choice lay, that David was left entire master of the field. His discomfited rival soon took his hat and withdrew, David thus was freed from all his embarrassments.

It was Saturday night. He remained at the cabin until Monday morning, making very diligent improvement of his time in the practice of all those arts of rural courtship which instinct teaches. He then returned home, not absolutely engaged, but with very sanguine hopes.

At that time, in that region, wolves were abundant and very destructive. The neighbors, for quite a distance, combined for a great wolf-hunt, which should explore the forest for many miles. By the hunters thus scattering on the same day, the wolves would have no place of retreat. If they fled before one hunter they would encounter another. Young Crockett, naturally confident, plunged recklessly into the forest, and wandered to and fro until, to his alarm, he found himself bewildered and utterly lost. There were no signs of human habitations near, and night was fast darkening around him.

Just as he was beginning to feel that he must look out for a night's encampment, he saw in the distance, through the gigantic trees, a young girl running at her utmost speed, or, as he expressed it in the Crockett vernacular, "streaking it along through the woods like all wrath." David gave chase, and soon overtook the terrified girl, whom he found, to his surprise and delight, to be his own sweetheart, who had also by some strange accident got lost.

Here was indeed a romantic and somewhat an embarrassing adventure. The situation was, however, by no means so embarrassing as it would have been to persons in a higher state of civilization. The cabin of the emigrant often consisted of but one room, where parents and children and the chance guest passed the night together. They could easily throw up a camp. David with his gun could kindle a fire and get some game. The girl could cook it. All their physical wants would thus be supplied. They had no material inconveniences to dread in camping out for a night. The delicacy of the situation would not be very keenly felt by persons who were at but one remove above the native Indian.

The girl had gone out in the morning into the woods, to hunt up one of her father's horses. She missed her way, became lost, and had been wandering all day long farther and farther from home. Soon after the two met they came across a path which they knew must lead to some house. Following this, just after dark they came within sight of the dim light of a cabin fire. They were kindly received by the inmates, and, tired as they were, they both sat up all night. Upon inquiry they found that David had wandered ten miles from his home, and the young girl seven from hers. Their paths lay in different directions, but the road was plain, and in the morning they separated, and without difficulty reached their destination.

David was now anxious to get married immediately. It will be remembered that he had bought a horse; but he had not paid for it. The only property he had, except the coarse clothes upon his back, was a rifle. All the land in that neighborhood was taken up. He did not even own an axe with which to build him a log cabin. It would be necessary for him to hire some deserted shanty, and borrow such articles as were indispensable. Nothing could be done to any advantage without a horse. To diminish the months which he had promised to work in payment for the animal, he threw in his rifle.

After a few weeks of toil the horse was his. He mounted his steed, deeming himself one of the richest men in the far West, and rode to see his girl and fix upon his wedding-day. He confesses that as he rode along, considering that he had been twice disappointed, he experienced no inconsiderable trepidation as to the result of this third matrimonial enterprise. He reached the cabin, and his worst fears were realized.

The nervous, voluble, irritable little woman, who with all of a termagant's energy governed both husband and family, had either become dissatisfied with young Crockett's poverty, or had formed the plan of some other more ambitious alliance for her daughter. She fell upon David in a perfect tornado of vituperation, and ordered him out of the house. She was "mighty wrathy," writes David, "and looked at me as savage as a meat-axe."

David was naturally amiable, and in the depressing circumstances had no heart to return railing for railing. He meekly reminded the infuriate woman that she had called him "son-in-law" before he had attempted to call her "mother-in-law," and that he certainly had been guilty of no conduct which should expose him to such treatment. He soon saw, to his great satisfaction, that the daughter remained faithful to him, and that the meek father was as decidedly on his side as his timid nature would permit him to be. Though

David felt much insulted, he restrained his temper, and, turning from the angry mother, told her daughter that he would come the next Thursday on horseback, leading another horse for her; and that then he would take her to a justice of the peace who lived at the distance of but a few miles from them, where they would be married. David writes of the mother:

"Her Irish was too high to do anything with her; so I quit trying. All I cared for was to have her daughter on my side, which I know'd was the case then. But how soon some other fellow might knock my nose out of joint again, I couldn't tell. Her mother declared I shouldn't have her. But I knowed I should, if somebody else didn't get her before Thursday."

The all-important wedding-day soon came David was resolved to crush out all opposition and consummate the momentous affair with very considerable splendor. He therefore rode to the cabin with a very imposing retinue. Mounted proudly upon his own horse, and leading a borrowed steed, with a blanket saddle, for his bride, and accompanied by his elder brother and wife and a younger brother and sister, each on horseback, he "cut out to her father's house to get her."

When this cavalcade of six horses had arrived within about two miles of the Irishman's cabin, quite a large party was found assembled from the log huts scattered several miles around. David, kind-hearted, generous, obliging, was very popular with his neighbors. They had heard of the approaching nuptials of the brave boy of but eighteen years, and of the wrath of the brawling, ill-tempered mother. They anticipated a scene, and wished to render David the support of their presence and sympathy. This large party, some on foot and some on horseback, proceeded together to the Irishman's cabin. The old man met them with smiles, whiskey bottle in hand, ready to offer them all a drink. The wife, however, was obdurate as ever. She stood at the cabin door, her eyes flashing fire, and quite bewildered to decide in what way to attempt to repel and drive off her foe.

She expected that the boy would come alone, and that, with her all-potent tongue, she would so fiercely assail him and so frighten her young girl as still to prevent the marriage. But here was quite an army of the neighbors, from miles around, assembled. They were all evidently the friends of David. Every eye was fixed upon her. Every ear was listening to hear what she would say. Every tongue was itching to cry out shame to her opposition, and to overwhelm her with reproaches. For once the termagant found herself baffled, and at her wits' end.

The etiquette of courts and cabins are quite different. David paid no attention to the mother, but riding up to the door of the log house, leading the horse for his bride, he shouted to her to come out. The girl had enjoyed no opportunity to pay any attention to her bridal trousseau. But undoubtedly she had contrived to put on her best attire. We do not know her age, but she was ever spoken of as a remarkably pretty little girl, and was probably about seventeen years old.

David did not deem it necessary to dismount, but called upon his "girl" to jump upon the horse he was leading. She did so. The mother was powerless. It was a waterloo defeat. In another moment they would disappear, riding away along the road, which wound through the gigantic trees of the forest. In another hour they would be married. And then they would forever be beyond the reach of the clamor of her voluble tongue. She began to relent. The old man, accustomed to her wayward humors, instinctively perceived it. Stepping up to David, and placing his hand upon the neck of his horse, he said:

"I wish you would stay and be married here. My woman has too much tongue. You oughtn't mind her."

Having thus, for a moment, arrested their departure, he stepped back to the door, where his discomfited wife stood, and entreated her to consent to their being married there. After much persuasion, common sense triumphed over uncommon stubbornness. She consented. David and his expectant bride were both on horseback, all ready to go. The woman rather sullenly came forward and said:

"I am sorry for the words I have spoken. This girl is the only child I have ever had to marry. I cannot bear to see her go off in this way. If you'll come into the house and be married here, I will do the best I can for you."

The good-natured David consented. They alighted from their horses, and the bridal party entered the log hut. The room was not large, and the uninvited guests thronged it and crowded around the door. The justice of peace was sent for, and the nuptial knot was tied.

The wedding ceremonies on such occasions were sufficiently curious to be worthy of record. They certainly were in very wide contrast with the pomp and splendor of nuptials in the palatial mansions of the present day. A large party usually met at some appointed place, some mounted and others on foot, to escort the bridegroom to the house of the bride. The horses were decorated with all sorts of caparisons, with ropes for bridles, with blankets or furs for saddles. The men were dressed in deerskin moccasins, leather breeches, leggins, coarse hunting-shirts of all conceivable styles of material, and all homemade.

The women wore gowns of very coarse homespun and home-woven cloth, composed of linen and wool, and called linsey-woolsey, very coarse shoes, and sometimes with buckskin gloves of their own manufacture. If any one chanced to have a ring or pretty buckle, it was a relic of former times.

There were no carriages, for there were no roads. The narrow trail they traversed in single file was generally a mere horse-path, often so contracted in width that two horses could not pass along abreast. As they marched along in straggling line, with shouts and jokes, and with the interchange of many gallant acts of rustic love-making between the coquettish maidens and the awkward swains, they encountered frequent obstacles on the way. It was a part of the frolic for the young men to throw obstructions in their path, and thus to create surprises. There were brooks to be forded. Sometimes large trees were mischievously felled across the trail. Grape-vines were tied across from tree to tree, to trip up the passers-by or to sweep off their caps. It was a great joke for half a dozen young men to play Indian. They would lie in ambuscade, and suddenly, as the procession was passing, would raise the war-whoop, discharge their guns, and raise shouts of laughter in view of the real or feigned consternation thus excited.

The maidens would of course shriek. The frightened horses would spring aside. The swains would gallantly rush to the rescue of their sweethearts. When the party had arrived within about a mile of the house where the marriage ceremony was to take place, two of the most daring riders among the young men who had been previously selected for the purpose, set out on horseback on a race for "the bottle." The master of the house was expected to be standing at his door, with a jug of whiskey in his hand. This was the prize which the victor in the race was to seize and take back in triumph to his companions.

The start was announced by a general Indian yell. The more rough the road—the more full of logs, stumps, rocks, precipitous hills, and steep glens, the better. This afforded a better opportunity for the display of intrepidity and horsemanship. It was a veritable steeple-chase. The victor announced his success by one of those shrill, savage yells, which would almost split the ears of the listener. Grasping the bottle, he returned in triumph. On approaching the party, he again gave forth the Indian war-whoop.

The bottle or jug was first presented to the bridegroom. He applied the mouth of the bottle to his lips, and took a dram of raw whiskey. He then handed it to his next of kin, and so the bottle passed through the whole company. It is to be supposed that the young women did not burn their throats with very copious drafts of the poisonous fire-water.

When they arrived at the house, the brief ceremony of marriage immediately took place, and then came the marriage feast. It was a very substantial repast of pork, poultry, wild turkeys, venison, and bear's meat. There was usually the accompaniment of corn-bread, potatoes, and other vegetables. Great hilarity prevailed on these occasions, with wonderful freedom of manners, coarse jokes, and shouts of laughter.

The table was often a large slab of timber, hewn out with a broad-axe, and supported by four stakes driven into auger-holes. The table furniture consisted of a few pewter dishes, with wooden plates and bowls. There were generally a few pewter spoons, much battered about the edges, but most of the spoons were of horn, homemade. Crockery, so easily broken, was almost unknown. Table knives were seldom seen. The deficiency was made up by the hunting-knives which all the men carried in sheaths attached to their hunting-shirts.

After dinner the dancing began. There was invariably some musical genius present who could play the fiddle. The dances were what were called three or four handed reels, or square sets and jigs. With all sorts of grotesque attitudes, pantomime and athletic displays, the revelry continued until late into the night, and often until the dawn of the morning. As there could be no sleeping accommodations for so large a company in the cabin of but one room, the guests made up for sleep in merriment.

The bridal party stole away in the midst of the uproar, one after another, up a ladder into the loft or garret above, which was floored with loose boards made often of split timber. This furnished a very rude sleeping apartment. As the revelry below continued, seats being scarce, every young man offered his lap as a seat for the girls; and the offer was always promptly accepted; Always, toward morning, some one was sent up into the loft with a bottle of whiskey, to offer the bridegroom and his bride a drink. The familiar name of the bottle was "Black Betty." One of the witticisms ever prominent on the occasion was, "Where is Black Betty? I want to kiss her sweet lips." At some splendid weddings, where the larder was abundantly stored with game, this feasting and dancing was continued for several days.

Such, in the main, was the wedding of David Crockett with the Irishman's daughter. In the morning the company dispersed. David also and his young bride left, during the day, for his father's cabin. As the families of the nuptial party both belonged to the aristocracy of the region, quite a splendid marriage reception was held at John Crockett's. There were feasting and dancing; and "Black Betty received many a cordial kiss. The bridegroom's heart was full of exultant joy. David writes:

"Having gotten my wife, I thought I was completely made up, and needed nothing more in the whole world."

He soon found his mistake, and awoke to the consciousness that he needed everything, and had nothing. He had no furniture, no cabin, no land, no money. And he had a wife to support. His only property consisted of a cheap horse. He did not even own a rifle, an article at that time so indispensable to the backwoodsman.

After spending a few days at David's father's, the bridegroom and bride returned to the cabin of her father, the Irishman. Here they found that a wonderful change had taken place in the mother's feelings and conduct. She had concluded to submit good-naturedly to the inevitable. Her "conversational powers" were wonderful. With the most marvellous volubility of honeyed words she greeted them. She even consented to have two cows given them, each with a calf. This was the dowry of the bride—her only dowry. David, who had not expected anything, felt exceedingly rich with this herd.

Near by there was a vacated log cabin with a few acres of land attached to it. Our boy bridegroom and bride hired the cabin at a very small rent. But then they had nothing whatever to put into it. They had not a bed, or a table or a chair; no cooking utensils; not even a knife or a fork. He had no farming tools; not a spade or a hoe. The whole capital with which they commenced life consisted of the clothes they had on, a farm-horse, two cows, and two calves.

In this emergence the good old Quaker, for whom David had worked, came forward, and loaned him fifteen dollars. In that wilderness, food, that is game and corn, was cheap. But as nearly everything else had to be brought from beyond the mountains, all tools and furniture commanded high prices. With the fifteen dollars, David and his little wife repaired to a country store a few miles distant, to furnish their house and farm. Under these circumstances, the china-closet of the bride must have been a curiosity. David says, "With this fifteen dollars we fixed up pretty grand, as we thought."

After a while, in some unexplained way, they succeeded in getting a spinning-wheel. The little wife, says David, "knowed exactly how to use it. She was also a good weaver. Being very industrious, she had, in little or no time, a fine web of cloth ready to make up. She was good at that too, and at almost anything else a woman could do."

Here this humble family remained for two years. They were both as contented with their lot as other people are. They were about as well off as most of their neighbors. Neither of them ever cherished a doubt that they belonged to the aristocracy of the region. They did not want for food or clothing, or shelter, or a warm fireside. They had their merry-makings, their dances, and their shooting-matches. Let it be remembered that this was three quarters of a century ago, far away in the wilds of an almost untamed wilderness.

Two children were born in this log cabin. David began to feel the responsibilities of a father who had children to provide for. Both of the children were sons. Though David's family was increasing, there was scarcely any increase of his fortune. He therefore decided that the interests of his little household demanded that he should move still farther back into the almost pathless wilderness, where the land was not yet taken up, and where he could get a settler's title to four hundred acres, simply by rearing a cabin and planting some corn.

He had one old horse, and a couple of colts, each two years old. The colts were broken, as it was called, to the halter; that is, they could be led, with light burdens upon their backs, but could not be ridden. Mrs.

Crockett mounted the old horse, with her babe in her arms, and the little boy, two years old, sitting in front of her, astride the horse's neck, and occasionally carried on his father's shoulders. Their few articles of household goods were fastened upon the backs of the two colts. David led one, and his kind-hearted father-in-law, who had very generously offered to help him move, led the other. Thus this party set out for a journey of two hundred and fifty miles, over unbridged rivers, across rugged mountains, and through dense forests, whose Indian trails had seldom if ever been trodden by the feet of white men.

This was about the year 1806. The whole population of the State then amounted to but about one hundred thousand. They were generally widely dispersed through the extensive regions of East Tennessee. But very few emigrants had ventured across the broad and rugged cliffs of the Cumberland Mountains into the rich and sunny plains of Western Tennessee. But a few years before, terrible Indian wars desolated the State. The powerful tribes of the Creeks and Cherokees had combined all their energies for the utter extermination of the white men, seeking to destroy all their hamlets and scattered cabins.

At a slow foot-pace the pioneers followed down the wild valley of the Holston River, often with towering mountains rising upon each side of them. If they chanced, at nightfall, to approach the lonely hut of a settler, it was especial good fortune, as they thus found shelter provided, and a fire built, and hospitable entertainment ready for them. If, however, they were overtaken in the wilderness by darkness, and even a menacing storm, it was a matter of but little moment, and caused no anxiety. A shelter, of logs and bark, was soon thrown up, with a crackling fire, illuminating the wilderness, blazing before it. A couch, as soft as they had ever been accustomed to, could speedily be spread from the pliant boughs of trees. Upon the pack-colts there were warm blankets. And during the journey of the day they had enjoyed ample opportunity to take such game as they might need for their supper and their morning breakfast.

At length they reached the majestic flood of the Tennessee River, and crossed it, we know not how. Then, directing their steps toward the setting sun, they pressed on, league after league, and day after day, in toilsome journey, over prairies and through forests and across mountain-ridges, for a distance of nearly four hundred miles from their starting-place, until they reached a small stream, called Mulberry Creek which flows into the Elk River, in what is now Lincoln County.

At the mouth of Mulberry Creek the adventurous emigrant found his promised land. It was indeed a beautiful region. The sun shines upon none more so. The scenery, which, however, probably had but few attractions for David Crockett's uncultivated eye, was charming. The soil was fertile. The streams abounded with fish and waterfowl; and prairie and forest were stocked with game. No family need suffer from hunger here, if the husband had a rifle and knew how to use it. A few hours' labor would rear a cabin which would shut out wind and rain as effectually as the gorgeous walls of Windsor or Versailles.

No jets of gas or gleam of wax candles ever illumined an apartment more brilliantly than the flashing blaze of the wood fire. And though the refectories of the Palais Royal may furnish more scientific cookery than the emigrant's hut, they cannot furnish fatter turkeys, or more tender venison, or more delicious cuts from the buffalo and the bear than are often found browning before the coals of the log cabin. And when we take into consideration the voracious appetites engendered in those wilds, we shall see that the emigrant needed not to look with envy upon the luxuriantly spread tables of Paris or New York.

Upon the crystal banks of the Mulberry River, David, aided by his father-in-law, reared his log cabin. It is a remote and uncultivated region even now. Then it was an almost unbroken wilderness, the axe of the settler having rarely disturbed its solitude.

A suitable spot for the cabin was selected, and a space of about fifteen feet by twenty feet was marked out and smoothed down for the floor. There was no cellar. Trees near by, of straight trunks, were felled and trimmed, and cut into logs of suitable length. These were piled one above another, in such a way as to enclose the space, and were held in their place by being notched at the corners. Rough boards were made for the roof by splitting straight-grained logs about four feet long.

The door was made by cutting or sawing the logs on one side of the hut, about three feet in width. This opening was secured by upright pieces of timber pinned to the end of the logs. A similar opening was left in the end for the chimney, which was built of logs outside of the hut. The back and jambs of the fireplace was of stone. A hole about two feet square constituted the window. Frequently the floor was the smooth, solid earth. A split slab supported by sticks driven into auger-holes, formed a table. A few three-legged stools supplied the place of chairs. Some wooden pins, driven into holes bored in the logs, supported shelves. A bedstead was framed by a network of poles in one corner.

Such was the home which David and his kind father reared in a few days. It will be perceived that it was but little in advance of the wigwam of the Indian. Still it afforded a comfortable shelter for men, women, and children who had no aspirations above a mere animal life; who thought only of warmth, food, and clothing; who had no conception of intellectual, moral, or religious cravings.

The kind-hearted father-in-law, who had accompanied his children on foot upon this long journey, that he might see them settled in their own home, now bade them adieu, and retraced the forest trails back to his own far-distant cabin. A man who could develop, unostentatiously, such generosity and such self-sacrifice, must have possessed some rare virtues. We regret our inability to record the name of one who thus commands our esteem and affection.

In this humble home, David Crockett and his family resided two years. He appears to have taken very little interest in the improvement of his homestead. It must be admitted that Crockett belonged to the class of what is called loafers. He was a sort of Rip Van Winkle. The forest and the mountain stream had great charms for him. He loved to wander in busy idleness all the day, with fishing-rod and rifle; and he would often return at night with a very ample supply of game. He would then lounge about his hut, tanning deerskins for moccasins and breeches, performing other little jobs, and entirely neglecting all endeavors to improve his farm, or to add to the appearance or comfort of the miserable shanty which he called his home.

He had an active mind, and a very singular command of the language of low, illiterate life, and especially of backwoodman's slang. Though not exactly a vain man, his self-confidence was imperturbable, and there was perhaps not an individual in the world to whom he looked up as in any sense his superior. In hunting, his skill became very remarkable, and few, even of the best marksmen, could throw the bullet with more unerring aim.

At the close of two years of this listless, solitary life, Crockett, without any assigned reason, probably influenced only by that vagrancy of spirit which had taken entire possession of the man, made another move. Abandoning his crumbling shanty and untilled fields, he directed his steps eastwardly through the forest, a distance of about forty miles, to what is now Franklin County. Here he reared another hut, on the banks of a little stream called Bear's Creek. This location was about ten miles below the present hamlet of Winchester.

An event now took place which changed the whole current of David Crockett's life, leading him from his lonely cabin and the peaceful scenes of a hunter's life to the field of battle, and to all the cruel and demoralizing influences of horrid war.

For many years there had been peace with the Indians in all that region. But unprincipled and vagabond white men, whom no law in the wilderness could restrain, were ever plundering them, insulting them, and wantonly shooting them down on the slightest provocation. The constituted authorities deplored this state of things, but could no more prevent it than the restraints of justice can prevent robberies and assassinations in London or New York.

The Indians were disposed to be friendly. There can be no question that, but for these unendurable outrages, inflicted upon them by vile and fiend-like men, many of whom had fled from the avenging arm of law, peace between the white man and the red man would have remained undisturbed. In the extreme southern region of Alabama, near the junction of the Alabama River with the almost equally majestic Tombeckbee River, there had been erected, several years before, for the protection of the emigrants, a fort called Mimms. It consisted of several strong log huts, surrounded by palisades which enclosed several acres. A strongly barred gate afforded entrance to the area within. Loop-holes were cut through the palisades, just sufficiently large to allow the barrel of a musket to be thrust through, and aim to be taken at any approaching foe.

The space within was sufficient to accommodate several families, who were thus united for mutual protection. Their horses and other cattle could be driven within the enclosure at night. In case of a general alarm, the pioneers, occupying huts scattered through the region for miles around, could assemble in the fort. Their corn-fields were outside, to cultivate which, even in times of war, they could resort in armed bands, setting a watch to give warning of any signs of danger.

The fort was in the middle of a small and fertile prairie. The forest-trees were cut down around, and every obstacle removed which could conceal the approach of a foe or protect him from the fire of the garrison. The long-continued peace had caused vigilance to slumber. A number of families resided in the fort, unapprehensive of danger.

One evening, a negro boy, who had been out into the forest at some distance from the fort in search of cattle, came back saying that he saw far in the distance quite a number of Indians, apparently armed warriors. As it was known that the Creek Indians had been greatly exasperated by recent outrages inflicted upon them, this intelligence created some anxiety. The gate was carefully closed. A guard was set through the night, and some slight preparations were made to repel an assault, should one be made.

Thus several days were passed, and there was no attack, and no signs of Indians being near. The general impression was that the timid negro boy was the victim of his own fears. Many jokes were perpetrated at his expense. With wonted carelessness, all precautions were forgotten, and the men sallied thoughtlessly forth to disperse through the fields in their labors.

But after several days, the boy was again sent out into the woods upon the same errand as before. He was a timid little fellow, and had a great dread of the Indian. Tremblingly and cautiously he threaded the paths of the forest for several miles, keeping a vigilant lookout for any signs of the savage foe, when his eye fell upon a sight which appalled him. At but a short distance, as he stood concealed by the thickets through which he was moving, he saw several hundred Indian warriors, plumed and painted, and armed to the teeth. They had probably just broken up from a council, and were moving about among the trees. His fears magnified their numbers to thousands. Terror-stricken, he turned for the fort, and with almost the fleetness of a deer entered the gate with his tidings. Even his black face was pallid with fright, as he breathlessly told his story. "The Indians," said he, "were as many, and as close together as the trees. There were thousands." The alarm was sounded in the garrison. All the outsiders were called in. The sun shone serenely, the gentle breeze swept over the fertile prairie; not a sight was to be seen but what was peaceful, not a sound came from the forest but the songs of birds.

It was generally believed that the silly, cowardly boy had given a false alarm. They cross-examined him. He was so frightened that he could not tell a straight story. The men, indignant at being thus a second time duped, as they supposed, actually tied the poor boy to the whipping-post and commenced whipping him. But a few lashes had left their bloody marks upon his back when the uplifted arm of the executioner was arrested.The awful Indian war-whoop, the precursor of blood and flame and torture, which even the boldest heart could seldom hear without terror, burst as it were simultaneously from a hundred warrior lips. The wary savages had provided themselves with sharpened sticks. Rending the skies with their yells, they rushed forward from the gloom of the woods upon the totally unprovided garrison, and very speedily plugged up the loop-holes, so that not a musket could be discharged through them.

Then with their hatchets they commenced cutting down the palisades. The bewilderment and consternation within was indescribable. A few of the assailants hewing at the barricades were shot down, but others instantly took their places. Soon a breach was cut through, and the howling warriors like maddened demons rushed in. There was no mercy shown. The gleaming tomahawk, wielded by hundreds of brawny arms, expeditiously did its work. Men, women, and children were indiscriminately cut down and scalped. It was an awful scene of butchery. Scarcely an individual escaped. One athletic boy, after having seen his father, mother, four sisters, and four brothers tomahawked and scalped, pursued by the savages, with frantic energy succeeded in leaping the palisades. Several Indians gave chase. He rushed for the woods. They hotly pursued. He reached a sluggish stream, upon the shore of which, half-imbedded in sand and water, there was a mouldering log, which he chanced to know was hollow beneath. He had but just time to slip into this retreat, when the baffled Indians came up. They actually walked over the log in their unavailing search for him. Here he remained until night, when he stole from his hiding-place, and in safety reached Fort Montgomery, which was distant about two miles from Fort Mimms.

CHAPTER IV.

The Soldier Life.

War with the Creeks.—Patriotism of Crockett.—Remonstrances of his Wife.—Enlistment.—The Rendezvous.—Adventure of the Scouts.—Friendlier Indians.—A March through the Forest.—Picturesque Scene.—The Midnight Alarm.—March by Moon-light.—Chagrin of Crockett.—Advance into Alabama.— War's Desolations.—Indian Stoicism.—Anecdotes of Andrew Jackson.—Battles, Carnage, and Woe.

The awful massacre at Fort Mimms, by the Creek Indians, summoned, as with a trumpet peal, the whole region to war. David Crockett had listened eagerly to stories of Indian warfare in former years, and as he listened to the tales of midnight conflagration and slaughter, his naturally peaceful spirit had no yearnings for the renewal of such sanguinary scenes. Crockett was not a quarrelsome man. He was not fond of brawls and fighting. Nothing in his life had thus far occurred to test his courage. Though there was great excitement to be found in hunting, there was but little if any danger. The deer and all smaller game were harmless. And even the grizzly bear had but few terrors for a marksman who, with unerring aim, could strike him with the deadly bullet at the distance of many rods.

But the massacre at Fort Mimms roused a new spirit in David Crockett. He perceived at once, that unless the savages were speedily quelled, they would ravage the whole region; and that his family as well as that of every other pioneer must inevitably perish. It was manifest to him that every man was bound immediately to take arms for the general defence. In a few days a summons was issued for every able-bodied man in all that region to repair to Winchester, which, as we have said, was a small cluster of houses about ten miles from Crockett's cabin.

When he informed his wife of his intention, her womanly heart was appalled at the thought of being left alone and unprotected in the vast wilderness. She was at a distance of hundreds of miles from all her connections. She had no neighbors near. Her children were too young to be of any service to her. If the dreadful Indians should attack them, she had no one to look to for protection. If anything should happen to him in battle so that he should not return, they must all perish of starvation. These obvious considerations she urged with many tears.

"It was mighty hard," writes Crockett, "to go against such arguments as these. But my countrymen had been murdered, and I knew that the next thing would be that the Indians would be scalping the women and children all about there, if we didn't put a stop to it. I reasoned the case with her as well as I could, and told her that if every man would wait till his wife got willing for him to go to war, there would be no fighting done until we all should be killed in our own houses; that as I was as able to go as any man in the world, and that I believed it was a duty I owed to my country. Whether she was satisfied with this reasoning or not she did not tell me, but seeing I was bent on it, all she did was to cry a little, and turn about to her work."

David Crockett hastened to Winchester. There was a large gathering there from all the hamlets and cabins for many miles around. The excitement was intense. The nation of Creek Indians was a very powerful one, and in intelligence and military skill far in advance of most of the Indian tribes. Mr. Crockett was one of the first to volunteer to form a company to serve for sixty days, under Captain Jones, who subsequently was a member of Congress from Tennessee. In a week the whole company was organized, and commenced its march to join others for the invasion of the Creek country. It was thought that by carrying the war directly into the Indian towns, their warriors might be detained at home to protect their wives and children, and could thus be prevented from carrying desolation into the settlements of the whites.

In the mean time David Crockett revisited his humble home, where his good but anxious and afflicted wife fitted him out as well as she could for the campaign. David was not a man of sentiment and was never disposed to contemplate the possibility of failure in any of his plans. With a light heart he bade adieu to his wife and his children, and mounting his horse, set out for his two months' absence to hunt up and shoot the Indians. He took only the amount of clothing he wore, as he wished to be entirely unencumbered when he should meet the sinewy and athletic foe on the battle-field.

This company, of about one hundred mounted men, commenced its march for an appointed rendezvous called Beatty's Spring. Here they encamped for several days, waiting the arrival of other companies from distant quarters. Ere long there was collected quite an imposing army of thirteen hundred men, all on horseback, and all hardy backwoodsmen, armed with the deadly rifle. A more determined set of men was perhaps never assembled. While they were thus gathering from far and near, and making all preparations to burst upon the foe in one of war's most terrific tempests, Major Gibson came, and wanted a few men, of tried sagacity and hardihood, to accompany him on a reconnoitring tour across the Tennessee River, down through the wilderness, into the country of the Creek Indians. It was a very hazardous enterprise. The region swarmed with savages. They were very vigilant. They were greatly and justly exasperated. If the reconnoitring party were captured, the certain doom of its members would be death by the most dreadful tortures.

Captain Jones pointed out David Crockett as one of the most suitable men for this enterprise. Crockett unhesitatingly consented to go, and, by permission, chose a companion by the name of George Russel, a young man whose courage and sagacity were far in advance of his years.

"I called him up," writes Crockett, "but Major Gibson said he thought he hadn't beard enough to please him; he wanted men, not boys. I must confess I was a little nettled at this; for I know'd George Russel, and I know'd there was no mistake in him; and I didn't think that courage ought to be measured by the beard, for fear a goat would have the preference over a man. I told the Major he was on the wrong scent; that Russel could go as far as he could, and I must have him along. He saw I was a little wrathy, and said I had the best chance of knowing, and agreed that it should be as I wanted it."

The heroic little band, thirteen in number, well armed and well mounted, set out early in the morning on their perilous enterprise. They crossed the Tennessee River, and directing their steps south, through a region almost entirely uninhabited by white men, journeyed cautiously along, keeping themselves concealed as much as possible in the fastnesses of the forest. They crossed the river, at what was called Ditto's Landing, and advancing about seven miles beyond, found a very secluded spot, one of nature's hiding-places, where they took up their encampment for the night.

Here they chanced to come across a man by the name of John Haynes, who for several years had been a trader among the Indians. He was thoroughly acquainted with the whole region about to be traversed, and consented to act as a guide. For the next day's march, instructed by their guide, the party divided into two bands, following along two obscure trails, which came together again after winding through the wilderness a distance of about twenty miles. Major Gibson led a party of seven, and David Crockett the other party of six.

The Cherokee Indians, a neighboring nation, powerful and warlike, were not in alliance with the Creeks in this war. They were, at that time, in general friendly to the whites. Many of their warriors were even induced to join the whites and march under their banners. On each of the trails that day to be passed over, there was the lodge of a Cherokee Indian. Both of them were friendly. Each of the parties was to collect all the information possible from these Indians, and then to meet where the trails came together again.

When Crockett arrived at the wigwam of the Indian he met with a very friendly reception. He also found there a half-breed Cherokee, by the name of Jack Thompson. This man, of savage birth and training, but with the white man's blood in his veins, offered to join the reconnoitring party. He however was not ready just then to set out, but in a few hours would follow and overtake the band at its night's encampment.

It was not safe to encamp directly upon the trail, lest some Creek war-party should be passing along, and should discover them. It was necessary to seek concealment where even the prying eyes of the savage would with difficulty search them out. The cry of the shriek-owl is exceedingly shrill, and can be heard at a great distance. A particular spot on the trail was designated, near which Crockett would seek his secret encampment. When Jack Thompson reached that spot, he was to imitate the cry of the owl. Crockett would respond, and thus guide the Indian to his retreat. As night approached, Crockett, with his party, found a deep and dark ravine, where, encircled by almost impenetrable thickets, he hid his men and the horses. No campfires could be built. It was ten o'clock in the night when, in the distance, he heard the signal shriek of the owl, a cry too common to arrest the attention of any Indian bands who might be in the vicinity. Jack, guided by a responsive cry, soon found the place of concealment, and there the party remained through the night.

The next morning after breakfast they set out to join Major Gibson and his band; but, in some way, they had lost track of him, and he could not be found. Some were alarmed, as, in so small a band, they were entering the domains of their powerful foe. Crockett taunted them with their fears; and indeed fear kept them together. The party consisted now of seven, including the Indian guide. Most of them determined to press on. The two or three who were in favor of going back dared not separate from the rest.

At the distance of about twenty miles, Jack Thompson told them that there was a village of friendly Cherokee Indians. As he was leading them through obscure trails toward that place, they came across the hut of a white man, by the name of Radcliff, who had married a Creek woman, and had been adopted into their tribe. The man had two nearly grown-up boys, stout, burly fellows, half-breeds by birth, and more than half savage in character and training. The old man's cabin was slightly above the usual style of Indian wigwams. It was in a region of utter solitude.

There Radcliff had taught his barbarian boys some of the arts of industry. He had cleared quite a space of ground around his hut, and was raising a supply of corn and potatoes ample for his family wants. With these vegetable productions, and with the game which the rifle supplied them, they lived in abundance, and free from most of those cares which agitate a higher civilization.

But the old man was quite agitated in receiving and entertaining his unwelcome guests. He was an adopted Creek, and ought to be in sympathy with his nation. He was bound to regard the white men as his enemies, to withhold from them all important information, and to deliver them up to the Creeks if possible. Should he be suspected of sympathy with the white men, the tomahawk of the savage would soon cleave his brain. He entreated Crockett immediately to leave him.

"Only an hour ago," said he, "there were ten Creek warriors here, all on horseback, and painted and armed. Should they come back and discover you here, they would certainly kill you all, and put me and my family to death also."

But Crockett, instead of being alarmed by this intelligence, was only animated by it. He assured Radcliff that he could desire no better luck than to meet a dozen Indians on the war-path. He considered his party quite strong enough to meet, at any time, three times their number. Evening was approaching, and the full moon, in cloudless brilliance, was rising over the forest, flooding the whole landscape with extraordinary splendor. After feeding their horses abundantly and feasting themselves from the fat larder of their host, they saddled their steeds and resumed their journey by moonlight.

The trail still led through the silent forest. It was, as usual, very narrow, so that the horses walked along in single file. As there was danger of falling into an ambush, not a word was spoken, and, as noiselessly as possible, they moved onward, every eye on the eager lookout. They had been thus riding along when Crockett, in the advance, heard the noise of some animals or persons apparently approaching. At a given signal, instantly the whole party stopped. Every man grasped his rifle, ready in case of need, to leap from his horse, and select the largest tree near him as a rampart for the battle.

All solicitude was, however, soon dispelled by seeing simply two persons advancing along the trail on Indian ponies. They proved to be two negro slaves who had been captured by the Indians, and who, having escaped, were endeavoring to make their way back to their former master. They were brothers, and being both very stout men, and able to speak the Indian as well as the English language, were esteemed quite a powerful reinforcement to the Crockett party.

They rode quietly along another hour and a half, when toward midnight they saw in the distance the gleam of camp-fires, and heard shouts of merriment and revelry. They knew that these must come from the camp of the friendly Cherokees, to which their Indian guide, Jack Thompson, was leading them. Soon a spectacle of wonderful picturesque beauty was opened to their view.

Upon the banks of a beautiful mountain stream there was a wide plateau, carpeted with the renowned blue-grass, as verdant and soft as could be found in any gentleman's park. There was no underbrush. The trees were two or three yards from each other, composing a luxuriant overhanging canopy of green leaves, more beautiful than art could possibly create. Beneath this charming grove, and illumined by the moonshine which, in golden tracery, pierced the foliage, there were six or eight Indian lodges scattered about.

An immense bonfire was crackling and blazing, throwing its rays far and wide through the forest. Moving around, in various engagements and sports, were about forty men, women, and children, in the fringed, plumed, and brilliantly colored attire of which the Indians were so fond. Quite a number of them, with bows and arrows, were shooting at a mark, which was made perfectly distinct by the blaze of pitch-pine knots, a light which no flame of candle or gas could outvie. It was a scene of sublimity and beauty, of peace and loveliness, which no artist could adequately transfer to canvas.

34

The Cherokees received very cordially the newcomers, took care of their horses, and introduced them to their sports. Many of the Indians had guns, but powder and bullets were too precious to be expended in mere amusements. Indeed, the Indians were so careful of their ammunition, that they rarely put more than half as much powder into a charge as a white man used. They endeavored to make up for the deficiency by creeping nearer to their prey.

Crockett and his men joined these barbarians, merry in their pleasant sports. Such are the joys of peace, so different from the miseries of demoniac war. At length the festivities were closed, and all began to prepare to retire to sleep.

The Cherokees were neutral in the war between the whites and the Creek Indians. It was very important for them to maintain this neutrality strictly, that they might not draw down upon themselves the vengeance of either party. Some of the Cherokees now began to feel anxious lest a war-party of the Creeks should come along and find them entertaining a war-party of whites, who were entering their country as spies. They therefore held an interview with one of the negroes, and requested him to inform Mr. Crockett that should a war-party come and find his men in the Cherokee village, not only would they put all the white men to death, but there would be also the indiscriminate massacre of all the men, women, and children in the Cherokee lodges.

Crockett, wrapped in his blanket, was half asleep when this message was brought to him. Raising his head, he said to the negro, in terms rather savoring of the spirit of the braggadocio than that of a high-minded and sympathetic man:

"Tell the Cherokees that I will keep a sharp lookout, and if a single Creek comes near the camp to-night, I will carry the skin of his head home to make me a moccasin."

When this answer was reported to the Indians they laughed aloud and dispersed. It was not at all improbable that there might be an alarm before morning. The horses were therefore, after being well fed, tied up with their saddles upon them, that they might be instantly mounted in case of emergence. They all slept, also, with their arms in their hands.

Just as Crockett was again falling into a doze, a very shrill Indian yell was heard in the forest, the yell of alarm. Every man, white and red, was instantly upon his feet. An Indian runner soon made his appearance, with the tidings that more than a thousand Creek warriors had, that day, crossed the Coosa River, but a few leagues south of them, at what was called the Ten Islands, and were on the march to attack an American force, which, under General Jackson, was assembling on another portion of the Coosa River.

The friendly Indians were so greatly alarmed that they immediately fled. Crockett felt bound to carry back this intelligence as speedily as possible to the headquarters from which he had come. He had traversed a distance of about sixty miles in a southerly direction. They returned, by the same route over which they had passed. But they found that a general alarm had pervaded the country, Radcliff and his family, abandoning everything, had fled, they knew not where. When they reached the Cherokee town of which we have before spoken, not a single Indian was to be seen. Their fires were still burning, which showed the precipitancy with which they had taken flight. This rather alarmed the party of the whites. They feared that the Indian warriors were assembling from all quarters, at some secret rendezvous, and would soon fall upon them in overwhelming numbers. They therefore did not venture to replenish the Indian fires and lie down by the warmth of them, but pushed rapidly on their way.

It chanced to be a serene, moonlight night. The trail through the forest, which the Indian's foot for countless generations had trodden smooth, illumined by the soft rays of the moon, was exceedingly beautiful. They travelled in single file, every nerve at its extreme tension in anticipation of falling into some ambush. Before morning they had accomplished about thirty miles. In the grey dawn they again reached Mr. Brown's. Here they found grazing for their horses, and corn and game for them selves.

Horses and riders were equally fatigued. The weary adventurers were in no mood for talking. After dozing for an hour or two, they again set out, and about noon reached the general rendezvous, from which they had departed but a few days before. Here Crockett was not a little disappointed in the reception he encountered. He was a young, raw backwoodsman, nearly on a level with the ordinary savage. He was exceedingly illiterate, and ignorant. And yet he had the most amazing self-confidence, with not a particle of reverence for any man, whatever his rank or culture. He thought no one his superior. Colonel Coffee paid very little respect to his vainglorious report. In the following characteristic strain Crockett comments on the event:

"He didn't seem to mind my report a bit. This raised my dander higher than ever. But I know'd that I had to be on my best behavior, and so I kept it all to myself; though I was so mad that I was burning inside like a tar-kiln, and I wonder that the smoke had not been pouring out of me at all points. The next day, Major Gibson got in. He brought a worse tale than I had, though he stated the same facts as far as I went. This seemed to put our Colonel all in a fidget; and it convinced me clearly of one of the hateful ways of the world. When I made my report I was not believed, because I was no officer. I was no great man, but just a poor soldier. But when the same thing was reported by Major Gibson, why then it was all true as preaching, and the Colonel believed it every word."

There was indeed cause for alarm. Many of the Indian chiefs displayed military ability of a very high order. Our officers were frequently outgeneralled by their savage antagonists. This was so signally the case that the Indians frequently amused themselves in laughing to scorn the folly of the white men. Every able-bodied man was called to work in throwing up breastworks. A line of ramparts was speedily constructed, nearly a quarter of a mile in circuit. An express was sent to Fayetteville, where General Jackson was assembling an army, to summon him to the rescue. With characteristic energy he rushed forward, by forced marches day and night, until his troops stood, with blistered feet, behind the newly erected ramparts.

They felt now safe from attack by the Indians. An expedition of eight hundred volunteers, of which Crockett was one, was fitted out to recross the Tennessee River, and marching by the way of Huntsville, to attack the Indians from an unexpected quarter. This movement involved a double crossing of the Tennessee. They pressed rapidly along the northern bank of this majestic stream, about forty or fifty miles, due west, until they came to a point where the stream expands into a width of nearly two miles. This place was called Muscle Shoals. The river could here be forded, though the bottom was exceedingly rough. The men were all mounted. Several horses got their feet so entangled in the crevices of the rocks that they could not be disengaged, and they perished there. The men, thus dismounted, were compelled to perform the rest of the campaign on foot.

A hundred miles south of this point, in the State of Alabama, the Indians had a large village, called Black Warrior. The lodges of the Indians were spread over the ground where the city of Tuscaloosa now stands. The wary Indians kept their scouts out in all directions. The runners conveyed to the warriors prompt warning of the approach of their foes. These Indians were quite in advance of the northern tribes. Their lodges were full as comfortable as the log huts of the pioneers, and in their interior arrangements more tasteful. The buildings were quite numerous. Upon many of them much labor had been expended. Luxuriant corn-fields spread widely around, and in well-cultivated gardens they raised beans and other vegetables in considerable abundance.

The hungry army found a good supply of dried beans for themselves, and carefully housed corn for their horses. They feasted themselves, loaded their pack-horses with corn and beans, applied the torch to every lodge, laying the whole town in ashes, and then commenced their backward march. Fresh Indian tracks indicated that many of them had remained until the last moment of safety.

The next day the army marched back about fifteen miles to the spot where it had held its last encampment. Eight hundred men, on a campaign, consume a vast amount of food. Their meat was all devoured. They had now only corn and beans. The soldiers were living mostly on parched corn. Crockett went to Colonel Coffee, then in command, and stating, very truthfully, that he was an experienced hunter, asked permission to draw aside from the ranks, and hunt as they marched along. The Colonel gave his consent, but warned him to be watchful in the extreme, lest he should fall into an Indian ambush.

Crockett was brave, but not reckless. He plunged into the forest, with vigilant gaze piercing the solitary space in all directions. He was alone, on horseback. He had not gone far when he found a deer just killed by a noiseless arrow. The animal was but partially skinned, and still warm and smoking. The deer had certainly been killed by an Indian; and it was equally certain that the savage, seeing his approach, had fled. The first thought of Crockett was one of alarm. The Indian might be hidden behind some one of the gigantic trees, and the next moment a bullet, from the Indian's rifle, might pierce his heart.

But a second thought reassured him. The deer had been killed by an arrow. Had the Indian been armed with a rifle, nothing would have been easier, as he saw the approach of Crockett in the distance than for him to have concealed himself, and then to have taken such deliberate aim at his victim as to be sure of his death. Mounting the horse which Crockett rode, the savage might have disappeared in the wilderness beyond all possibility of pursuit. But this adventure taught Crockett that he might not enjoy such good luck the next time. Another Indian might be armed with a rifle, and Crockett, self-confident as he was, could not pretend to be wiser in woodcraft than were the savages.

Crockett dismounted, took up the body of the deer, laid it upon the mane of his horse, in front of the saddle, and remounting, with increasing vigilance made his way, as rapidly as he could, to the trail along which the army was advancing. He confesses to some qualms of conscience as to the right of one hunter thus to steal away the game killed by another.

It was late in the afternoon when he reached the rear. He pressed along to overtake his own company. The soldiers looked wistfully at the venison. They offered him almost any price for it. Crockett was by nature a generous man. There was not a mean hair in his head. This generosity was one of the virtues which gave him so many friends. Rather boastfully, and yet it must be admitted truthfully, he writes, in reference to this adventure:

"I could have sold it for almost any price I would have asked. But this wasn't my rule, neither in peace nor war. Whenever I had anything and saw a fellow-being suffering, I was more anxious to relieve him than to benefit myself. And this is one of the true secrets of my being a poor man to the present day. But it is my way. And while it has often left me with an empty purse, yet it has never left my heart empty of consolations which money couldn't buy; the consolation of having sometimes fed the hungry and covered the naked. I gave all my deer away except a small part, which I kept for myself, and just sufficient to make a good supper for my mess."

The next day, in their march, they came upon a drove of swine, which belonged to a Cherokee farmer. The whites were as little disposed as were the Indians, in this war, to pay any respect to private property. Hundreds of rifles were aimed at the poor pigs, and their squealing indicated that they had a very hard time of it. The army, in its encampment that night, feasted very joyously upon fresh pork. This thrifty Cherokee was also the possessor of a milch cow. The animal was speedily slaughtered and devoured.

They soon came upon another detachment of the army, and uniting, marched to Ten Islands, on the Coosa River, where they established a fort, which they called Fort Strother, as a depot for provisions and ammunition. They were here not far from the centre of the country inhabited by the hostile Indians. This fort stood on the left bank of the river, in what is now St. Clair County, Alabama. It was a region but little explored, and the whites had but little acquaintance with the nature of the country around them, or with the places occupied by the Indians. Some scouts, from the friendly Creeks, brought the intelligence that, at the distance of about eight miles from the fort, there was an Indian town, where a large party of warriors was assembled in preparation for some secret expedition. A large and select band was immediately dispatched, on horseback, to attack them by surprise. Two friendly Creeks led them with Indian sagacity through circuitous trails. Stealthily they approached the town, and dividing their force, marched on each side so as to encircle it completely. Aided by their Creek guides, this important movement was accomplished without the warriors discovering their approach. The number of the whites was so great that they were enabled to surround the town with so continuous a line that escape was impossible for any enclosed within that fearful barrier of loaded rifles wielded by unerring marksmen. Closer and more compactly the fatal line was drawn. These movements were accomplished in the dim morning twilight.

All being ready, Captain Hammond, and a few rangers, were sent forward to show themselves, and to bring on the fight. The moment the warriors caught sight of them, one general war-whoop rose from every throat. Grasping their rifles, they rushed headlong upon the rangers, who retired before them. They soon reached one portion of the compact line, and were received with a terrible fire, which struck many of them down in instant death. The troops then closed rapidly upon the doomed Indians, and from the north, the south, the east, and the west, they were assailed by a deadly storm of bullets.

Almost immediately the Indians saw that they were lost. There was no possibility of escape. This was alike manifest to every one, to warrior, squaw, and pappoose. All surrendered themselves to despair. The warriors threw down their weapons, in sign of surrender. Some rushed into the lodges. Some rushed toward the soldiers, stretching out their unarmed hands in supplication for life. The women in particular, panic-stricken, ran to the soldiers, clasped them about the knees, and looked up into their faces with piteous supplications for life. Crockett writes:

"I saw seven squaws have hold of one man. So I hollered out the Scriptures was fulfilling; that there was seven women holding to one man's coat-tail. But I believe it was a hunting-shirt all the time. We took them all prisoners that came out to us in this way."

Forty-six warriors, by count, threw down their arms in token of surrender, and ran into one of the large houses. A band of soldiers pursued them, with the apparent intent of shooting them down. It was considered rare sport to shoot an Indian. A woman came to the door, bow and arrow in hand. Fixing the arrow upon the string, she drew the bow with all the strength of her muscular arm, and let the arrow fly into the midst of the approaching foe. It nearly passed through the body of Lieutenant Moore, killing him instantly. The woman made no attempt to evade the penalty which she knew weald follow this act. In an instant twenty bullets pierced her body, and she fell dead at the door of the house.

The infuriate soldiers rushed in and shot the defenceless warriors mercilessly, until every one was fatally wounded or dead. They then set the house on fire and burned it up, with the forty-six warriors in it. It mattered not to them whether the flames consumed the flesh of the living or of the dead.

There was something very remarkable in the stoicism which the Indians ever manifested. There was a bright-looking little Indian boy, not more than twelve years of age, whose arm was shattered by one bullet and his thigh-bone by another. Thus terribly wounded, the poor child crept from the flames of the burning house. There was no pity in that awful hour to come to his relief. The heat was so intense that his almost naked body could be seen blistering and frying by the fire. The heroic boy, striving in vain to crawl along, was literally roasted alive; and yet he did not utter an audible groan.

The slaughter was awful. But five of the Americans were killed. One hundred and eighty-six of the Indians were either killed or taken prisoners. The party returned with their captives the same day to Fort Strother. The army had so far consumed its food that it was placed on half rations. The next day a party was sent back to the smouldering town to see if any food could be found. Even these hardy pioneers were shocked at the awful spectacle which was presented. The whole place was in ruins. The half-burned bodies of the dead, in awful mutilation, were scattered around. Demoniac war had performed one of its most fiend-like deeds.

On this bloody field an Indian babe was found clinging to the bosom of its dead mother. Jackson urged some of the Indian women who were captives to give it nourishment. They replied:

"All the child's friends are killed. There is no one to care for the helpless babe. It is much better that it should die."

Jackson took the child under his own care, ordered it to be conveyed to his tent, nursed it with sugar and water, took it eventually with him to the Hermitage, and brought it up as his son. He gave the boy the name of Lincoyer. He grew up a finely formed young man, and died of consumption at the age of seventeen.

Jackson was a very stern man. The appeals of pity could seldom move his heart. Still there were traits of heroism which marked his character. On the return march, a half-starved soldier came to Jackson with a piteous story of his famished condition. Jackson drew from his pocket a handful of acorns, and presenting a portion to the man, said:

"This is all the fare I have. I will share it with you."

Beneath one of the houses was found quite a large cellar, well stored with potatoes. These were eagerly seized. All the other stores of the Indians the insatiable flames had consumed. Starvation now began to threaten the army. The sparsely settled country afforded no scope for forage. There were no herds of cattle, no well-replenished magazines near at hand. Neither was there game enough in the spreading wilderness to supply so many hungry mouths. The troops were compelled to eat even the very hides of the cattle whom they had driven before them, and who were now all slaughtered.

While in this forlorn condition, awaiting the arrival of food, and keeping very vigilant guard against surprise, one night an Indian, cautiously approaching from the forest, shouted out that he wished to see General Jackson, for he had important information to communicate. He was conducted to the General's tent. The soldiers knew not the news which he brought. But immediately the beat of drums summoned all to arms. In less than an hour a strong party of cavalry and infantry, in the darkness, were on the march. General Andrew Jackson was one of the most energetic of men. The troops crossed the Coosa River to the eastern shore, and as rapidly as possible pressed forward in a southerly direction toward Talladega, which was distant about thirty miles. Gradually the rumor spread through the ranks that General Jackson had received the following intelligence: At Talladega there was a pretty strong fort, occupied by friendly Indians. They had resolutely refused to take part in the war against the Americans. Eleven hundred hostile warriors, of the Creek nation, marched upon the fort, encamped before it, and sent word to the friendly Indians within the palisades, that if they did not come out and join them in an expedition against the whites, they would utterly demolish the fort and take all their provisions and ammunition. The Creeks were in sufficient strength to accomplish their threat.

The friendly Indians asked for three days to consider the proposition. They stated that if, at the end of this time, they did not come out to join them in an expedition against the whites, they would surrender the fort. The request was granted. Instantly an Indian runner was dispatched to inform General Jackson, at Fort Strother, of their danger and to entreat him to come to their aid. Hence the sudden movement.

The Creek warriors had their scouts out, carefully watching, and were speedily apprised of the approach of General Jackson's band. Immediately they sent word into the fort, to the friendly Indians there, that the American soldiers were coming, with many fine horses, and richly stored with guns, blankets, powder, bullets, and almost everything else desirable. They promised that if the Indians would come out from the fort, and help them attack and conquer the whites, they would divide the rich plunder with them. They assured them that, by thus uniting, they could easily gain the victory over the whites, who were the deadly foes of their whole race. The appeal was not responded to.

A little south of the fort there was a stream, which, in its circuitous course, partially encircled it. The bank was high, leaving a slight level space or meadow between it and the stream. Here the hostile Indians were encamped, and concealed from any approaches from the north. It was at midnight, on the 7th of

December, that Jackson set out on this expedition. He had with him, for the occasion, a very strong force, consisting of twelve hundred infantry and eight hundred cavalry.

When they reached the fort, the army divided, passing on each side, and again uniting beyond, as they approached the concealed encampment of the enemy. While passing the fort, the friendly Indians clambered the palisades, and shouted out joyously to the soldiers "How-de-do, brother—how-de-do, brother?"

The lines, meeting beyond the fort, formed for battle. No foe was visible. Nearly a thousand warriors, some armed with arrows, but many with rifles, were hidden, but a few rods before them, beneath the curving bank, which was fringed with bushes. Major Russel, with a small party, was sent cautiously forward to feel for the enemy, and to bring on the battle. He was moving directly into the curve, where a concentric fire would soon cut down every one of his men.

The Indians in the fort perceived his danger, and shouted warning to him. He did not understand their language. They made the most earnest gestures. He did not comprehend their meaning. Two Indians then leaped from the fort, and running toward him, seized his horse by the bridle. They made him understand that more than a thousand warriors, with rifle in hand and arrows on the string, were hidden, at but a short distance before him, ready to assail him with a deadly fire. The account which Crockett gives of the battle, though neither very graphic nor classic, is worthy of insertion here, as illustrative of the intellectual and moral traits of that singular man.

"This brought them to a halt; and about this moment the Indians fired upon them, and came rushing forth like a cloud of Egyptian locusts, and screaming like all the young devils had been turned loose with the old devil of all at their head. Russel's company quit their arses and took into the fort. Their horses ran up to our line, which was then in view. The warriors then came yelling on, meeting us, and continued till they were within shot of us, when we fired and killed a considerable number of them. They broke like a gang of steers, and ran across to the other line.

"And so we kept them running, from one line to the other, constantly under a heavy fire, till we had killed upwards of four hundred of them. They fought with guns and also with bow and arrows. But at length they made their escape through a part of our line, which was made up of drafted militia, which broke ranks, and they passed. We lost fifteen of our men, as brave fellows as ever lived or died. We buried them all in one grave, and started back to our fort. But before we got there, two more of our men died of wounds they had received, making our total loss seventeen good fellows in that battle."

CHAPTER V.

Indian Warfare.

The Army at Fort Strother.—Crockett's Regiment.—Crockett at Home.—His Reenlistment.—Jackson Surprised.—Military Ability of the Indians.—Humiliation of the Creeks.—March to Florida.—Affairs at Pensacola.—Capture of the City.—Characteristics of Crockett.—The Weary March,—Inglorious Expedition.—Murder of Two Indians.—Adventures at the Island.—The Continued March.—Severe Sufferings.—Charge upon the Uninhabited Village.

The army, upon its return to Fort Strother, found itself still in a starving condition. Though the expedition had been eminently successful in the destruction of Indian warriors, it had consumed their provisions, without affording them any additional supply. The weather had become intensely cold. The clothing of the soldiers, from hard usage, had become nearly worn out. The horses were also emaciate and feeble. There was danger that many of the soldiers must perish from destitution and hunger.

The regiment to which Crockett belonged had enlisted for sixty days. Their time had long since expired. The officers proposed to Jackson that they and their soldiers might be permitted to return to their homes, promising that they would immediately re-enlist after having obtained fresh horses and fresh clothing. Andrew Jackson was by nature one of the most unyielding of men. His will was law, and must be obeyed, right or wrong. He was at that time one of the most profane of men. He swore by all that was sacred that they should not go; that the departure of so many of the men would endanger the possession of the fort and the lives of the remaining soldiers. There were many of the soldiers in the same condition, whose term of service had expired. They felt that they were free and enlightened Americans, and resented the idea of being thus enslaved and driven, like cattle, at the will of a single man. Mutinous feelings were excited. The camp was filled with clamor. The soldiers generally were in sympathy with those who demanded their discharge, having faithfully served out the term of their enlistment. Others felt that their own turn might come when they too might be thus enslaved.

There was a bridge which it was necessary for the soldiers to cross on the homeward route. The inflexible General, supposing that the regulars would be obedient to military discipline, and that it would be for their interest to retain in the camp those whose departure would endanger all their lives placed them upon the bridge, with cannon loaded to the muzzle with grape-shot. They were ordered mercilessly to shoot down any who should attempt to cross without his permission. In Crockett's ludicrous account of this adventure, he writes:

"The General refused to let us go. We were, however, determined to go. With this, the General issued his orders against it. We began to fix for a start. The General went and placed his cannon on a bridge we had to cross, and ordered out his regulars and drafted men to prevent our crossing. But when the militia started to guard the bridge, they would holler back to us to bring their knapsacks along when we came; for they wanted to go as bad as we did. We got ready, and moved on till we came near the bridge, where the General's men were all strung along on both sides. But we all had our flints ready picked and our guns ready primed, that, if we were fired on, we might fight our way through, or all die together.

"When we came still nearer the bridge we heard the guards cocking their guns, and we did the same. But we marched boldly on, and not a gun was fired, nor a life lost. When we had passed, no further attempt

43

was made to stop us. We went on, and near Huntsville we met a reinforcement who were going on to join the army. It consisted of a regiment of sixty-day volunteers. We got home pretty safely, and in a short time we had procured fresh horses, and a supply of clothing better suited for the season."

The officers and soldiers ere long rendezvoused again at Fort Deposit. Personally interested as every one was in subduing the Creeks, whose hostility menaced every hamlet with flames and the inmates of those hamlets with massacre, still the officers were so annoyed by the arrogance of General Jackson that they were exceedingly unwilling to serve again under his command.

Just as they came together, a message came from General Jackson, demanding that, on their return, they should engage to serve for six months. He regarded enlistment merely for sixty days as absurd. With such soldiers, he justly argued that no comprehensive campaign could be entered upon. The officers held a meeting to decide upon this question. In the morning, at drum-beat, they informed the soldiers of the conclusion they had formed. Quite unanimously they decided that they would not go back on a six-months term of service, but that each soldier might do as he pleased. Crockett writes:

"I know'd if I went back home I wouldn't rest for I felt it my duty to be out. And when out, I was somehow or other always delighted to be in the thickest of the danger. A few of us, therefore, determined to push on and join the army. The number I do not recollect, but it was very small."

When Crockett reached Fort Strother he was placed in a company of scouts under Major Russel. Just before they reached the fort, General Jackson had set out on an expedition in a southeasterly direction, to what was called Horseshoe Bend, on the Tallapoosa River. The party of scouts soon overtook him and led the way. As they approached the spot through the silent trails which threaded the wide solitudes, they came upon many signs of Indians being around. The scouts gave the alarm, and the main body of the army came up. The troops under Jackson amounted to about one thousand men. It was the evening of January 23d, 1814.

The camp-fires were built, supper prepared, and sentinels being carefully stationed all around to prevent surprise, the soldiers, protected from the wintry wind only by the gigantic forest, wrapped themselves in their blankets and threw themselves down on the withered leaves for sleep. The Indians crept noiselessly along from tree to tree, each man searching for a sentinel, until about too hours before day, when they opened a well-aimed fire from the impenetrable darkness in which they stood. The sentinels retreated back to the encampment, and the whole army was roused.

The troops were encamped in the form of a hollow square, and thus were necessarily between the Indians and the light of their own camp-fires. Not a warrior was to be seen. The only guide the Americans had in shooting, was to notice the flash of the enemy's guns. They fired at the flash. But as every Indian stood behind a tree, it is not probable that many, if any, were harmed. The Indians were very wary not to expose themselves. They kept at a great distance, and were not very successful in their fire. Though they wounded quite a number, only four men were killed. With the dawn of the morning they all vanished.

General Jackson did not wish to leave the corpses of the slain to be dug up and scalped by the savages. He therefore erected a large funeral pyre, placed the bodies upon it, and they were soon consumed to ashes. Some litters were made of long and flexible poles, attached to two horses, one at each end, and upon these the wounded were conveyed over the rough and narrow way. The Indians, thus far, had manifestly been the victors They had inflicted serious injury upon the Americans; and there is no evidence that a single one of their warriors had received the slightest harm. This was the great object of Indian strategy. In the wars of civilization, a great general has ever been willing to sacrifice the lives of ten thousand of his own troops if, by so doing, he could kill twenty thousand of the enemy. But it was never so with the Indians. They prized the lives of their warriors too highly.

On their march the troops came to a wide creek, which it was necessary to cross. Here the Indians again prepared for battle. They concealed themselves so effectually as to elude all the vigilance of the scouts. When about half the troops had crossed the stream, the almost invisible Indians commenced their assault, opening a very rapid but scattering fire. Occasionally a warrior was seen darting from one point to another, to obtain better vantage-ground.

Major Russel was in command of a small rear-guard. His soldiers soon appeared running almost breathless to join the main body, pursued by a large number of Indians. The savages had chosen the very best moment for their attack. The artillery-men were in an open field surrounded by the forest. The Indians, from behind stumps, logs, and trees, took deliberate aim, and almost every bullet laid a soldier prostrate. Quite a panic ensued. Two of the colonels, abandoning their regiments, rushed across the creek to escape the deadly fire. There is no evidence that the Indians were superior in numbers to the Americans. But it cannot be denied that the Americans, though under the leadership of Andrew Jackson, were again outgeneralled. General Jackson lost, in this short conflict, in killed and wounded, nearly one hundred men. His disorganized troops at length effected the passage of the creek, beyond which the Indians did not pursue them. Crockett writes:

"I will not say exactly that the old General was whipped. But I think he would say himself that he was nearer whipped this time than any other; for I know that all the world couldn't make him acknowledge that he was pointedly whipped. I know I was mighty glad when it was over, and the savages quit us, for I began to think there was one behind every tree in the woods."

Crockett, having served out his term, returned home. But he was restless there. Having once experienced the excitements of the camp, his wild, untrained nature could not repose in the quietude of domestic life. The conflict between the United States and a small band of Indians was very unequal. The loss of a single warrior was to the Creeks irreparable. General Jackson was not a man to yield to difficulties. On the 27th of March, 1814, he drove twelve hundred Creek warriors into their fort at Tohopeka. They were then surrounded, so that escape was impossible, and the fort was set on fire. The carnage was awful. Almost every warrior perished by the bullet or in the flames. The military power of the tribe was at an end. The remnant, utterly dispirited, sued for peace.

Quite a number of the Creek warriors fled to Florida, and joined the hostile Indian tribes there. We were at this time involved in our second war with Great Britain. The Government of our mother country was doing everything in its power to rouse the savages against us. The armies in Canada rallied most of the Northern tribes beneath their banners. Florida, at that time, belonged to Spain. The Spanish Government was nominally neutral in the conflict between England and the United States. But the Spanish governor in Florida was in cordial sympathy with the British officers. He lent them all the aid and comfort in his power, carefully avoiding any positive violation of the laws of neutrality. He extended very liberal hospitality to the refugee Creek warriors, and in many ways facilitated their cooperation with the English.

A small British fleet entered the mouth of the Apalachicola River and landed three hundred soldiers. Here they engaged vigorously in constructing a fort, and in summoning all the surrounding Indian tribes to join them in the invasion of the Southern States. General Jackson, with a force of between one and two thousand men, was in Northern Alabama, but a few days' march north of the Florida line. He wrote to the Secretary of War, in substance, as follows:

"The hostile Creeks have taken refuge in Florida. They are there fed, clothed, and protected. The British have armed a large force with munitions of war, and are fortifying and stirring up the savages. If you will permit me to raise a few hundred militia, which can easily be done, I will unite them with such a force of regulars as can easily be collected, and will make a descent on Pensacola, and will reduce it. I promise you I will bring the war in the South to a speedy termination; and English influence with the savages, in this quarter, shall be forever destroyed."

The President was not prepared thus to provoke war with Spain, by the invasion of Florida. Andrew Jackson assumed the responsibility. The British had recently made an attack upon Mobile, and being repulsed, had retired with their squadron to the harbor of Pensacola. Jackson called for volunteers to march upon Pensacola. Crockett roused himself at the summons, like the war-horse who snuffs the battle from afar. "I wanted," he wrote, "a small taste of British fighting, and I supposed they would be there."

His wife again entered her tearful remonstrance. She pointed to her little children, in their lonely hut far away in the wilderness, remote from all neighborhood, and entreated the husband and the father not again to abandon them. Rather unfeelingly he writes, "The entreaties of my wife were thrown in the way of my going, but all in vain; for I always had a way of just going ahead at whatever I had a mind to."

Many who have perused this sketch thus far, may inquire, with some surprise, "What is it which has given this man such fame as is even national? He certainly does not develop a very attractive character; and there is but little of the romance of chivalry thrown around his exploits. The secret is probably to be found in the following considerations, the truth of which the continuation of this narrative will be continually unfolding."

Without education, without refinement, without wealth or social position, or any special claims to personal beauty, he was entirely self-possessed and at home under all circumstances. He never manifested the slightest embarrassment. The idea seemed never to have entered his mind that there could be any person superior to David Crockett, or any one so humble that Crockett was entitled to look down upon him with condescension. He was a genuine democrat. All were in his view equal. And this was not the result of thought, of any political or moral principle. It was a part of his nature, which belonged to him without any volition, like his stature or complexion. This is one of the rarest qualities to be found in any man. We do not here condemn it, or applaud it. We simply state the fact.

In the army he acquired boundless popularity from his fun-making qualities. In these days he was always merry. Bursts of laughter generally greeted Crockett's approach and followed his departure. He was blessed with a memory which seemed absolutely never to have forgotten anything. His mind was an inexhaustable store-house of anecdote. These he had ever at command. Though they were not always,

46

indeed were seldom, of the most refined nature, they were none the less adapted to raise shouts of merriment in cabin and camp. What Sydney Smith was at the banqueting board in the palatial saloon, such was David Crockett at the campfire and in the log hut. If ever in want of an illustrative anecdote he found no difficulty in manufacturing one.

His thoughtless kindness of heart and good nature were inexhaustible. Those in want never appealed to him in vain. He would even go hungry himself that he might feed others who were more hungry. He would, without a moment's consideration, spend his last dollar to buy a blanket for a shivering soldier, and, without taking any merit for the deed, would never think of it again. He did it without reflection, as he breathed.

Such was the David Crockett who, from the mere love of adventure, left wife and children, in the awful solitude of the wilderness, to follow General Jackson in a march to Pensacola. He seems fully to have understood the character of the General, his merits and his defects. The main body of the army, consisting of a little more than two thousand men, had already commenced its march, when Crockett repaired to a rendezvous, in the northern frontiers of Alabama, where another company was being formed, under Major Russel, soon to follow. The company numbered one hundred and thirty men, and commenced its march.

They forded the Tennessee River at Muscle Shoals, and marched south unmolested, through the heart of the Choctaw and Chickasaw nations, and pressed rapidly forward two or three hundred miles, until they reached the junction of the Tombeckbee and Alabama rivers, in the southern section of the State. The main army was now but two days' march before them. The troops, thus far, had been mounted, finding sufficient grazing for their horses by the way. But learning that there was no forage to be found between there and Pensacola, they left their animals behind them, under a sufficient guard, at a place called Cut-off, and set out for the rest of the march, a distance of about eighty miles, on foot. The slight protective works they threw up here, they called Fort Stoddart.

These light troops, hardy men of iron nerves, accomplished the distance in about two days. On the evening of the second day, they reached an eminence but a short distance out from Pensacola, where they found the army encamped. Not a little to Crockett's disappointment, he learned that Pensacola was already captured. Thus he lost his chance of having "a small taste of British fighting."

The British and Spaniards had obtained intelligence of Jackson's approach, and had made every preparation to drive him back. The forts were strongly garrisoned, and all the principal streets of the little Spanish city were barricaded. Several British war-vessels were anchored in the bay, and so placed as to command with their guns the principal entrance to the town. Jackson, who had invaded the Spanish province unsanctioned by the Government, was anxious to impress upon the Spanish authorities that the measure had been reluctantly adopted, on his own authority, as a military necessity; that he had no disposition to violate their neutral rights; but that it was indispensable that the British should be dislodged and driven away.

The pride of the Spaniard was roused, and there was no friendly response to this appeal. But the Spanish garrison was small, and, united with the English fleet, could present no effectual opposition to the three thousand men under such a lion-hearted leader as General Jackson. On the 7th of January the General opened fire upon the foe. The conflict was short. The Spaniards were compelled to surrender their works.

The British fled to the ships. The guns were turned upon them. They spread sail and disappeared. Jackson was severely censured, at the time, for invading the territory of a neutral power. The final verdict of his countrymen has been decidedly in his favor.

It was supposed that the British would move for the attack of Mobile. This place then consisted of a settlement of but about one hundred and fifty houses. General Jackson, with about two thousand men, marched rapidly for its defence. A few small, broken bands of hostile, yet despairing Creeks, fled back from Florida into the wilds of Alabama. A detachment of nearly a thousand men, under Major Russell, were sent in pursuit of these fleas among the mountains. Crockett made part of this expedition. The pursuing soldiers directed their steps northwest about a hundred miles to Fort Montgomery, on the Alabama, just above its confluence with the Tornbeckbee, about twelve miles above Fort Stoddart. Not far from there was Fort Mimms, where the awful massacre had taken place which opened the Creek war.

There were many cattle grazing in the vicinity of the fort at the time of the massacre, which belonged to the garrison. These animals were now running wild. A thousand hungry men gave them chase. The fatal bullet soon laid them all low, and there was great feasting and hilarity in the camp. The carouse was much promoted by the arrival that evening of a large barge, which had sailed up the Alabama River from Mobile, with sugar, coffee, and,—best of all, as the soldiers said—worst of all, as humanity cries,—with a large amount of intoxicating liquors.

The scene presented that night was wild and picturesque in the extreme. The horses of the army were scattered about over the plain grazing upon the rich herbage. There was wood in abundance near, and the camp-fires for a thousand men threw up their forked flames, illumining the whole region with almost the light of day. The white tents of the officers, the varied groups of the soldiers, running here and there, in all possible attitudes, the cooking and feasting, often whole quarters of beef roasting on enormous spits before the vast fires, afforded a spectacle such as is rarely seen.

One picture instantly arrested the eye of every beholder. There were one hundred and eighty-six friendly Chickasaw and Choctaw Indians, who had enlisted in the army. They formed a band by themselves under their own chiefs. They were all nearly naked, gorgeously painted, and decorated with the very brilliant attire of the warrior, with crimson-colored plumes, and moccasins and leggins richly fringed, and dyed in bright and strongly contrasting hues. These savages were in the enjoyment of their greatest delight, drinking to frenzy, and performing their most convulsive dances, around the flaming fires.

In addition to this spectacle which met the eye, there were sounds of revelry which fell almost appallingly upon the ear. The wide expanse reverberated with bacchanal songs, and drunken shouts, and frenzied war-whoops. These were all blended in an inextricable clamor. With the unrefined eminently, and in a considerable degree with the most refined, noise is one of the essential elements of festivity. A thousand men were making all the noise they could in this midnight revel. Probably never before, since the dawn of creation, had the banks of the Alabama echoed with such a clamor as in this great carouse, which had so suddenly burst forth from the silence of the almost uninhabited wilderness.

This is the poetry of war. This it is which lures so many from the tameness of ordinary life to the ranks of the army. In such scenes, Crockett, bursting with fun, the incarnation of wit and good nature, was in his element. Here he was chief. All did him homage. His pride was gratified by his distinction. Life in his lonely hut, with wife and children, seemed, in comparison, too spiritless to be endured.

The Alabama here runs nearly west. The army was on the south side of the river. The next day the Indians asked permission to cross to the northern bank on an exploring expedition. Consent was given; but Major Russel decided to go with them, taking a company of sixteen men, of whom Crockett was one. They crossed the river and encamped upon the other side, seeing no foe and encountering no alarm. They soon came to a spot where the winding river, overflowing its banks, spread over a wide extent of the flat country. It was about a mile and a half across this inundated meadow. To journey around it would require a march of many miles. They waded the meadow. The water was very cold, often up to their armpits, and they stumbled over the rough ground. This was not the poetry of war. But still there is a certain degree of civilization in which the monotony of life is relieved by such adventures.

When they reached the other side they built large fires, and warmed and dried themselves. They were in search of a few fugitive Indian warriors, who, fleeing from Pensacola, had scattered themselves over a wilderness many hundred square miles in extent. This pursuit of them, by a thousand soldiers, seems now very foolish. But it is hardly safe for us, seated by our quiet firesides, and with but a limited knowledge of the circumstances, to pass judgment upon the measure.

The exploring party consisted, as we have mentioned, of nearly two hundred Indians, and sixteen white men. They advanced very cautiously. Two scouts were kept some distance in the advance, two on the side nearest the river, and five on their right. In this way they had moved along about six miles, when the two spies in front came rushing breathlessly back, with the tidings that they had discovered a camp of Creek Indians. They halted for a few moments while all examined their guns and their priming and prepared for battle.

The Indians went through certain religious ceremonies, and getting out their war-paint, colored their bodies anew. They then came to Major Russell, and told him that, as he was to lead them in the battle, he must be painted too. He humored them, and was painted in the most approved style of an Indian warrior. The plan of battle was arranged to strike the Indian camp by surprise, when they were utterly unprepared for any resistance. The white men were cautiously to proceed in the advance, and pour in a deadly fire to kill as many as possible. The Indians were then, taking advantage of the panic, to rush in with tomahawk and scalping-knife, and finish the scene according to their style of battle, which spared neither women nor children. It is not pleasant to record such a measure. They crept along, concealed by the forest, and guided by the sound of pounding, till they caught sight of the camp. A little to their chagrin they found that it consisted of two peaceful wigwams, where there was a man, a woman, and several children. The wigwams were also on an island of the river, which could not be approached without boats. There could not be much glory won by an army of two hundred men routing such a party and destroying their home. There was also nothing to indicate that these Indians had even any unfriendly feelings. The man and woman were employed in bruising what was called brier root, which they had dug from the forest, for food. It seems that this was the principal subsistence used by the Indians in that vicinity.

While the soldiers were deliberating what next to do, they heard a gun fired in the direction of the scouts, at some distance on the right, followed by a single shrill war-whoop. This satisfied them that if the scouts

49

had met with a foe, it was indeed war on a small scale. There seemed no need for any special caution. They all broke and ran toward the spot from which the sounds came. They soon met two of the spies, who told the following not very creditable story, but one highly characteristic of the times.

As they were creeping along through the forest, they found two Indians, who they said were Creeks, out hunting. As they were approaching each other, it so happened that there was a dense cluster of bushes between them, so that they were within a few feet of meeting before either party was discovered. The two spies were Choctaws. They advanced directly to the Indians, and addressed them in the most friendly manner; stating that they had belonged to General Jackson's army, but had escaped, and were on their way home. They shook hands, kindled a fire, and sat down and smoked in apparent perfect cordiality.

One of the Creeks had a gun. The other had only a bow and arrows. After this friendly interview, they rose and took leave of each other, each going in opposite directions. As soon as their backs were turned, and they were but a few feet from each other, one of the Choctaws turned around and shot the unsuspecting Creek who had the gun. He fell dead, without a groan. The other Creek attempted to escape, while the other Choctaw snapped his gun at him repeatedly, but it missed fire. They then pursued him, overtook him, knocked him down with the butt of their guns, and battered his head until he also was motionless in death. One of the Choctaws, in his frenzied blows, broke the stock of his rifle. They then fired off the gun of the Creek who was killed, and one of them uttered the war-whoop which was heard by the rest of the party.

These two savages drew their scalping-knives and cut off the heads of both their victims. As the whole body came rushing up, they found the gory corpses of the slain, with their dissevered heads near by. Each Indian had a war-club. With these massive weapons each savage, in his turn, gave the mutilated heads a severe blow. When they had all performed this barbaric deed, Crockett, whose peculiar type of good nature led him not only to desire to please the savages, but also to know what would please them, seized a war-club, and, in his turn, smote with all his strength the mangled, blood-stained heads. The Indians were quite delighted. They gathered around him with very expressive grunts of satisfaction, and patting him upon the back, exclaimed, "Good warrior! Good warrior!"

The Indians then scalped the heads, and, leaving the bodies unburied, the whole party entered a trail which led to the river, near the point where the two wigwams were standing. As they followed the narrow path they came upon the vestiges of a cruel and bloody tragedy. The mouldering corpses of a Spaniard, his wife, and four children lay scattered around, all scalped. Our hero Crockett, who had so valiantly smitten the dissevered heads of the two Creeks who had been so treacherously murdered, confesses that the revolting spectacle of the whites, scalped and half devoured, caused him to shudder. He writes:

"I began to feel mighty ticklish along about this time; for I knowed if there was no danger then, there had been, and I felt exactly like there still was."

The white soldiers, leading the Indians, continued their course until they reached the river. Following it down, they came opposite the point where the wigwams stood upon the island. The two Indian hunters who had been killed had gone out from this peaceful little encampment. Several Indian children were playing around, and the man and woman whom they had before seen were still beating their roots. Another Indian woman was also there seen. These peaceful families had no conception of the disaster

50

which had befallen their companions who were hunting in the woods. Even if they had heard the report of the rifles, they could only have supposed that it was from the guns of the hunters firing at game.

The evening twilight was fading away. The whole party was concealed in a dense canebrake which fringed the stream. Two of the Indians were sent forward as a decoy—a shameful decoy—to lure into the hands of two hundred warriors an unarmed man, two women, and eight or ten children. The Indians picked out some of their best marksmen and hid them behind trees and logs near the river. They were to shoot down the Indians whom others should lure to cross the stream.

The creek which separated the island from the mainland was deep, but not so wide but that persons without much difficulty could make themselves heard across it. Two of the Indians went down to the river-side, and hailed those at the wigwams, asking them to send a canoe across to take them over. An Indian woman came down to the bank and informed them that the canoe was on their side, that two hunters had crossed the creek that morning, and had not yet returned. These were the two men who had been so inhumanly murdered. Immediate search was made for the canoe, and it was found a little above the spot where the men were hiding. It was a very large buoyant birch canoe, constructed for the transportation of a numerous household, with all their goods, and such game as they might take.

This they loaded with warriors to the water's edge, and they began vigorously to paddle over to the island. When the one solitary Indian man there saw this formidable array approaching he fled into the woods. The warriors landed, and captured the two women and the little children, ten in number, and conveyed their prisoners, with the plunder of the wigwams, back across the creek to their own encampment. This was not a very brilliant achievement to be accomplished by an army of two hundred warriors aided by a detachment of sixteen white men under Major Russel. What finally became of these captives we know not. It is gratifying to be informed by David Crockett that they did not kill either the squaws or the pappooses.

The company then marched through the silent wilderness, a distance of about thirty miles east, to the Conecuh River. This stream, in its picturesque windings through a region where even the Indian seldom roved, flowed into the Scambia, the principal river which pours its floods, swollen by many tributaries, into Pensacola Bay. It was several miles above the point where the detachment struck the river that the Indian encampment, to which the two murdered men had alluded, was located. But the provisions of the party were exhausted. There was scarcely any game to be found. Major Russel did not deem it prudent to march to the attack of the encampment, until he had obtained a fresh supply of provisions. The main body of the army, which had remained in Florida, moving slowly about, without any very definite object, waiting for something to turn up was then upon the banks of the Scambia. Colonel Blue was in command.

David Crockett was ordered to take a light birch canoe, and two men, one a friendly Creek Indian, and paddle down the stream about twenty miles to the main camp. Here he was to inform Colonel Blue of Major Russel's intention to ascend the Conecuh to attack the Creeks, and to request the Colonel immediately to dispatch some boats up the river with the needful supplies.

It was a romantic adventure descending in the darkness that wild and lonely stream, winding through the dense forest of wonderful exuberance of vegetation. In the early evening he set out. The night proved very dark. The river, swollen by recent rains, overflowed its banks and spread far and wide over the low bottoms. The river was extremely crooked, and it was with great difficulty that they could keep the channel. But the instinct of the Indian guide led them safely along, through overhanging boughs and forest glooms, until, a little before midnight, they reached the camp. There was no time to be lost. Major Russel was anxious to have the supplies that very night dispatched to him, lest the Indians should hear of their danger and should escape.

But Colonel Blue did not approve of the expedition. There was no evidence that the Indian encampment consisted of anything more than half a dozen wigwams, where a few inoffensive savages, with their wives and children, were eking out a half-starved existence by hunting, fishing, and digging up roots from the forest. It did not seem wise to send an army of two hundred and sixteen men to carry desolation and woe to such humble homes. Crockett was ordered to return with this message to the Major. Military discipline, then and there, was not very rigid. He hired another man to carry back the unwelcome answer in his place. In the light canoe the three men rapidly ascended the sluggish stream. Just as the sun was rising over the forest, they reached the camp of Major Russell. The detachment then immediately commenced its march down the River Scambia, and joined the main body at a point called Miller's Landing. Here learning that some fugitive Indians were on the eastern side of the stream, a mounted party was sent across, swimming their horses, and several Indians were hunted down and shot.

Soon after this, the whole party, numbering nearly twelve hundred in all, commenced a toilsome march of about two or three hundred miles across the State to the Chattahoochee River, which constitutes the boundary-line between Southern Alabama and Georgia. Their route led through pathless wilds. No provisions, of any importance, could be found by the way. They therefore took with them rations for twenty-eight days. But their progress was far more slow and toilsome than they had anticipated. Dense forests were to be threaded, where it was necessary for them to cut their way through almost tropical entanglement of vegetation. Deep and broad marshes were to be waded, where the horses sank almost to their saddle-girths. There were rivers to be crossed, which could only be forded by ascending the banks through weary leagues of wilderness.

Thus, when twenty-eight days had passed, and their provisions were nearly expended, though they had for some time been put on short allowance, they found that they had accomplished but three-quarters of their journey. Actual starvation threatened them. But twice in nineteen days did Crockett Taste of any bread. Despondency spread its gloom over the half-famished army. Still they toiled along, almost hopeless, with tottering footsteps. War may have its excitements and its charms. But such a march as this, of woe-begone, emaciate, skeleton bands, is not to be counted as among war's pomps and glories.

One evening, in the deepening twilight, when they had been out thirty-four days, the Indian scouts, ever sent in advance, came into camp with the announcement, that at the distance of but a few hours' march before them, the Chattahoochee River was to be found, with a large Indian village upon its banks. We know not what reason there was to suppose that the Indians inhabiting this remote village were hostile. But as the American officers decided immediately upon attacking them, we ought to suppose that they, on the ground, had sufficient reason to justify this course.

The army was immediately put in motion. The rifles were loaded and primed, and the flints carefully examined, that they might not fall into ambush unprepared. The sun was just rising as they cautiously approached the doomed village. There was a smooth green meadow a few rods in width on the western bank of the river, skirted by the boundless forest. The Indian wigwams and lodges, of varied structure, were clustered together on this treeless, grassy plain, in much picturesque beauty. The Indians had apparently not been apprised of the approach of the terrible tempest of war about to descend upon them. Apparently, at that early hour, they were soundly asleep. Not a man, woman, or child was to be seen.

Silently, screened by thick woods, the army formed in line of battle. The two hundred Indian warriors, rifle in hand and tomahawk at belt, stealthily took their position. The white men took theirs. At a given signal, the war-whoop burst from the lips of the savages, and the wild halloo of the backwoodsmen reverberated through the forest, as both parties rushed forward in the impetuous charge. "We were all so furious," writes Crockett, "that even the certainty of a pretty hard fight could not have restrained us."

But to the intense mortification of these valiant men, not a single living being was to be found as food for bullet or tomahawk. The huts were all deserted, and despoiled of every article of any value. There was not a skin, or an unpicked bone, or a kernel of corn left behind. The Indians had watched the march of the foe, and, with their wives and little ones, had retired to regions where the famishing army could not follow them.

CHAPTER VI.

The Camp and the Cabin.

Deplorable Condition of the Army.—Its wanderings.—Crockett's Benevolence.—Cruel Treatment of the Indians.—A Gleam of Good Luck.—The Joyful Feast.—Crockett's Trade with the Indian.—Visit to the Old Battlefield.—Bold Adventure of Crockett.—His Arrival Home.—Death of his Wife.—Second Marriage.—Restlessness.—Exploring Tour.—Wild Adventures.—Dangerous Sickness.—Removal to the West.—His New Home.

The army, far away in the wilds of Southern Alabama, on the banks of the almost unknown Chattahoochee, without provisions, and with leagues of unexplored wilderness around, found itself in truly a deplorable condition. The soldiers had hoped to find, in the Indian village, stores of beans and corn, and quantities of preserved game. In the impotence of their disappointment they applied the torch, and laid the little village in ashes.

A council was held, and it was deemed best to divide their forces. Major Childs took one-half of the army and retraced their steps westward, directing their course toward Baton Rouge, where they hoped to find General Jackson with a portion of the army with which he was returning from New Orleans. The other division, under Major Russel, pressed forward, as rapidly as possible, nearly north, aiming for Fort Decatur, on the Tallapoosa River, where they expected to find shelter and provisions. Crockett accompanied Major Russel's party. Indian sagacity was now in great requisition. The friendly savages led the way through scenes of difficulty and entanglement where, but for their aid, the troops might all have perished. So great was the destitution of food that the soldiers were permitted to stray, almost at pleasure, on either side of the line of march. Happy was the man who could shoot a raccoon or a squirrel, or even the smallest bird. Implicit confidence was placed in the guidance of the friendly Indians, and the army followed in single file, along the narrow trail which the Indians trod before them.

Crockett, in this march, had acquired so much the confidence of the officers that he seems to have enjoyed quite unlimited license. He went where he pleased and did what he would. Almost invariably at night, keeping pace with the army, he would bring in some small game, a bird or a squirrel, and frequently several of these puny animals. It was a rule, when night came, for all the hunters to throw down what they had killed in one pile. This was then divided among the messes as equitably as possible.

One night, Crockett returned empty-handed. He had killed nothing, and he was very hungry. But there was a sick man in his mess, who was suffering far more than he. Crockett, with his invariable unselfishness and generosity, forgot his own hunger in his solicitude for his sick comrade. He went to the fire of Captain Cowen, who was commandant of the company to which Crockett belonged, and told him his story. Captain Cowen was broiling, for his supper, the gizzard of a turkey. He told Crockett that the turkey was all that had fallen to the share of his company that night, and that the bird had already been divided, in very small fragments, among the sick. There was nothing left for Crockett's friend.

On this march the army was divided into messes of eight or ten men, who cooked and ate their food together. This led Crockett to decide that he and his mess would separate themselves from the rest of the army, and make a small and independent band. The Indian scouts, well armed and very wary, took the lead. They kept several miles in advance of the main body of the troops, that they might give timely warning should they encounter any danger. Crockett and his mess kept close after them, following their trail, and leaving the army one or two miles behind.

One day the scouts came across nine Indians. We are not informed whether they were friends or enemies, whether they were hunters or warriors, whether they were men, women, or children, whether they were in their wigwams or wandering through the forest, whether they were all together or were found separately: we are simply told that they were all shot down. The circumstances of the case are such, that the probabilities are very strong that they were shot as a wolf or a bear would be shot, at sight, without asking any questions. The next day the scouts found a frail encampment where there were three Indians. They shot them all.

The sufferings of the army, as it toiled along through these vast realms of unknown rivers and forest glooms, and marshes and wide-spread, flower-bespangled prairies, became more and more severe. Game was very scarce. For three days, Crockett's party killed barely enough to sustain life. He writes:

"At last we all began to get nearly ready to give up the ghost, and lie down and die, for we had no prospect of provision, and we knowed we couldn't go much farther without it."

While in this condition they came upon one of those wide and beautiful prairies which frequently embellish the landscape of the South and the West This plain was about six miles in width, smooth as a floor, and waving with tall grass and the most brilliantly colored flowers. It was bordered with a forest of luxuriant growth, but not a tree dotted its surface. They came upon a trail leading through the tall, thick grass. Crockett's practised eye saw at once that it was not a trail made by human foot-steps, but the narrow path along which deer strolled and turkeys hobbled in their movement across the field from forest to forest.

Following this trail, they soon came to a creek of sluggish water. The lowlands on each side were waving with a rank growth of wild rye, presenting a very green and beautiful aspect. The men were all mounted, as indeed was nearly the whole army. By grazing and browsing, the horses, as they moved slowly along at a foot-pace, kept in comfortable flesh. This rye-field presented the most admirable pasturage for the horses. Crockett and his comrades dismounted, and turned the animals loose. There was no danger of their straying far in so fat a field.

Crockett and another man, Vanzant by name, leaving the horses to feed, pushed across the plain to the forest, in search of some food for themselves They wandered for some time, and found nothing. At length, Crockett espied a squirrel on the limb of a tall tree. He shot at the animal and wounded it but it succeeded in creeping into a small hole in the tree, thirty feet from the ground. There was not a limb for that distance to aid in climbing. Still the wants of the party were such that Crockett climbed the tree to get the squirrel, and felt that he had gained quite a treasure.

"I shouldn't relate such small matters," he writes, "only to show what lengths a hungry man will go to, to get something to eat."

Soon after, he killed two more squirrels. Just as he was reloading his gun, a large flock of fat turkeys rose from the marshy banks of the creek along which they were wandering, and flying but a short distance, relighted. Vanzant crept forward, and aiming at a large gobbler, fired, and brought him down. The flock immediately flew back to near the spot where Crockett stood. He levelled his rifle, took deliberate aim, and another fine turkey fell. The flock then disappeared.

The two hunters made the forest resound with shouts of triumph. They had two large, fat turkeys, which would be looked at wistfully upon any gourmand's table, and for side-dishes they had three squirrels. Thus they were prepared for truly a thanksgiving feast. Hastily they returned with their treasure, when they learned that the others of their party had found a bee-tree, that is, a tree where a swarm of bees had taken lodgment, and were laying in their winter stores. They cut down the tree with their hatchets, and obtained an ample supply of wild honey. They all felt that they had indeed fallen upon a vein of good luck.

It was but a short distance from the creek to the gigantic forest, rising sublimely in its luxuriance, with scarcely an encumbering shrub of undergrowth. They entered the edge of the forest, built a hot fire, roasted their game, and, while their horses were enjoying the richest of pasturage, they, with their keen appetites, enjoyed a more delicious feast than far-famed Delmonico ever provided for his epicurean guests.

The happy party, rejoicing in the present, and taking no thought for the morrow, spent the night in this camp of feasting. The next morning they were reluctant to leave such an inviting hunting-ground. Crockett and Vanzant again took to their rifles, and strolled into the forest in search of game. Soon they came across a fine buck, which seemed to have tarried behind to watch the foe, while the rest of the herd, of which he was protector, had taken to flight. The beautiful creature, with erect head and spreading antlers, gallantly stopping to investigate the danger to which his family was exposed, would have moved the sympathies of any one but a professed hunter. Crockett's bullet struck him, wounded him severely, and he limped away. Hotly the two hunters pursued. They came to a large tree which had been blown down, and was partly decayed. An immense grizzly bear crept growling from the hollow of this tree, and plunged into the forest. It was in vain to pursue him, without dogs to retard his flight. They however soon overtook the wounded buck, and shot him. With this treasure of venison upon their shoulders, they had but just returned to their camp when the main body of the army came up. The game which Crockett had taken, and upon which they had feasted so abundantly, if divided among twelve hundred men, would not have afforded a mouthful apiece.

The army was in the most deplorable condition of weakness and hunger. Ere long they reached the Coosa, and followed up its eastern bank. About twenty miles above the spot where they struck the river there was a small military post, called Fort Decatur. They hoped to find some food there. And yet, in that remote, almost inaccessible station, they could hardly expect to meet with anything like a supply for twelve hundred half-famished men.

Upon reaching the river, Crockett took a canoe and paddled across. On the other shore he found an Indian. Instead of shooting him, he much more sensibly entered into relations of friendly trade with the savage. The Indian had a little household in his solitary wigwam, and a small quantity of corn in store. Crockett wore a large hat. Taking it from his head, he offered the Indian a silver dollar if he would fill it with corn. But the little bit of silver, with enigmatical characters stamped upon it, was worth nothing to the Indian. He declined the offer. Speaking a little broken English, he inquired, "You got any powder? You got any bullets?" Crockett told him he had. He promptly replied, "Me will swap my corn for powder and bullets."

Eagerly the man gave a hatful of corn for ten bullets and ten charges of powder. He then offered another hatful at the same price. Crockett took off his hunting-shirt, tied it up so as to make a sort of bag, into which he poured his two hatfuls of corn. With this great treasure he joyfully paddled across the stream to rejoin his companions. It is pleasant to think that the poor Indian was not shot, that his wigwam was not burned over his head, and that he was left with means to provide his wife and children with many luxurious meals.

The army reached Fort Decatur. One single meal consumed all the provisions which the garrison could by any possibility spare. They had now entered upon a rough, hilly, broken country. The horses found but little food, and began to give out. About fifty miles farther up the Coosa River there was another military station, in the lonely wilds, called Fort William. Still starving, and with tottering horses, they toiled on. Parched corn, and but a scanty supply of that, was now almost their only subsistence.

They reached the fort. One ration of pork and one ration of flour were mercifully given them. It was all which could be spared. To remain where they were was certain starvation. Forty miles above them on the same stream was Fort Strother. Sadly they toiled along. The skeleton horses dropped beneath their riders, and were left, saddled and bridled, for the vultures and the wolves. On their route to Fort Strother they passed directly by the ancient Indian fort of Talladega. It will be remembered that a terrible battle had been fought here by General Jackson with the Indians, on the 7th of December, 1813. In the carnage of that bloody day nearly five hundred Indians fell. Those who escaped scattered far and wide. A few of them sought refuge in distant Florida.

The bodies of the slain were left unburied. Slowly the flesh disappeared from the bones, either devoured by wild beasts or decomposed by the action of the atmosphere. The field, as now visited, presented an appalling aspect. Crockett writes:

"We went through the old battle-ground, and it looked like a great gourd-patch. The skulls of the Indians who were killed, still lay scattered all about. Many of their frames were still perfect, as their bones had not separated."

As they were thus despairingly tottering along, they came across a narrow Indian trail, with fresh footmarks, indicating that moccasined Indians had recently passed along. It shows how little they had cause to fear from the Indians, that Crockett, entirely alone, should have followed that trail, trusting that it would lead him to some Indian village, where he could hope to buy some more corn. He was not deceived in his expectation. After threading the narrow and winding path about five miles, he came to a cluster of Indian wigwams. Boldly he entered the little village, without apparently the slightest apprehension that he should meet with any unfriendly reception.

He was entirely at the mercy of the savages Even if he were murdered, it would never be known by whom. And if it were known, the starving army, miles away, pressing along in its flight, was in no condition to send a detachment to endeavor to avenge the deed. The savages received him as though he had been one of their own kith and kin, and readily exchanged corn with him, for powder and bullets. He then returned, but did not overtake the rest of the army until late in the night.

The next morning they were so fortunate as to encounter a detachment of United States troops on the march to Mobile. These troops, having just commenced their journey, were well supplied; and they liberally distributed their corn and provisions. Here Crockett found his youngest brother, who had enlisted for the campaign. There were also in the band many others of his old friends and neighbors. The succeeding day, the weary troops, much refreshed, reached a point on the River Coosa opposite Fort Strother, and crossing the stream, found there shelter and plenty of provisions.

We know not, and do not care to know, who was responsible for this military movement, which seems to us now as senseless as it was cruel and disastrous. But it is thus that poor humanity has ever gone blundering on, displaying but little wisdom in its affairs. Here Crockett had permission to visit his home, though he still owed the country a month of service. In his exceeding rude, unpolished style which pictures the man, he writes:

"Once more I was safely landed at home with my wife and children. I found them all well and doing well; and though I was only a rough sort of backwoodsman, they seemed mighty glad to see me, however little the quality folks might suppose it. For I do reckon we love as hard in the backwood country as any people in the whole creation.

"But I had been home only a few days, when we received orders to start again, and go on to the Black Warrior and Cahaula rivers, to see if there were no Indians there. I know'd well enough there was none, and I wasn't willing to trust my craw any more where there was neither any fighting to do, nor anything to go on. So I agreed to give a young man, who wanted to go, the balance of my wages, if he would serve out my time, which was about a month.

"He did so. And when they returned, sure enough they hadn't seen an Indian any more than if they had been, all the time, chopping wood in my clearing. This closed my career as a warrior; and I am glad of it; for I like life now a heap better than I did then. And I am glad all over that I lived to see these times, which I should not have done if I had kept fooling along in war, and got used up at it. When I say I am glad, I just mean that I am glad that I am alive, for there is a confounded heap of things I ain't glad of at all."

When Crockett wrote the above he was a member of Congress, and a very earnest politician. He was much opposed to the measure of President Jackson in removing the deposits from the United States Bank—a movement which greatly agitated the whole country at that time. In speaking of things of which he was not glad, he writes:

"I ain't glad, for example, that the Government moved the deposits; and if my military glory should take such a turn as to make me President after the General's time, I will move them back. Yes, I the Government, will take the responsibility, and move them back again. If I don't I wish I may be shot."

The hardships of war had blighted Crockett's enthusiasm for wild adventures, and had very considerably sobered him. He remained at home for two years, diligently at work upon his farm. The battle of New Orleans was fought. The war with England closed, and peace was made with the poor Indians, who, by British intrigue, had been goaded to the disastrous fight. Death came to the cabin of Crockett; and his faithful wife, the tender mother of his children, was taken from him. We cannot refrain from quoting his own account of this event as it does much honor to his heart.

"In this time I met with the hardest trial which ever falls to the lot of man. Death, that cruel leveller of all distinctions, to whom the prayers and tears of husbands, and even of helpless infancy, are addressed in vain, entered my humble cottage, and tore from my children an affectionate, good mother, and from me a tender and loving wife. It is a scene long gone by, and one which it would be supposed I had almost forgotten. Yet when I turn my memory back upon it, it seems but as the work of yesterday.

"It was the doing of the Almighty, whose ways are always right, though we sometimes think they fall heavily on us. And as painful as even yet is the remembrance of her sufferings, and the loss sustained by my little children and myself, yet I have no wish to lift up the voice of complaint. I was left with three children. The two eldest were sons, the youngest a daughter, and at that time a mere infant. It appeared to me, at that moment, that my situation was the worst in the world.

"I couldn't bear the thought of scattering my children; and so I got my youngest brother, who was also married, and his family, to live with me. They took as good care of my children as they well could; but yet it wasn't all like the care of a mother. And though their company was to me, in every respect, like that of a brother and sister, yet it fell far short of being like that of a wife. So I came to the conclusion that it wouldn't do, but that I must have another wife."

One sees strikingly, in the above quotation, the softening effect of affliction on the human heart There was a widow in the neighborhood, a very worthy woman, who had lost her husband in the war. She had two children, a son and a daughter, both quite young. She owned a snug little farm, and being a very capable woman, was getting along quite comfortably. Crockett decided that he should make a good step-father to her children, and she a good step-mother for his. The courtship was in accordance with the most approved style of country love-making. It proved to be a congenial marriage. The two families came very harmoniously together, and in their lowly hut enjoyed peace and contentment such as frequently is not found in more ambitious homes.

But the wandering propensity was inherent in the very nature of Crockett. He soon tired of the monotony of a farmer's life, and longed for change. A few months after his marriage he set out, with three of his neighbors, all well mounted, on an exploring tour into Central Alabama, hoping to find new homes there. Taking a southerly course, they crossed the Tennessee River, and striking the upper waters of the Black Warrior, followed down that stream a distance of about two hundred miles from their starting-point, till they came near to the place where Tuscaloosa, the capital of the State, now stands.

This region was then almost an unbroken wilderness. But during the war Crockett had frequently traversed it, and was familiar with its general character. On the route they came to the hut of a man who was a comrade of Crockett in the Florida campaign. They spent a day with the retired soldier, and all went out in the woods together to hunt. Frazier unfortunately stepped upon a venomous snake, partially covered with leaves. The reptile struck its deadly fangs into his leg. The effect was instantaneous and awful. They carried the wounded man, with his bloated and throbbing limb, back to the hut. Here such remedies were applied as backwoods medical science suggested; but it was evident that many weeks would elapse ere the man could move, even should he eventually recover. Sadly they were constrained to leave their suffering companion there. What became of him is not recorded.

The three others, Crockett, Robinson, and Rich, continued their journey. Their route led them through a very fertile and beautiful region, called Jones's Valley. Several emigrants had penetrated and reared their log huts upon its rich and blooming meadows.

When they reached the spot where the capital of the State now stands, with its spacious streets, its public edifices, its halls of learning, its churches, and its refined and cultivated society, they found only the silence, solitude, and gloom of the wilderness. With their hatchets they constructed a rude camp to shelter them from the night air and the heavy dew. It was open in front. Here they built their camp-fire, whose cheerful glow illumined the forest far and wide, and which converted midnight glooms into almost midday radiance. The horses were hobbled and turned out to graze on a luxuriant meadow. It was supposed that the animals, weary of the day's journey, and finding abundant pasturage, would not stray far. The travellers cooked their supper, and throwing themselves upon their couch of leaves, enjoyed that sound sleep which fatigue, health, and comfort give.

When they awoke in the morning the horses were all gone. By examining the trail it seemed that they had taken the back-track in search of their homes. Crockett, who was the most vigorous and athletic of the three, leaving Robinson and Rich in the camp, set out in pursuit of the runaways. It was a rough and dreary path he had to tread. There was no comfortable road to traverse, but a mere path through forest, bog, and ravine, which, at times, it was difficult to discern. He had hills to climb, creeks to ford, swamps to wade through. Hour after hour he pressed on, but the horses could walk faster than he could. There was nothing in their foot-prints which indicated that he was approaching any nearer to them.

At last, when night came, and Crockett judged that he had walked fifty miles, he gave up the chase as hopeless. Fortunately he reached the cabin of a settler, where he remained until morning. A rapid walk, almost a run, of fifty miles in one day, is a very severe operation even for the most hardy of men. When Crockett awoke, after his night's sleep, he found himself so lame that he could scarcely move. He was, however, anxious to get back with his discouraging report to his companions. He therefore set out, and hobbled slowly and painfully along, hoping that exercise would gradually loosen his stiffened joints.

But, mile after mile, he grew worse rather than better. His head began to ache very severely. A burning fever spread through his veins. He tottered in his walk, and his rifle seemed so heavy that he could scarcely bear its weight. He was toiling through a dark and gloomy ravine, damp and cold, and thrown into shade by the thick foliage of the overhanging trees. So far as he knew, no human habitation was near. Night was approaching. He could go no farther. He had no food; but he did not need any, for a deathly nausea oppressed him. Utterly exhausted, he threw himself down upon the grass and withered leaves, on a small dry mound formed by the roots of a large tree.

Crockett had no wish to die. He clung very tenaciously to life, and yet he was very apprehensive that then and there he was to linger through a few hours of pain, and then die, leaving his unburied body to be devoured by wild beasts, and his friends probably forever ignorant of his fate. Consumed by fever, and agitated by these painful thoughts, he remained for an hour or two, when he heard the sound of approaching footsteps and of human voices. His sensibilities were so stupefied by his sickness that these sounds excited but little emotion.

Soon three or four Indians made their appearance walking along the narrow trail in single file. They saw the prostrate form of the poor, sick white man, and immediately gathered around him. The rifle of Crockett, and the powder and bullets which he had, were, to these Indians, articles of almost inestimable value. One blow of the tomahawk would send the helpless man to realms where rifles and ammunition were no longer needed, and his priceless treasures would fall into their hands. Indeed, it was not necessary even to strike that blow. They had but to pick up the rifle, and unbuckle the belt which contained the powder-horn and bullet-pouch, and leave the dying man to his fate.

But these savages, who had never read our Saviour's beautiful parable of the good Samaritan, acted the Samaritan's part to the white man whom they found in utter helplessness and destitution. They kneeled around him, trying to minister to his wants. One of them had a watermelon. He cut from it a slice of the rich and juicy fruit, and entreated him to eat it. But his stomach rejected even that delicate food.

They then, by very expressive signs, told him that if he did not take some nourishment he would die and be buried there—"a thing," Crockett writes, "I was confoundedly afraid of, myself." Crockett inquired how far it was to any house. They signified to him, by signs, that there was a white man's cabin about a mile and a half from where they then were, and urged him to let them conduct him to that house. He rose to make the attempt. But he was so weak that he could with difficulty stand, and unsupported could not walk a step.

One of these kind Indians offered to go with him; and relieving Crockett of the burden of his rifle, and with his strong arm supporting and half carrying him, at length succeeded in getting him to the log hut of the pioneer. The shades of night were falling. The sick man was so far gone that it seemed to him that he could scarcely move another step. A woman came to the door of the lowly hut and received them with a woman's sympathy. There was a cheerful fire blazing in one corner, giving quite a pleasing aspect to the room. In another corner there was a rude bed, with bed-clothing of the skins of animals. Crockett's benefactor laid him tenderly upon the bed, and leaving him in the charge of his countrywoman, bade him adieu, and hastened away to overtake his companions.

What a different world would this be from what it has been, did the spirit of kindness, manifested by this poor Indian, universally animate human hearts!

"O brother man! fold to thy heart thy brother: Where pity dwells the peace of God is there; To worship rightly is to love each other, Each smile a hymn, each kindly word a prayer."

The woman's husband was, at the time, absent. But she carefully nursed her patient, preparing for him some soothing herb-tea. Delirium came, and for several hours, Crockett, in a state of unconsciousness, dwelt in the land of troubled dreams. The next morning he was a little more comfortable, but still in a high fever, and often delirious.

It so happened that two white men, on an exploring tour, as they passed along the trail, met the Indians, who informed them that one of their sick countrymen was at a settler's cabin at but a few miles' distance. With humanity characteristic of a new and sparsely settled country they turned aside to visit him. They proved to be old acquaintances of Crockett. He was so very anxious to get back to the camp where he had left his companions, and who, knowing nothing of his fate, must think it very strange that he had thus deserted them, that they, very reluctantly, in view of his dangerous condition, consented to help him on his way.

They made as comfortable a seat as they could, of blankets and skins, which they buckled on the neck of one of the horses just before the saddle. Upon this Crockett was seated. One of the men then mounted the saddle behind him, threw both arms around the patient, and thus they commenced their journey. The sagacious horse was left to pick out his own way along the narrow trail at a slow foot-pace. As the horse thus bore a double burden, after journeying an hour or two, Crockett's seat was changed to the other horse. Thus alternating, the painful journey of nearly fifty miles was accomplished in about two days.

When they reached the camp, Crockett, as was to have been expected, was in a far worse condition than when they commenced the journey. It was evident that he was to pass through a long run of fever, and that his recovery was very doubtful. His companions could not thus be delayed. They had already left Frazier, one of their company, perhaps to die of the bite of a venomous snake; and now they were constrained to leave Crockett, perhaps to die of malarial fever.

They ascertained that, at the distance of a few miles from them, there was another log cabin in the wilderness. They succeeded in purchasing a couple of horses, and in transporting the sick man to this humble house of refuge. Here Crockett was left to await the result of his sickness, unaided by any medical skill. Fortunately he fell into the hands of a family who treated him with the utmost kindness. For a fortnight he was in delirium, and knew nothing of what was transpiring around him.

Crockett was a very amiable man. Even the delirium of disease developed itself in kindly words and grateful feelings. He always won the love of those around him. He did not miss delicacies and luxuries of which he had never known anything. Coarse as he was when measured by the standard of a higher civilization, he was not coarse at all in the estimation of the society in the midst of which he moved. In this humble cabin of Jesse Jones, with all its aspect of penury, Crockett was nursed with brotherly and sisterly kindness, and had every alleviation in his sickness which his nature craved.

The visitor to Versailles is shown the magnificent apartment, and the regal couch, with its gorgeous hangings, upon which Louis XIV., the proudest and most pampered man on earth, languished and died. Crockett, on his pallet in the log cabin, with unglazed window and earthern floor, was a far less unhappy man, than the dying monarch surrounded with regal splendors.

At the end of a fortnight the patient began slowly to mend. His emaciation was extreme, and his recovery very gradual. After a few weeks he was able to travel. He was then on a route where wagons passed over a rough road, teaming the articles needed in a new country. Crockett hired a wagoner to give him a seat in his wagon and to convey him to the wagoner's house, which was about twenty miles distant. Gaining strength by the way, when he arrived there he hired a horse of the wagoner, and set out for home.

Great was the astonishment of his family upon his arrival, for they had given him up as dead. The neighbors who set out on this journey with him had returned and so reported; for they had been misinformed. They told Mrs. Crockett that they had seen those who were with him when he died, and had assisted in burying him.

Still the love of change had not been dispelled from the bosom of Crockett. He did not like the place where he resided. After spending a few months at home, he set out, in the autumn, upon another exploring tour. Our National Government had recently purchased, of the Chickasaw Indians, a large extent of territory in Southern Tennessee. Crockett thought that in those new lands he would find the earthly paradise of which he was in search. The region was unsurveyed, a savage wilderness, and there were no recognized laws and no organized government there.

Crockett mounted his horse, lashed his rifle to his back, filled his powder-horn and bullet-pouch, and journeying westward nearly a hundred miles, through pathless wilds whose solitudes had a peculiar charm for him, came to a romantic spot, called Shoal Creek, in what is now Giles County, in the extreme southern part of Tennessee. He found other adventurers pressing into the new country, where land was abundant and fertile, and could be had almost for nothing.

Log cabins were rising in all directions, in what they deemed quite near neighborhood, for they were not separated more than a mile or two from each other. Crockett, having selected his location on the banks of a crystal stream, summoned, as was the custom, some neighbors to his aid, and speedily constructed the cabin, of one apartment, to shield his family from the wind and the rain. Moving with such a family is not a very arduous undertaking. One or two pack-horses convey all the household utensils. There are no mirrors, bedsteads, bureaus, or chairs to be transported. With an auger and a hatchet, these articles are soon constructed in their new home. The wife, with the youngest child, rides. The husband, with his rifle upon his shoulder, and followed by the rest of the children, trudges along on foot.

Should night or storm overtake them, an hour's work would throw up a camp, with a cheerful fire in front, affording them about the same cohorts which they enjoyed in the home they had left. A little meal, baked in the ashes, supplied them with bread. And during the journey of the day the rifle of the father would be pretty sure to pick up some game to add to the evening repast.

Crockett and his family reached their new home in safety. Here quite a new sphere of life opened before the adventurer, and he became so firmly settled that he remained in that location for three years. In the mean time, pioneers from all parts were rapidly rearing their cabins upon the fertile territory, which was then called The New Purchase.

CHAPTER VII.

The Justice of Peace and the Legislator.

Vagabondage.—Measures of Protection.—Measures of Government.—Crockett's Confession.—A Candidate for Military Honors.—Curious Display of Moral Courage.—The Squirrel Hunt.—A Candidate for the Legislature.—Characteristic Electioneering.—Specimens of his Eloquence.—Great Pecuniary Calamity.—Expedition to the Far West.—Wild Adventures.—The Midnight Carouse.—A Cabin Reared.

The wealthy and the prosperous are not disposed to leave the comforts of a high civilization for the hardships of the wilderness. Most of the pioneers who crowded to the New Purchase were either energetic young men who had their fortunes to make, or families who by misfortune had encountered impoverishment. But there was still another class. There were the vile, the unprincipled, the desperate; vagabonds seeking whom they might devour; criminals escaping the penalty of the laws which they had violated.

These were the men who shot down an Indian at sight, as they would shoot a wolf; merely for the fun of it; who robbed the Indian of his gun and game, burned his wigwam, and atrociously insulted his wife and daughters. These were the men whom no law could restrain; who brought disgrace upon the name of a white man, and who often provoked the ignorant savage to the most dreadful and indiscriminate retaliation.

So many of these infamous men flocked to this New Purchase that life there became quite undesirable. There were no legally appointed officers of justice, no organized laws. Every man did what was pleasing in his own sight. There was no collecting of debts, no redress for violence, no punishment for cheating or theft.

Under these circumstances, there was a general gathering of the well-disposed inhabitants of the cabins scattered around, to adopt some measures for their mutual protection. Several men were appointed justices of peace, with a set of resolute young men, as constables, to execute their commissions. These justices were invested with almost dictatorial power. They did not pretend to know anything about written law or common law. They were merely men of good sound sense, who could judge as to what was right in all ordinary intercourse between man and man.

A complaint would be entered to Crockett that one man owed another money and refused to pay him. Crockett would send his constables to arrest the man, and bring him to his cabin. After hearing both parties, if Crockett judged the debt to be justly due, and that it could be paid, he would order the man's horse, cow, rifle, or any other property he owned, to be seized and sold, and the debt to be paid. If the man made any resistance he would be very sure to have his cabin burned down over his head; and he would be very lucky if he escaped a bullet through his own body.

One of the most common and annoying crimes committed by these desperadoes was shooting an emigrant's swine. These animals, regarded as so invaluable in a new country, each had its owner's mark, and ranged the woods, fattening upon acorns and other nuts. Nothing was easier than for a lazy man to wander into the woods, shoot one of these animals, take it to his cabin, devour it there, and obliterate all possible traces of the deed. Thus a large and valuable herd would gradually disappear. This crime was consequently deemed to merit the most severe punishment. It was regarded as so disgraceful that no respectable man was liable to suspicion.

The punishment for the crime was very severe, and very summary. If one of these swine-thieves was brought before Justice Crockett, and in his judgment the charge was proved against him, the sentence was—

"Take the thief, strip off his shirt, tie him to a tree, and give him a severe flogging. Then burn down his cabin, and drive him out of the country."

There was no appeal from this verdict, and no evading its execution. Such was the justice which prevailed, in this remote region, until the Legislature of Alabama annexed the territory to Giles County, and brought the region under the dominion of organized law. Crockett, who had performed his functions to the entire satisfaction of the community, then was legally appointed a justice of peace, and became fully entitled to the appellation of esquire. He certainly could not then pretend to any profound legal erudition, for at this time he could neither read nor write.

Esquire Crockett, commenting upon this transaction, says, "I was made a Squire, according to law; though now the honor rested more heavily upon me than before. For, at first, whenever I told my constable, says I, 'Catch that fellow, and bring him up for trial,' away he went, and the fellow must come, dead or alive. For we considered this a good warrant, though it was only in verbal writing.

"But after I was appointed by the Assembly, they told me that my warrants must be in real writing and signed; and that I must keep a book and write my proceedings in it. This was a hard business on me, for I could just barely write my own name. But to do this, and write the warrants too, was at least a huckleberry over my persimmon. I had a pretty well informed constable, however, and he aided me very much in this business. Indeed, I told him, when he should happen to be out anywhere, and see that a warrant was necessary, and would have a good effect, he needn't take the trouble to come all the way to me to get one, but he could just fill out one; and then, on the trial, I could correct the whole business if he had committed any error.

"In this way I got on pretty well, till, by care and attention, I improved my handwriting in such a manner as to be able to prepare my warrants and keep my record-books without much difficulty. My judgments were never appealed from; and if they had been, they would have stuck like wax, as I gave my decisions on the principles of common justice and honesty between man and man, and relied on natural-born sense, and not on law-learning, to guide me; for I had never read a page in a law-book in all my life."

Esquire Crockett was now a rising man. He was by no means diffident. With strong native sense, imperturbable self-confidence, a memory almost miraculously stored with rude anecdotes, and an astonishing command of colloquial and slang language, he was never embarrassed, and never at a loss as to what to say or to do.

They were about getting up a new regiment of militia there, and a Captain Mathews, an ambitious, well-to-do settler, with cribs full of corn, was a candidate for the colonelship. He came to Crockett to insure his support, and endeavored to animate him to more cordial cooperation by promising to do what he could to have him elected major of the regiment. Esquire Crockett at first declined, saying that he was thoroughly disgusted with all military operations, and that he had no desire for any such honors. But as Captain Mathews urged the question, and Crockett reflected that the office would give him some additional respect and influence with his neighbors, and that Major Crockett was a very pleasantly sounding title, he finally consented, and, of course, very soon became deeply interested in the enterprise.

Captain Mathews, as an electioneering measure, invited all his neighbors, far and near, to a very magnificent corn-husking frolic. There was to be a great treat on the occasion, and "all the world," as the French say, were eager to be there. Crockett and his family were of course among the invited guests. When Crockett got there he found an immense gathering, all in high glee, and was informed, much to his surprise and chagrin, that Captain Mathews's son had offered himself for the office of major, in opposition to Crockett.

The once had, in reality, but few charms for Crockett, and he did not care much for it. But this unworthy treatment roused his indignation. He was by nature one of the most frank and open-hearted of men, and never attempted to do anything by guile. Immediately he called Captain Mathews aside, and inquired what this all meant. The Captain was much embarrassed, and made many lame excuses, saying that he would rather his son would run against any man in the county than against Squire Crockett.

"You need give yourself no uneasiness about that," Crockett replied. "I care nothing for the office of major; I shall not allow my name to be used against your son for that office. But I shall do everything in my power to prevent his father from being colonel."

In accordance with the custom of the region and the times, after the feasting and the frolicking, Captain Mathews mounted a stump, and addressed the assembly in what was appropriately called a stump speech, advocating his election.

The moment he closed, Squire Crockett mounted the stump, and on the Captain's own grounds, addressing the Captain's guests, and himself one of those guests, totally unabashed, made his first stump speech. He was at no loss for words or ideas. He was full to the brim of fun. He could, without any effort, keep the whole assembly in roars of laughter. And there, in the presence of Captain Mathews and his family, he argued his total unfitness to be the commander of a regiment.

It is to be regretted that there was no reporter present to transmit to us that speech. It must have been a peculiar performance. It certainly added much to Crockett's reputation as an able man and an orator. When the election came, both father and son were badly beaten. Soon after, a committee waited upon Crockett, soliciting him to stand as candidate for the State Legislature, to represent the two counties of Lawrence and Hickman.

Crockett was beginning to be ambitious. He consented. But he had already engaged to take a drove of horses from Central Tennessee to the lower part of North Carolina. This was a long journey, and going and coming would take three months. He set out early in March, 1821. Upon his return in June, he commenced with all zeal his electioneering campaign. Characteristically he says:

"It was a bran-fire new business to me. It now became necessary that I should tell the people something about the Government, and an eternal sight of other things that I know'd nothing more about than I did about Latin, and law, and such things as that. I have said before, that in those days none of us called

General Jackson the Government. But I know'd so little about it that if any one had told me that he was the Government, I should have believed it; for I had never read even a newspaper in my life, or anything else on the subject."

Lawrence County bounded Giles County on the west. Just north of Lawrence came Hickman County. Crockett first directed his steps to Hickman County, to engage in his "bran-fire" new work of electioneering for himself as a candidate for the Legislature. What ensued cannot be more graphically told than in Crockett's own language:

"Here they told me that they wanted to move their town nearer to the centre of the county, and I must come out in favor of it. There's no devil if I know'd what this meant, or how the town was to be moved. And so I kept dark, going on the identical same plan that I now find is called non-committal.

"About this time there was a great squirrel-hunt, on Duck River, which was among my people. They were to hunt two days; then to meet and count the scalps, and have a big barbecue, and what might be called a tip-top country frolic. The dinners and a general treat was all to be paid for by the party having taken the fewest scalps. I joined one side, and got a gun ready for the hunt. I killed a great many squirrels, and when we counted scalps my party was victorious.

"The company had everything to eat and drink that could be furnished in a new country; and much fun and good humor prevailed. But before the regular frolic commenced, I was called on to make a speech as a candidate, which was a business I was as ignorant of as an outlandish negro.

"A public document I had never seen. How to begin I couldn't tell. I made many apologies, and tried to get off, for I know'd I had a man to run against who could speak prime. And I know'd, too that I wasn't able to cut and thrust with him. He was there, and knowing my ignorance as well as I did myself, he urged me to make a speech. The truth is, he thought my being a candidate was a mere matter of sport, and didn't think for a moment that he was in any danger from an ignorant back woods bear-hunter.

"But I found I couldn't get off. So I determined to go ahead, and leave it to chance what I should say. I got up and told the people I reckoned they know'd what I had come for; but if not, I could tell them. I had come for their votes, and if they didn't watch mighty close I'd get them too. But the worst of all was, that I could not tell them anything about Government. I tried to speak about something, and I cared very little what, until I choked up as bad as if my mouth had been jamm'd and cramm'd chock-full of dry mush. There the people stood, listening all the while, with their eyes, mouths, and ears all open to catch every word I could speak.

"At last I told them I was like a fellow I had heard of not long before. He was beating on the head of an empty barrel on the roadside, when a traveller, who was passing along, asked him what he was doing that for? The fellow replied that there was some cider in that barrel a few days before, and he was trying to see if there was any then; but if there was, he couldn't get at it. I told them that there had been a little bit of a speech in me a while ago, but I believed I couldn't get it out.

"They all roared out in a mighty laugh, and I told some other anecdotes, equally amusing to them, and believing I had them in a first-rate way, I quit and got down, thanking the people for their attention. But I took care to remark that I was as dry as a powder-horn, and that I thought that it was time for us all to wet our whistles a little. And so I put off to a liquor-stand, and was followed by the greater part of the crowd.

"I felt certain this was necessary, for I know'd my competitor could talk Government matters to them as easy as he pleased. He had, however, mighty few left to hear him, as I continued with the crowd, now and then taking a horn, and telling good-humored stories till he was done speaking. I found I was good for the votes at the hunt; and when we broke up I went on to the town of Vernon, which was the same they wanted me to move. Here they pressed me again on the subject. I found I could get either party by agreeing with them. But I told them I didn't know whether it would be right or not, and so couldn't promise either way."

This famous barbecue was on Saturday. The next Monday the county court held its session at Vernon. There was a great gathering of the pioneers from all parts of the county. The candidates for the Governor of the State, for a representative in Congress, and for the State Legislature, were all present. Some of these men were of considerable ability, and certainly of very fluent speech. The backwoodsmen, from their huts, where there were no books, no newspapers, no intelligent companionship, found this a rich intellectual treat. Their minds were greatly excited as they listened to the impassioned and glowing utterances of speaker after speaker; for many of these stump orators had command of a rude but very effective eloquence.

Crockett listened also, with increasing anxiety. He knew that his turn was to come; that he must mount the stump and address the listening throng. He perceived that he could not speak as these men were speaking; and perhaps for the first time in his life began to experience some sense of inferiority. He writes:

"The thought of having to make a speech made my knees feel mighty weak, and set my heart to fluttering almost as bad as my first love-scrape with the Quaker's niece. But as good luck would have it, these big candidates spoke nearly all day, and when they quit the people were worn out with fatigue, which afforded me a good apology for not discussing the Government. But I listened mighty close to them, and was learning pretty fast about political matters. When they were all done, I got up and told some laughable story, and quit. I found I was safe in those parts; and so I went home, and did not go back again till after the election was over. But to cut this matter short, I was elected, doubling my competitor, and nine votes over.

"A short time after this, I was at Pulaski, where I met with Colonel Polk, now a member of Congress from Tennessee. He was at that time a member elected to the Legislature, as well as myself. In a large company he said to me, 'Well, Colonel, I suppose we shall have a radical change of the judiciary at the next session of the Legislature.' 'Very likely, sir,' says I. And I put out quicker, for I was afraid some one would ask me what the judiciary was; and if I know'd I wish I may be shot. I don't indeed believe I had ever before heard that there was any such thing in all nature. But still I was not willing that the people there should know how ignorant I was about it."

At length the day arrived for the meeting of the Legislature. Crockett repaired to the seat of government. With all his self-complacency he began to appreciate that he had much to learn. The two first items of intelligence which he deemed it important that he, as a member of the Legislature, should acquire, were the meaning of the words government and judiciary. By adroit questioning and fixed thought, he ere long stored up those intellectual treasures. Though with but little capacity to obtain knowledge from books, he became an earnest student of the ideas of his fellow-legislators as elicited in conversation or debate. Quite a heavy disaster, just at this time, came upon Crockett. We must again quote his own words, for it is our wish, in this volume, to give the reader a correct idea of the man. Whatever Crockett says, ever comes fresh from his heart. He writes:

"About this time I met with a very severe misfortune, which I may be pardoned for naming, as it made a great change in my circumstances, and kept me back very much in the world. I had built an extensive grist-mill and powder-mill, all connected together, and also a large distillery. They had cost me upward of three thousand dollars; more than I was worth in the world. The first news that I heard, after I got to the Legislature, was that my mills were all swept to smash by a large freshet that came soon after I left home.

"I had, of course, to stop my distillery, as my grinding was broken up. And indeed I may say that the misfortune just made a complete mash of me. I had some likely negroes, and a good stock of almost everything about me, and, best of all, I had an honest wife. She didn't advise me, as is too fashionable, to smuggle up this, and that, and t'other, to go on at home. But she told me, says she, 'Just pay up as long as you have a bit's worth in the world; and then everybody will be satisfied, and we will scuffle for more.'

"This was just such talk as I wanted to hear, for a man's wife can hold him devilish uneasy if she begins to scold and fret, and perplex him, at a time when he has a full load for a railroad car on his mind already. And so, you see, I determined not to break full-handed, but thought it better to keep a good conscience with an empty purse, than to get a bad opinion of myself with a full one. I therefore gave up all I had, and took a bran-fire new start."

Crockett's legislative career was by no means brilliant, but characteristic. He was the fun-maker of the house, and, like Falstaff, could boast that he was not only witty himself, but the cause of wit in others. His stories were irresistibly comic; but they almost always contained expressions of profanity or coarseness which renders it impossible for us to transmit them to these pages. He was an inimitable mimic, and had perfect command of a Dutchman's brogue. One of the least objectionable of his humorous stories we will venture to record.

There were, he said, in Virginia, two Dutchmen, brothers, George and Jake Fulwiler. They were both well to do in the world, and each owned a grist mill. There was another Dutchman near by, by the name of Henry Snyder. He was a mono-maniac, but a harmless man, occasionally thinking himself to be God. He built a throne, and would often sit upon it, pronouncing judgment upon others, and also upon himself. He would send the culprits to heaven or to hell, as his humor prompted.

One day he had a little difficulty with the two Fulwilers. He took his seat upon his throne, and in imagination summoning the culprits before him, thus addressed them:

"Shorge Fulwiler, stand up. What hash you been dain in dis lower world?"

"Ah! Lort, ich does not know."

"Well, Shorge Fulwiler, hasn't you got a mill?"

"Yes, Lort, ich hash."

"Well, Shorge Fulwiler, didn't you never take too much toll?"

"Yes, Lort, ich hash; when der water wash low, and mein stones wash dull, ich take leetle too much toll."

"Well, den, Shorge Fulwiler, you must go to der left mid der goats."

"Well, Shake Fulwiler, now you stand up. What hash you been doin in dis lower world?"

"Ah! Lort, ich does not know."

"Well, Shake Fulwiler, hasn't you got a mill?"

"Yes, Lort, ich hash."

"Well, Shake Fulwiler hasn't you never taken too much toll?"

"Yes Lort, ich hash; when der water wash low, and mein stones wash dull, ich take leetle too much toll."

"Well, den, Shake Fuhviler, you must go to der left mid der goats."

"Now ich try menself. Henry Snyder, Henry Snyder, stand up. What hash you bin dain in die lower world?"

"Ah, Lort, ich does not know."

"Well, Henry Snyder, hasn't you got a mill?"

"Yes, Lort, ich hash."

"Well, Henry Snyder, didn't you never take too much toll?"

"Yes, Lort, ich hash; when der water wash low, and mein stones wash dull, ich hash taken leetle too much toll."

"But, Henry Snyder, vat did you do mid der toll?"

"Ah, Lort, ich gives it to der poor."

The judge paused for a moment, and then said, "Well, Henry Snyder, you must go to der right mid der sheep. But it is a tight squeeze."

Another specimen of his more sober forensic eloquence is to be found in the following speech. There was a bill before the house for the creation of a new county, and there was a dispute about the boundary-line. The author of the bill wished to run the line in a direction which would manifestly promote his own interest. Crockett arose and said:

"Mr. Speaker: Do you know what that man's bill reminds me of? Well, I s'pose you don't, so I'll tell you. Well, Mr. Speaker, when I first came to this country a blacksmith was a rare thing. But there happened to be one in my neighborhood. He had no striker; and whenever one of the neighbors wanted any work done, he had to go over and strike until his work was finished. These were hard times, Mr. Speaker, but we had to do the best we could.

"It happened that one of my neighbors wanted an axe. So he took along with him a piece of iron, and went over to the blacksmith's to strike till his axe was done. The iron was heated, and my neighbor fell to work,

71

and was striking there nearly all day; when the blacksmith concluded that the iron wouldn't make an axe, but 'twould make a fine mattock.

"So my neighbor, wanting a mattock, concluded that he would go over and strike till the mattock was done. Accordingly he went over the next day, and worked faithfully. But toward night the blacksmith concluded his iron wouldn't make a mattock but 'twould make a fine ploughshare.

"So my neighbor, wanting a ploughshare, agreed that he would go over the next day and strike till that was done. Accordingly he went over, and fell hard at work. But toward night the blacksmith concluded his iron wouldn't make a ploughshare, but 'twould make a fine skow. So my neighbor, tired of working, cried, 'A skow let it be;' and the blacksmith, taking up the red-hot iron, threw it into a trough of hot water near him, and as it fell in, it sung out skow. And this, Mr. Speaker, will be the way of that man's bill for a county. He'll keep you all here, doing nothing, and finally his bill will turn up a skow; now mind if it don't."

At this time, Crockett, by way of courtesy, was usually called colonel, as with us almost every respectable man takes the title of esquire. One of the members offended Colonel Crockett by speaking disrespectfully of him as from the back woods, or, as he expressed it, the gentleman from the cane. Crockett made a very bungling answer, which did not satisfy himself. After the house adjourned, he very pleasantly invited the gentleman to take a walk with him. They chatted very sociably by the way, till, at the distance of about a mile, they reached a very secluded spot, when the Colonel, turning to his opponent, said:

"Do you know what I brought you here for?"

"No," was the reply.

"Well," added the Colonel, "I brought you here for the express purpose of whipping you; and now I mean to do it."

"But," says the Colonel, in recording the event, "the fellow said he didn't mean anything, and kept 'pologizing till I got into good humor."

They walked back as good friends as ever, and no one but themselves knew of the affair.

After the adjournment of the Legislature, Crockett returned to his impoverished home. The pecuniary losses he had encountered, induced him to make another move, and one for which it is difficult to conceive of any adequate motive. He took his eldest son, a boy about eight years of age, and a young man by the name of Abram Henry, and with one pack-horse to carry their blankets and provisions, plunged into the vast wilderness west of them, on an exploring tour, in search of a new home.

Crockett and the young man shouldered their rifles. Day after day the three trudged along, fording streams, clambering hills, wading morasses, and threading ravines, each night constructing a frail shelter, and cooking by their camp-fire such game as they had taken by the way.

After traversing these almost pathless wilds a hundred and fifty miles, and having advanced nearly fifty miles beyond any white settlement, they reached the banks of a lonely stream, called Obion River, on the extreme western frontier of Tennessee. This river emptied into the Mississippi but a few miles from the spot where Crockett decided to rear his cabin. His nearest neighbor was seven miles distant, his next fifteen, his next twenty.

About ten years before, that whole region had been convulsed by one of the most terrible earthquakes recorded in history. One or two awful hurricanes had followed the earthquake, prostrating the gigantic forest, and scattering the trees in all directions. Appalling indications remained of the power expended by these tremendous forces of nature. The largest forest-trees were found split from their roots to their tops, and lying half on each side of a deep fissure. The opening abysses, the entanglement of the prostrate forest, and the dense underbrush which had sprung up, rendered the whole region almost impenetrable. The country was almost entirely uninhabited. It had, however, become quite celebrated as being the best hunting-ground in the West. The fear of earthquakes and the general desolation had prevented even the Indians from rearing their wigwams there. Consequently wild animals had greatly increased. The country was filled with bears, wolves, panthers, deer, elks, and other smaller game.

The Indians had recently made this discovery, and were, in ever-increasing numbers, exploring the regions in hunting-bands. Crockett does not seem to have had much appreciation of the beautiful. In selecting a spot for his hut, he wished to be near some crystal stream where he could get water, and to build his hut upon land sufficiently high to be above the reach of freshets. It was also desirable to find a small plain or meadow free from trees, where he could plant his corn; and to be in the edge of the forest, which would supply him with abundance of fuel. Crockett found such a place, exactly to his mind. Being very fond of hunting, he was the happiest of men. A few hours' labor threw up a rude hut which was all the home he desired. His rifle furnished him with food, and with the skins of animals for bed and bedding. Every frontiersman knew how to dress the skin of deer for moccasins and other garments. With a sharpened stick he punched holes through the rank sod, and planted corn, in soil so rich that it would return him several hundred-fold.

Thus his tastes, such as they were, were gratified, and he enjoyed what to him were life's luxuries. He probably would not have been willing to exchange places with the resident in the most costly mansion in our great cities. In a few days he got everything comfortable around him. Crockett's cabin, or rather camp, was on the eastern side of the Obion River. Seven miles farther up the stream, on the western bank, a Mr. Owen had reared his log house. One morning, Crockett, taking the young man Henry and his son with him, set out to visit Mr. Owen, his nearest neighbor. He hobbled his horse, leaving him to graze until he got back.

They followed along the banks of the river, through the forest, until they reached a point nearly opposite Owen's cabin. By crossing the stream there, and following up the western bank they would be sure to find his hut. There was no boat, and the stream must be swum or forded. Recent rains had caused it to overflow its banks and spread widely over the marshy bottoms and low country near by. The water was icy cold. And yet they took to it, says Crockett, "like so many beavers."

The expanse to be crossed was very wide, and they knew not how deep they should find the channel. For some distance the water continued quite shoal. Gradually it deepened. Crockett led the way, with a pole in his hand. Cautiously he sounded the depth before him, lest they should fall into any slough. A dense growth of young trees covered the inundated bottom over which they were wading. Occasionally they came to a deep but narrow gully. Crockett, with his hatchet, would cut down a small tree, and by its aid would cross.

At length the water became so deep that Crockett's little boy had to swim, though they evidently had not yet reached the channel of the stream. Having waded nearly half a mile, they came to the channel. The stream, within its natural banks, was but about forty feet wide. Large forest-trees fringed the shores. One immense tree, blown down by the wind, reached about halfway across. Crockett, with very arduous labor with his hatchet, cut down another, so that it fell with the branches of the two intertwining.

Thus aided they reached the opposite side. But still the lowlands beyond were overflowed as far as the eye could see through the dense forest. On they waded, for nearly a mile, when, to their great joy, they came in sight of dry land. Their garments were dripping and they were severely chilled as they reached the shore. But turning their steps up the stream, they soon came in sight of the cabin, which looked to them like a paradise of rest. It was one of the rudest of huts. The fenceless grounds around were rough and ungainly. The dismal forest, which chanced there to have escaped both earthquake and hurricane, spread apparently without limits in all directions.

Most men, most women, gazing upon a scene so wild, lonely, cheerless, would have said, "Let me sink into the grave rather than be doomed to such a home as that." But to Crockett and his companions it presented all the attractions their hearts could desire. Mr. Owen and several other men were just starting away from the cabin, when, to their surprise, they saw the party of strangers approaching. They waited until Crockett came up and introduced himself. The men with Mr. Owen were boatmen, who had entered the Obion River from the Mississippi with a boat-load of articles for trade. They were just leaving to continue their voyage.

Such men are seldom in a hurry. Time is to them of but very little value. Hospitality was a virtue which cost nothing. Any stranger, with his rifle, could easily pay his way in the procurement of food. They all turned back and entered the cabin together. Mrs. Owen was an excellent, motherly woman, about fifty years of age. Her sympathies were immediately excited for the poor little boy, whose garments were drenched, and who was shivering as if in an ague-fit. She replenished the fire, dried his clothes, and gave him some warm and nourishing food. The grateful father writes:

"Her kindness to my little boy did me ten times as much good as anything she could have done for me, if she had tried her best."

These were not the days of temperance. The whiskey-bottle was considered one of the indispensables of every log cabin which made any pretences to gentility. The boat, moored near the shore, was loaded with whiskey, flour, sugar, hardware, and other articles, valuable in the Indian trade in the purchase of furs, and in great demand in the huts of pioneers. There was a small trading-post at what was called McLemone's Bluff; about thirty miles farther up the river by land, and nearly one hundred in following the windings of the stream. This point the boatmen were endeavoring to reach.

For landing their cargo at this point the boatmen were to receive five hundred dollars, besides the profits of any articles they could sell in the scattered hamlets they might encounter by the way. The whiskey-bottle was of course brought out. Crockett drank deeply; he says, at least half a pint. His tongue was unloosed, and he became one of the most voluble and entertaining of men. His clothes having been dried by the fire, and all having with boisterous merriment partaken of a hearty supper, as night came on the little boy was left to the tender care of Mrs. Owen, while the rest of the party repaired to the cabin of the boat, to make a night of it in drinking and carousal.

They had indeed a wild time. There was whiskey in abundance. Crockett was in his element, and kept the whole company in a constant roar. Their shouts and bacchanal songs resounded through the solitudes, with clamor and profaneness which must have fallen painfully upon angels' ears, if any of heaven's pure and gentle spirits were within hearing distance.

"We had," writes Crockett, "a high night of it, as I took steam enough to drive out all the cold that was in me, and about three times as much more."

These boon companions became warm friends, according to the most approved style of backwoods friendship. Mr. Owen told the boatmen that a few miles farther up the river a hurricane had entirely prostrated the forest, and that the gigantic trees so encumbered the stream that he was doubtful whether the boat could pass, unless the water should rise higher. Consequently he, with Crockett and Henry, accompanied the boatmen up to that point to help them through, should it be possible to effect a passage. But it was found impossible, and the boat dropped down again to its moorings opposite Mr. Owen's cabin.

As it was now necessary to wait till the river should rise, the boatmen and Mr. Owen all consented to accompany Crockett to the place where he was to settle, and build his house for him. It seems very strange that, in that dismal wilderness, Crockett should not have preferred to build his cabin near so kind a neighbor. But so it was. He chose his lot at a distance of seven miles from any companionship.

"And so I got the boatmen," he writes, "all to go out with me to where I was going to settle, and we slipped up a cabin in little or no time. I got from the boat four barrels of meal, one of salt, and about ten gallons of whiskey."

For these he paid in labor, agreeing to accompany the boatmen up the river as far as their landing-place at McLemone's Bluff.

CHAPTER VIII.

Life on the Obion.

Hunting Adventures.—The Voyage up the River.—Scenes in the Cabin.—Return Home.—Removal of the Family.—Crockett's Riches.—A Perilous Enterprise.—Reasons for his Celebrity.—Crockett's Narrative.—A Bear-Hunt.—Visit to Jackson.—Again a Candidate for the Legislature.—Electioneering and Election.

The next day after building the cabin, to which Crockett intended to move his family, it began to rain, as he says, "rip-roariously." The river rapidly rose, and the boatmen were ready to resume their voyage. Crockett stepped out into the forest and shot a deer, which he left as food for Abram Henry and his little boy, who were to remain in the cabin until his return. He expected to be absent six or seven days. The stream was very sluggish. By poling, as it was called, that is, by pushing the boat with long poles, they reached the encumbrance caused by the hurricane, where they stopped for the night.

In the morning, as soon as the day dawned, Crockett, thinking it impossible for them to get through the fallen timber that day, took his rifle and went into the forest in search of game. He had gone but a short distance when he came across a fine buck. The animal fell before his unerring aim, and, taking the prize upon his shoulders, he commenced a return to the boat.

He had not proceeded far before he came upon the fresh tracks of a herd of elks. The temptation to follow their trail was to a veteran hunter irresistible. He threw down his buck, and had not gone far before he came upon two more bucks, very large and splendid animals. The beautiful creatures, though manifesting some timidity, did not seem disposed to run, but, with their soft, womanly eyes, gazed with wonder upon the approaching stranger. The bullet from Crockett's rifle struck between the eyes of one, and he fell dead. The other, his companion, exhibited almost human sympathy. Instead of taking to flight, he clung to his lifeless associate, looking down upon him as if some incomprehensible calamity had occurred. Crockett rapidly reloaded his rifle, and the other buck fell dead.

He hung them both upon the limb of a tree, so that they should not be devoured by the wolves, and followed on in the trail of the elks. He did not overtake them until nearly noon. They were then beyond rifle-shot, and kept so, luring him on quite a distance. At length he saw two other fine bucks, both of which he shot. The intellectual culture of the man may be inferred from the following characteristic description which he gives of these events:

"I saw two more bucks, very large fellows too. I took a blizzard at one of them, and up he tumbled. The other ran off a few jumps and stopped, and stood there until I loaded again and fired at him. I knocked his trotters from under him, and then I hung them both up. I pushed on again, and about sunset I saw three other bucks. I down'd with one of them, and the other two ran off. I hung this one up also, having killed six that day.

"I then pushed on till I got to the hurricane, and at the lower edge of it, about where I expected the boat was. Here I hollered as hard as I could roar, but could get no answer. I fired off my gun, and the men on the boat fired one too. But, quite contrary to my expectations, they had got through the timber, and were about two miles above me. It was now dark, and I had to crawl through the fallen timber the best way I could; and if the reader don't know it was bad enough, I am sure I do. For the vines and briers had grown all through it, and so thick that a good fat coon couldn't much more than get along. I got through at last, and went on to near where I had killed my last deer, and once more fired off my gun, which was again answered from the boat, which was a little above me. I moved on as fast as I could, but soon came to water; and not knowing how deep it was, I halted, and hollered till they came to me with a skiff. I now got to the boat without further difficulty. But the briers had worked on me at such a rate that I felt like I wanted sewing up all over. I took a pretty stiff horn, which soon made me feel much better. But I was so tired that I could scarcely work my jaws to eat."

The next morning, Crockett took a young man with him and went out into the woods to bring in the game he had shot. They brought in two of the bucks, which afforded them all the supply of venison they needed, and left the others hanging upon the trees. The boatmen then pushed their way up the river. The progress was slow, and eleven toilsome days passed before they reached their destination. Crockett had now discharged his debt, and prepared to return to his cabin. There was a light skiff attached to the large flat-bottomed boat in which they had ascended the river. This skiff Crockett took, and, accompanied by a young man by the name of Flavius Harris, who had decided to go back with him, speedily paddled their way down the stream to his cabin.

There were now four occupants of this lonely, dreary hut, which was surrounded by forests and fallen trees and briers and brambles. They all went to work vigorously in clearing some land for a corn field, that they might lay in a store for the coming winter. The spring was far advanced, and the season for planting nearly gone. They had brought some seed with them on their pack-horse, and they soon had the pleasure of seeing the tender sprouts pushing up vigorously through the luxuriant virgin soil. It was not necessary to fence their field. Crockett writes:

"There was no stock nor anything else to disturb our corn except the wild varmints; and the old serpent himself, with a fence to help him, couldn't keep them out."

Here Crockett and his three companions remained through the summer and into the autumn, until they could gather in their harvest of corn. During that time they lived, as they deemed, sumptuously, upon game. To kill a grizzly bear was ever considered an achievement of which any hunter might boast. During the summer, Crockett killed ten of these ferocious monsters. Their flesh was regarded as a great delicacy. And their shaggy skins were invaluable in the cabin for beds and bedding. He also shot deer in great abundance. The smaller game he took, of fat turkeys, partridges, pigeons, etc., he did not deem worth enumerating.

It was a very lazy, lounging, indolent life. Crockett could any morning go into the woods and shoot a deer. He would bring all the desirable parts of it home upon his shoulders, or he would take his pack-horse out with him for that purpose. At their glowing fire, outside of the cabin if the weather were pleasant, inside if it rained, they would cook the tender steaks. They had meal for corn bread; and it will also be remembered that they had sugar, and ten gallons of whiskey.

The deerskins were easily tanned into soft and pliant leather. They all knew how to cut these skins, and with tough sinews to sew them into hunting-shirts, moccasins, and other needed garments. Sitting Indian-fashion on mattresses or cushions of bearskin, with just enough to do gently to interest the mind, with no anxiety or thought even about the future, they would loiter listlessly through the long hours of the summer days.

Occasionally two or three Indians, on a hunting excursion, would visit the cabin. These Indians were invariably friendly. Crockett had no more apprehension that they would trouble him than he had that the elk or the deer would make a midnight attack upon his cabin. Not unfrequently they would have a visit from Mr. Owen's household; or they would all go up to his hut for a carouse. Two or three times, during the summer, small parties exploring the country came along, and would rest a day or two under Crockett's hospitable roof. Thus with these men, with their peculiar habits and tastes, the summer probably passed away as pleasantly as with most people in this world of care and trouble.

Early in the autumn, Crockett returned to Central Tennessee to fetch his family to the new home. Upon reaching his cabin in Giles County, he was met by a summons to attend a special session of the Legislature. He attended, and served out his time, though he took but little interest in legislative affairs. His thoughts were elsewhere, and he was impatient for removal, before cold weather should set in, to his far-distant home.

Late in October he set out with his little family on foot, for their long journey of one hundred and fifty miles through almost a pathless forest. His poverty was extreme. But the peculiar character of the man was such that he did net seem to regard that at all. Two pack-horses conveyed all their household goods. Crockett led the party, with a child on one arm and his rifle on the other. He walked gayly along, singing as merrily as the birds. Half a dozen dogs followed him. Then came the horses in single file. His wife and older children, following one after the other in single file along the narrow trail, closed up the rear. It was a very singular procession, thus winding its way, through forest and moor, over hills and prairies, to the silent shores of the Mississippi. The eventful journey was safely accomplished, and he found all things as he had left them. A rich harvest of golden ears was waving in his corn-field; and his comfortable cabin, in all respects as comfortable as the one he had left, was ready to receive its inmates.

He soon gathered in his harvest, and was thus amply supplied with bread for the winter. Fuel, directly at his hand, was abundant, and thus, as we may say, his coal-bin was full. Game of every kind, excepting buffaloes, was ranging the woods, which required no shelter or food at his expense, and from which he could, at pleasure, select any variety of the most delicious animal food he might desire. Thus his larder was full to repletion. The skins of animals furnished them with warm and comfortable clothing, easily decorated with fringes and some bright coloring, whose beauty was tasteful to every eye. Thus the family wardrobe was amply stored. Many might have deemed Crockett a poor man. He regarded himself as one of the lords of creation.

Christmas was drawing nigh. It may be doubted whether Crockett had the slightest appreciation of the sacred character of that day which commemorates the advent of the Son of God to suffer and die for the sins of the world. With Crockett it had ever been a day of jollification. He fired salutes with his rifle. He sung his merriest songs. He told his funniest stories. He indulged himself in the highest exhilaration which whiskey could induce.

As this holiday approached, Crockett was much troubled in finding that his powder was nearly expended, and that he had none "to fire Christmas guns." This seemed really to annoy him more than that he had none to hunt with.

In the mean time, a brother-in-law had moved to that region, and had reared his cabin at a distance of six miles from the hut of David Crockett, on the western bank of Rutherford's Fork, one of the tributaries of Obion River. He had brought with him a keg of powder for Crockett, which had not yet been delivered.

The region all around was low and swampy. The fall rains had so swollen the streams that vast extents of territory were inundated. All the river-bottoms were covered with water. The meadows which lined the Obion, where Crockett would have to pass, were so flooded that it was all of a mile from shore to shore.

The energy which Crockett displayed on the difficult and perilous journey, illustrates those remarkable traits of character which have given him such wide renown. There must be something very extraordinary about a man which can make his name known throughout a continent. And of the forty millions of people in the United States, there is scarcely one, of mature years, who has not heard the name of David Crockett.

When Crockett told his wife that he had decided to go to his brother's for the powder, she earnestly remonstrated, saying that it was at the imminent hazard of his life. The ground was covered with snow. He would have to walk at least a mile through icy water, up to his waist, and would probably have to swim the channel. He then, with dripping clothes, and through the cold wintry blast, would have to walk several miles before he could reach his brother's home. Crockett persisted in his determination, saying, "I have no powder for Christmas, and we are out of meat."

He put on some woollen wrappers and a pair of deerskin moccasins. He then tied up a small bundle; of clothes, with shoes and stockings, which he might exchange for his dripping garments when he should reach his brother's cabin. I quote from his own account of the adventure.

"I didn't before know how much a person could suffer and not die. The snow was about four inches deep when I started. And when I got to the water, which was only about a quarter of a mile off, it looked like an ocean. I put in, and waded on till I came to the channel, where I crossed that on a high log. I then took water again, having my gun and all my hunting tools along, and waded till I came to a deep slough, that was wider than the river itself. I had often crossed it on a log; but behold, when I got there no log was to be seen.

"I know'd of an island in the slough, and a sapling stood on it close to the side of that log, which was now entirely under water. I know'd further, that the water was about eight or ten feet deep under the log, and I judged it to be three feet deep over it. After studying a little what I should do, I determined to cut a forked sapling, which stood near me, so as to lodge it against the one that stood on the island. In this I succeeded very well. I then cut me a pole, and then crawled along on my sapling till I got to the one it was lodged against, which was about six feet above the water.

"I then felt about with the pole till I found the log, which was just about as deep under the water as I had judged. I then crawled back and got my gun, which I had left at the stump of the sapling I had cut, and again made my way to the place of lodgment, and then climbed down the other sapling so as to get on the log. I felt my way along with my feet in the water about waist-deep, but it was a mighty ticklish business.

However, I got over, and by this time I had very little feeling in my feet and legs, as I had been all the time in the water, except what time I was crossing the high log over the river and climbing my lodged sapling.

"I went but a short distance when I came to another slough, over which there was a log, but it was floating on the water. I thought I could walk it, so I mounted on it. But when I had got about the middle of the deep water, somehow or somehow else, it turned over, and in I went up to my head. I waded out of this deep water, and went ahead till I came to the highland, where I stopped to pull of my wet clothes, and put on the others which I held up with my gun above water when I fell in."

This exchanging of his dripping garments for dry clothes, standing in the snow four inches deep, and exposed to the wintry blast, must have been a pretty severe operation. Hardy as Crockett was, he was so chilled and numbed by the excessive cold that his flesh had scarcely any feeling. He tied his wet clothes together and hung them up on the limb of a tree, to drip and dry He thought he would then set out on the full run, and endeavor thus to warm himself by promoting the more rapid circulation of his blood. But to his surprise he could scarcely move. With his utmost exertions he could not take a step more than six inches in length. He had still five miles to walk, through a rough, pathless forest, encumbered with snow.

By great and painful effort he gradually recovered the use of his limbs, and toiling along for two or three hours, late in the evening was cheered by seeing the light of a bright fire shining through the chinks between the logs of his brother's lonely cabin. He was received with the utmost cordiality. Even his hardy pioneer brother listened with astonishment to the narrative of the perils he had surmounted and the sufferings he had endured. After the refreshment of a warm supper, Crockett wrapped himself in a bearskin, and lying down upon the floor, with his feet to the fire, slept the sweet, untroubled sleep of a babe. In the morning he awoke as well as ever, feeling no bad consequences from the hardships of the preceding day.

The next morning a freezing gale from the north wailed through the snow-whitened forest, and the cold was almost unendurable. The earnest persuasions of his brother and his wife induced him to remain with them for the day. But, with his accustomed energy, instead of enjoying the cosey comfort of the Fireside, he took his rifle, and went out into the woods, wading the snow and breasting the gale. After the absence of an hour or two, he returned tottering beneath the load of two deer, which he had shot, and which he brought to the cabin on his shoulders. Thus he made a very liberal contribution to the food of the family, so that his visit was a source of profit to them, not of loss.

All the day, and during the long wintry night, the freezing blasts blew fiercely, and the weather grew more severely cold. The next morning his friends urged him to remain another day. They all knew that the water would be frozen over, but not sufficiently hard to bear his weight, and this would add greatly to the difficulty and the danger of his return. It seemed impossible that any man could endure, on such a day, fording a swollen stream, a mile in breadth, the water most of the way up to his waist, in some places above his head, and breaking the ice at every step. The prospect appalled even Crockett himself. He therefore decided to remain till the next morning, though he knew that his family would be left in a state of great anxiety. He hoped that an additional day and night might so add to the thickness of the ice that it would bear his weight.

He therefore shouldered his musket and again went into the woods on a hunt. Though he saw an immense bear, and followed him for some distance, he was unable to shoot him. After several hours' absence, he returned empty-handed.

Another morning dawned, lurid and chill, over the gloomy forest. Again his friends entreated him not to run the risk of an attempt to return in such fearful weather. "It was bitter cold," he writes, "but I know'd my family was without meat, and I determined to get home to them, or die a-trying."

We will let Crockett tell his own story of his adventures in going back:

"I took my keg of powder and all my hunting tools and cut out. When I got to the water, it was a sheet of ice as far as I could see. I put on to it, but hadn't got far before it broke through with me; and so I took out my tomahawk, and broke my way along before me for a considerable distance.

"At last I got to where the ice would bear me for a short distance, and I mounted on it and went ahead. But it soon broke in again, and I had to wade on till I came to my floating log. I found it so tight this time, that I know'd it couldn't give me another fall, as it was frozen in with the ice. I crossed over it without much difficulty, and worked along till I came to my lodged sapling and my log under the water.

"The swiftness of the current prevented the water from freezing over it; and so I had to wade, just as I did when I crossed it before. When I got to my sapling, I left my gun, and climbed out with my powder-keg first, and then went back and got my gun. By this time, I was nearly frozen to death; but I saw all along before me where the ice had been fresh broke, and I thought it must be a bear struggling about in the water. I therefore fresh-primed my gun, and, cold as I was, I was determined to make war on him if we met. But I followed the trail till it led me home. Then I found that it had been made by my young man that lived with me, who had been sent by my distressed wife to see, if he could, what had become of me, for they all believed that I was dead. When I got home, I wasn't quite dead, but mighty nigh it; but had my powder, and that was what I went for."

The night after Crockett's return a heavy rain fell, which, toward morning, turned to sleet. But there was no meat in the cabin. There were at that time three men who were inmates of that lowly hut—Crockett, a young man, Flavius Harris, who had taken up his abode with the pioneer, and a brother in-law, who had recently emigrated to that wild country, and had reared his cabin not far distant from Crockett's. They all turned out hunting. Crockett, hoping to get a bear, went up the river into the dense and almost impenetrable thickets, where the gigantic forest had been swept low by the hurricane. The other two followed down the stream in search of turkeys, grouse, and such small game.

Crockett took with him three dogs, one of which was an old hound, faithful, sagacious, but whose most vigorous days were gone. The dogs were essential in hunting bears. By their keen scent they would find the animal, which fact they would announce to the hunter by their loud barking. Immediately a fierce running fight would ensue. By this attack the bear would be greatly retarded in his flight, so that the hunter could overtake him, and he would often be driven into a tree, where the unerring rifle-bullet would soon bring him down.

The storm of sleet still raged, and nothing could be more gloomy than the aspect of dreariness and desolation which the wrecked forest presented with its dense growth of briers and thorns. Crockett toiled through the storm and the brush about six miles up the river, and saw nothing. He then crossed over, about four miles, to another stream. Still no game appeared. The storm was growing more violent, the sleet growing worse and worse. Even the bears sought shelter from the pitiless wintry gale. The bushes were all bent down with the ice which clung to their branches, and were so bound together that it was almost impossible for any one to force his way through them.

The ice upon the stream would bear Crockett's weight. He followed it down a mile or two, when his dogs started up a large flock of turkeys. He shot two of them. They were immensely large, fat, and heavy. Tying their legs together, he slung them over his shoulder, and with this additional burden pressed on his toilsome way. Ere long he became so fatigued that he was compelled to sit down upon a log to rest.

Just then his dogs began to bark furiously. He was quite sure that they had found a bear. Eagerly he followed the direction they indicated, as fast as he could force his way along. To his surprise he found that the three dogs had stopped near a large tree, and were barking furiously at nothing. But as soon as they saw him approaching they started off again, making the woods resound with their baying. Having run about a quarter of a mile, he could perceive that again they had stopped. When Crockett reached them there was no game in sight. The dogs, barking furiously again, as soon as they saw him approaching plunged into the thicket.

For a third time, and a fourth time, this was repeated. Crockett could not understand what it meant. Crockett became angry at being thus deceived, and resolved that he would shoot the old hound, whom he considered the ringleader in the mischief, as soon as he got near enough to do so.

"With this intention," he says, "I pushed on the harder, till I came to the edge of an open prairie; and looking on before my dogs, I saw about the biggest bear that ever was seen in America. He looked, at the distance he was from me, like a large black bull. My dogs were afraid to attack him, and that was the reason they had stopped so often that I might overtake them."

This is certainly a remarkable instance of animal sagacity. The three dogs, by some inexplicable conference among themselves, decided that the enemy was too formidable for them to attack alone. They therefore summoned their master to their aid. As soon as they saw that he was near enough to lend his cooperation, then they fearlessly assailed the monster.

The sight inspired Crockett with new life. Through thickets, briers, and brambles they all rushed—bear, dogs, and hunter. At length, the shaggy monster, so fiercely assailed, climbed for refuge a large black-oak tree, and sitting among the branches, looked composedly down upon the dogs barking fiercely at its foot. Crockett crept up within about eighty yards, and taking deliberate aim at his breast, fired. The bullet struck and pierced the monster directly upon the spot at which it was aimed. The bear uttered a sharp cry, made a convulsive movement with one paw, and remained as before.

Speedily Crockett reloaded his rifle, and sent another bullet to follow the first. The shaggy brute shuddered in every limb, and then tumbled head-long to the icy ground. Still he was not killed. The dogs plunged upon him, and there was a tremendous fight. The howling of the bear, and the frenzied barking of the dogs, with their sharp cries of pain as the claws of the monster tore their flesh, and the deathly struggle witnessed as they rolled over and over each other in the fierce fight, presented a terrific spectacle.

Crockett hastened to the aid of his dogs. As soon as the bear saw him approach, he forsook the inferior, and turned with all fury upon the superior foe. Crockett was hurrying forward with his tomahawk in one hand and his big butcher-knife in the other, when the bear, with eyes flashing fire, rushed upon him. Crockett ran back, seized his rifle, and with a third bullet penetrated the monster's brain and he fell dead. The dogs and their master seemed to rejoice alike in their great achievement.

By the route which Crockett had pursued, he was about twelve miles from home. Leaving the huge carcass where the animal had fallen, he endeavored to make a straight line through the forest to his cabin. That he might find his way back again, he would, at every little distance, blaze, as it was called, a sapling, that is, chip off some of the bark with his hatchet. When he got within a mile of home this was no longer necessary.

The other two men had already returned to the cabin. As the wolves might devour the valuable meat before morning, they all three set out immediately, notwithstanding their fatigue and the still raging storm, and taking with them four pack-horses, hastened back to bring in their treasure. Crockett writes:

"We got there just before dark, and struck a fire, and commenced butchering my bear. It was some time in the night before we finished it. And I can assert, on my honor, that I believe he would have weighed six hundred pounds. It was the second largest I ever saw. I killed one, a few years after, that weighed six hundred and seventeen pounds. I now felt fully compensated for my sufferings in going back after my powder; and well satisfied that a dog might sometimes be doing a good business, even when he seemed to be barking up the wrong tree.

"We got our meat home, and I had the pleasure to know that we now had a plenty, and that of the best; and I continued through the winter to supply my family abundantly with bear-meat, and venison from the woods."

In the early spring, Crockett found that he had a large number of valuable skins on hand, which he had taken during the winter. About forty miles southeast from Crockett's cabin, in the heart of Madison County, was the thriving little settlement of Jackson. Crockett packed his skins on a horse, shouldered his rifle, and taking his hardy little son for a companion, set off there to barter his peltries for such articles of household use as he could convey back upon his horse. The journey was accomplished with no more than the ordinary difficulties. A successful trade was effected, and with a rich store of coffee, sugar, powder, lead, and salt, the father and son prepared for their return.

Crockett found there some of his old fellow-soldiers of the Creek War. When all things were ready for a start, he went to bid adieu to his friends and to take a parting dram with them. There were three men present who were candidates for the State Legislature. While they were having a very merry time, one, as though uttering a thought which had that moment occurred to him, exclaimed, "Why, Crockett, you ought to offer yourself for the Legislature for your district." Crockett replied, "I live at least forty miles from any white settlement." Here the matter dropped.

About ten days after Crockett's return home, a stranger, passing along, stopped at Crockett's cabin and told him that he was a candidate for Legislature, and took from his pocket a paper, and read to him the announcement of the fact. There was something in the style of the article which satisfied Crockett that there was a little disposition to make fun of him; and that his nomination was intended as a burlesque.

This roused him, and he resolved to put in his claim with all his zeal. He consequently hired a man to work upon his farm, and set out on an electioneering tour.

Though very few people had seen Crockett, he had obtained very considerable renown in that community of backwoodsmen as a great bear-hunter. Dr. Butler, a man of considerable pretensions, and, by marriage, a nephew of General Jackson, was the rival candidate, and a formidable one. Indeed, he and his friends quite amused themselves with the idea that "the gentleman from the cane," as they contemptuously designated Crockett, could be so infatuated as to think that there was the least chance for him. The population of that wilderness region was so scarce that the district for which a representative was to be chosen consisted of eleven counties.

A great political gathering was called, which was to be held in Madison County, which was the strongest of them all. Here speeches were to be made by the rival candidates and their friends, and electioneering was to be practised by all the arts customary in that rude community. The narrative of the events which ensued introduces us to a very singular state of society. At the day appointed there was a large assembly, in every variety of backwoods costume, among the stumps and the lowly cabins of Jackson. Crockett mingled with the crowd, watching events, listening to everything which was said, and keeping himself as far as possible unknown.

Dr. Butler, seeing a group of men, entered among them, and called for whiskey to treat them all. The Doctor had once met Crockett when a few weeks before he had been in Jackson selling his furs. He however did not recognize his rival among the crowd. As the whiskey was passing freely around, Crockett thought it a favorable moment to make himself known, and to try his skill at an electioneering speech. He was a good-looking man, with a face beaming with fun and smiles, and a clear, ringing voice. He jumped upon a stump and shouted out, in tones which sounded far and wide, and which speedily gathered all around him.

"Hallo! Doctor Butler; you don't know me do you? But I'll make you know me mighty well before August. I see they have weighed you out against me. But I'll beat you mighty badly."

Butler pleasantly replied, "Ah, Colonel Crockett, is that you? Where did you come from?"

Crockett rejoined, "Oh, I have just crept out from the cane, to see what discoveries I could make among the white folks. You think you have greatly the advantage of me, Butler. 'Tis true I live forty miles from any settlement. I am poor, and you are rich. You see it takes two coonskins here to buy a quart. But I've good dogs, and my little boys at home will go to their death to support my election. They are mighty industrious. They hunt every night till twelve o'clock. It keeps the little fellows mighty busy to keep me in whiskey. When they gets tired, I takes my rifle and goes out and kills a wolf, for which the State pays me three dollars. So one way or other I keeps knocking along."

Crockett perhaps judged correctly that the candidate who could furnish the most whiskey would get the most votes. He thus adroitly informed these thirsty men of his readiness and his ability to furnish them with all the liquor they might need. Strange as his speech seems to us, it was adapted to the occasion, and was received with roars of laughter and obstreperous applause.

"Well, Colonel," said Dr. Butler, endeavoring to clothe his own countenance with smiles, "I see you can beat me electioneering."

"My dear fellow," shouted out Crockett, "you don't call this electioneering, do you? When you see me electioneering, I goes fixed for the purpose. I've got a suit of deer-leather clothes, with two big pockets. So I puts a bottle of whiskey in one, and a twist of tobacco in t'other, and starts out. Then, if I meets a friend, why, I pulls out my bottle and gives him a drink. He'll be mighty apt, before he drinks, to throw away his tobacco. So when he's done, I pulls my twist out of t'other pocket and gives him a chaw. I never likes to leave a man worse off than when I found him. If I had given him a drink and he had lost his tobacco, he would not have made much. But give him tobacco, and a drink too, and you are mighty apt to get his vote."

With such speeches as these, interlarded with fun and anecdote, and a liberal supply of whiskey, Crockett soon made himself known through all the grounds, and he became immensely popular. The backwoodsmen regarded him as their man, belonging to their class and representing their interests.

Dr. Butler was a man of some culture, and a little proud and overbearing in his manners. He had acquired what those poor men deemed considerable property. He lived in a framed house, and in his best room he had a rug or carpet spread over the middle of the floor. This carpet was a luxury which many of the pioneers had never seen or conceived of. The Doctor, standing one day at his window, saw several persons, whose votes he desired, passing along, and he called them in to take a drink.

There was a table in the centre of the room, with choice liquors upon it. The carpet beneath the table covered only a small portion of the floor, leaving on each side a vacant space around the room. The men cautiously walked around this space, without daring to put their feet upon the carpet. After many solicitations from Dr. Butler, and seeing him upon the carpet, they ventured up to the table and drank. They, however, were under great restraint, and soon left, manifestly not pleased with their reception.

Calling in at the next log house to which they came, they found there one of Crockett's warm friends. They inquired of him what kind of a man the great bear-hunter was, and received in reply that he was a first-rate man, one of the best hunters in the world; that he was not a bit proud; that he lived in a log cabin, without any glass for his windows, and with the earth alone for his floor.

"Ah!" they exclaimed with one voice, "he's the fellow for us. We'll never give our votes for such a proud man as Butler. He called us into his house to take a drink, and spread down one of his best bed-quilts for us to walk on. It was nothing but a piece of pride."

The day of election came, and Crockett was victorious by a majority of two hundred and forty-seven votes. Thus he found himself a second time a member of the Legislature of the State of Tennessee, and with a celebrity which caused all eyes to be turned toward "the gentleman from the cane."

CHAPTER IX.

Adventures in the Forest, on the River, and in the City

The Bear Hunter's Story.—Service in the Legislature.—Candidate for Congress.—Electioneering.—The New Speculation.—Disastrous Voyage.—Narrow Escape.—New Electioneering Exploits.—Odd Speeches.—The Visit to Crockett's Cabin.—His Political Views.—His Honesty.—Opposition to Jackson.—Scene at Raleigh.—Dines with the President.—Gross Caricature.—His Annoyance.

Crockett was very fond of hunting-adventures, and told stories of these enterprises in a racy way, peculiarly characteristic of the man. The following narrative from his own lips, the reader will certainly peruse with much interest.

"I was sitting by a good fire in my little cabin, on a cool November evening, roasting potatoes I believe, and playing with my children, when some one halloed at the fence. I went out, and there were three strangers, who said they come to take an elk-hunt. I was glad to see 'em, invited 'em in, and after supper we cleaned our guns. I took down old Betsey, rubbed her up, greased her, and laid her away to rest. She is a mighty rough old piece, but I love her, for she and I have seen hard times. She mighty seldom tells me a lie. If I hold her right, she always sends the ball where I tell her, After we were all fixed, I told 'em hunting-stories till bedtime.

"Next morning was clear and cold, and by times I sounded my horn, and my dogs came howling 'bout me, ready for a chase. Old Rattler was a little lame—a bear bit him in the shoulder; but Soundwell, Tiger, and the rest of 'em were all mighty anxious. We got a bite, and saddled our horses. I went by to git a neighbor to drive for us, and off we started for the Harricane. My dogs looked mighty wolfish; they kept jumping on one another and growling. I knew they were run mad for a fight, for they hadn't had one for two or three days. We were in fine spirits, and going 'long through very open woods, when one of the strangers said, 'I would give my horse now to see a bear.'

"Said I, 'Well, give me your horse,' and I pointed to an old bear, about three or four hundred yards ahead of us, feeding on acorns.

"I had been looking at him some time, but he was so far off; I wasn't certain what it was. However, I hardly spoke before we all strained off; and the woods fairly echoed as we harked the dogs on. The old bear didn't want to run, and he never broke till we got most upon him; but then he buckled for it, I tell you. When they overhauled him he just rared up on his hind legs, and he boxed the dogs 'bout at a mighty rate. He hugged old Tiger and another, till he dropped 'em nearly lifeless; but the others worried him, and after a while they all come to, and they give him trouble. They are mighty apt, I tell you, to give a bear trouble before they leave him.

"'Twas a mighty pretty fight—'twould have done any one's soul good to see it, just to see how they all rolled about. It was as much as I could do to keep the strangers from shooting him; but I wouldn't let 'em, for fear they would kill some of my dogs. After we got tired seeing 'em fight, I went in among 'em, and the first time they got him down I socked my knife in the old bear. We then hung him up, and went on to take our elk-hunt. You never seed fellows so delighted as them strangers was. Blow me, if they didn't cut more capers, jumping about, than the old bear. 'Twas a mighty pretty fight, but I believe I seed more fun looking at them than at the bear.

"By the time we got to the Harricane, we were all rested, and ripe for a drive. My dogs were in a better humor, for the fight had just taken off the wiry edge. So I placed the strangers at the stands through which I thought the elk would pass, sent the driver way up ahead, and I went down below.

"Everything was quiet, and I leaned old Betsey 'gin a tree, and laid down. I s'pose I had been lying there nearly an hour, when I heard old Tiger open. He opened once or twice, and old Rattler gave a long howl; the balance joined in, and I knew the elk were up. I jumped up and seized my rifle. I could hear nothing but one continued roar of all my dogs, coming right towards me. Though I was an old hunter, the music made my hair stand on end. Soon after they first started, I heard one gun go off, and my dogs stopped, but not long, for they took a little tack towards where I had placed the strangers. One of them fired, and they dashed back, and circled round way to my left. I run down 'bout a quarter of a mile, and I heard my dogs make a bend like they were coming to me. While I was listening, I heard the bushes breaking still lower down, and started to run there.

"As I was going 'long, I seed two elks burst out of the Harricane 'bout one hundred and thirty or forty yards below me. There was an old buck and a doe. I stopped, waited till they got into a clear place, and as the old fellow made a leap, I raised old Bet, pulled trigger, and she spoke out. The smoke blinded me so, that I couldn't see what I did; but as it cleared away, I caught a glimpse of only one of them going through the bushes; so I thought I had the other. I went up, and there lay the old buck kicking. I cut his throat, and by that time, Tiger and two of my dogs came up. I thought it singular that all my dogs wasn't there, and I began to think they had killed another. After the dogs had bit him, and found out he was dead, old Tiger began to growl, and curled himself up between his legs. Everything had to stand off then, for he wouldn't let the devil himself touch him.

"I started off to look for the strangers. My two dogs followed me. After gitting away a piece, I looked back, and once in a while I could see old Tiger git up and shake the elk, to see if he was really dead, and then curl up between his legs agin. I found the strangers round a doe elk the driver had killed; and one of 'em said he was sure he had killed one lower down. I asked him if he had horns. He said he didn't see any. I put the dogs on where he said he had shot, and they didn't go fur before they came to a halt. I went up, and there lay a fine buck elk; and though his horns were four or five feet long, the fellow who shot him was so scared that he never saw them. We had three elk, and a bear; and we managed to git it home, then butchered our game, talked over our hunt, and had a glorious frolic."

Crockett served in the Legislature for two years, during which time nothing occurred of special interest. These were the years of 1823 and 1824. Colonel Alexander was then the representative, in the National Legislature, of the district in which Crockett lived. He had offended his constituents by voting for the Tariff. It was proposed to run Crockett for Congress in opposition to him. Crockett says:

"I told the people that I could not stand that. It was a step above my knowledge; and I know'd nothing about Congress matters."

They persisted; but he lost the election; for cotton was very high, and Alexander urged that it was in consequence of the Tariff. Two years passed away, which Crockett spent in the wildest adventures of hunting. He was a true man of the woods with no ambition for any better home than the log cabin he occupied. There was no excitement so dear to him as the pursuit and capture of a grizzly bear. There is nothing on record, in the way of hunting, which surpasses the exploits of this renowned bear-hunter. But there is a certain degree of sameness in these narratives of skill and endurance which would weary the reader.

In the fall of 1825, Crockett built two large flat-boats, to load with staves for the making of casks, which he intended to take down the river to market. He employed a number of hands in building the boat and splitting out the staves, and engaged himself in these labors "till the bears got fat." He then plunged into the woods, and in two weeks killed fifteen. The whole winter was spent in hunting with his son and his dogs. His workmen continued busy getting the staves, and when the rivers rose with the spring floods, he had thirty thousand ready for the market.

With this load he embarked for New Orleans. His boats without difficulty floated down the Obion into the majestic Mississippi. It was the first time he had seen the rush of these mighty waters. There was before him a boat voyage of nearly fifteen hundred miles, through regions to him entirely unknown. In his own account of this adventure he writes:

"When I got into the Mississippi I found all my hands were bad scared. In fact, I believe I was scared a little the worst of any; for I had never been down the river, and I soon discovered that my pilot was as ignorant of the business as myself. I hadn't gone far before I determined to lash the two boats together. We did so; but it made them so heavy and obstinate that it was next akin to impossible to do any thing at all with them, or to guide them right in the river.

"That evening we fell in company with some Ohio boats, and about night we tried to land, but we could not. The Ohio men hollered to us to go on and run all night. We took their advice, though we had a good deal rather not. But we couldn't do any other way. In a short distance we got into what is called the Devil's Elbow. And if any place in the wide creation has its own proper name I thought it was this. Here we had about the hardest work that I was ever engaged in in my life, to keep out of danger. And even then we were in it all the while. We twice attempted to land at Wood Yards, which we could see, but couldn't reach.

"The people would run out with lights, and try to instruct us how to get to shore; but all in vain. Our boats were so heavy that we could not take them much any way except the way they wanted to go, and just the way the current would carry them. At last we quit trying to land, and concluded just to go ahead as well as we could, for we found we couldn't do any better.

"Some time in the night I was down in the cabin of one of the boats, sitting by the fire, thinking on what a hobble we had got into; and how much better bear-hunting was on hard land, than floating along on the water, when a fellow had to go ahead whether he was exactly willing or not. The hatch-way of the cabin came slap down, right through the top of the boat; and it was the only way out, except a small hole in the side which we had used for putting our arms through to dip up water before we lashed the boats together.

"We were now floating sideways, and the boat I was in was the hindmost as we went. All at once I heard the hands begin to run over the top of the boat in great confusion, and pull with all their might. And the first thing I know'd after this we went broadside full tilt against the head of an island, where a large raft of drift timber had lodged. The nature of such a place would be, as everybody knows, to suck the boats down and turn them right under this raft; and the uppermost boat would, of course, be suck'd down and go under first. As soon as we struck, I bulged for my hatchway, as the boat was turning under sure enough. But when I got to it, the water was pouring through in a current as large as the hole would let it, and as strong as the weight of the river would force it. I found I couldn't get out here, for the boat was now turned down in such a way that it was steeper than a house-top. I now thought of the hole in the side, and made my way in a hurry for that.

"With difficulty I got to it, and when I got there, I found it was too small for me to get out by my own power, and I began to think that I was in a worse box than ever. But I put my arms through, and hollered as loud as I could roar, as the boat I was in hadn't yet quite filled with water up to my head; and the hands who were next to the raft, seeing my arms out, and hearing me holler, seized them, and began to pull. I told them I was sinking, and to pull my arms off, or force me through, for now I know'd well enough it was neck or nothing, come out or sink.

"By a violent effort they jerked me through; but I was in a pretty pickle when I got through. I had been sitting without any clothing over my shirt; this was tom off, and I was literally skinn'd like a rabbit. I was, however, well pleased to get out in any way, even without shirt or hide; as before I could straighten myself on the boat next to the raft, the one they pull'd me out of went entirely under, and I have never seen it any more to this day. We all escaped on to the raft, where we were compelled to sit all night, about a mile from land on either side. Four of my company were bareheaded, and three barefooted; and of that number I was one. I reckon I looked like a pretty cracklin ever to get to Congress!

"We had now lost all our loading, and every particle of our clothing, except what little we had on; but over all this, while I was sitting there, in the night, floating about on the drift, I felt happier and better off than I ever had in my life before, for I had just made such a marvellous escape, that I had forgot almost everything else in that; and so I felt prime.

"In the morning about sunrise, we saw a boat coming down, and we hailed her. They sent a large skiff, and took us all on board, and carried us down as far as Memphis. Here I met with a friend, that I never can forget as long as I am able to go ahead at anything; it was a Major Winchester, a merchant of that place; he let us all have hats, and shoes, and some little money to go upon, and so we all parted.

"A young man and myself concluded to go on down to Natchez, to see if we could hear anything of our boats; for we supposed they would float out from the raft, and keep on down the river. We got on a boat at Memphis, that was going down, and so cut out. Our largest boat, we were informed, had been seen about fifty miles below where we stove, and an attempt had been made to land her, but without success, as she was as hard-headed as ever.

"This was the last of my boats, and of my boating; for it went so badly with me along at the first, that I had not much mind to try it any more. I now returned home again, and, as the next August was the Congressional election, I began to turn my attention a little to that matter, as it was beginning to be talked of a good deal among the people."

Cotton was down very low. Crockett could now say to the people: "You see the effects of the Tariff." There were two rival candidates for the office, Colonel Alexander and General Arnold. Money was needed to carry the election, and Crockett had no money. He resolved, however, to try his chances. A friend loaned him a little money to start with; which sum Crockett, of course, expended in whiskey, as the most potent influence, then and there, to secure an election.

"So I was able," writes Crockett, "to buy a little of the 'creature,' to put my friends in a good humor, as well as the other gentlemen, for they all treat in that country; not to get elected, of course, for that would be against the law, but just to make themselves and their friends feel their keeping a little."

The contest was, as usual, made up of drinking, feasting, and speeches. Colonel Alexander was an intelligent and worthy man, who had been public surveyor. General Arnold was a lawyer of very respectable attainments. Neither of these men considered Crockett a candidate in the slightest degree to be feared. They only feared each other, and tried to circumvent each other.

On one occasion there was a large gathering, where all three of the candidates were present, and each one was expected to make a speech. It came Crockett's lot to speak first. He knew nothing of Congressional affairs, and had sense enough to be aware that it was not best for him to attempt to speak upon subjects of which he was entirely ignorant. He made one of his funny speeches, very short and entirely non-committal. Colonel Alexander followed, endeavoring to grapple with the great questions of tariffs, finance, and internal improvements, which were then agitating the nation.

General Arnold then, in his turn, took the stump, opposing the measures which Colonel Alexander had left. He seemed entirely to ignore the fact that Crockett was a candidate. Not the slightest allusion was made to him in his speech. The nervous temperament predominated in the man, and he was easily annoyed. While speaking, a large flock of guinea-hens came along, whose peculiar and noisy cry all will remember who have ever heard it. Arnold was greatly disturbed, and at last requested some one to drive the fowls away. As soon as he had finished his speech, Crockett again mounted the stump, and ostensibly addressing Arnold, but really addressing the crowd, said, in a loud voice, but very jocosely:

"Well, General, you are the first man I ever saw that understood the language of fowls. You had not the politeness even to allude to me in your speech. But when my little friends the guinea-hens came up, and began to holler 'Crockett, Crockett, Crockett,' you were ungenerous enough to drive them all away."

This raised such a universal laugh that even Crockett's opponents feared that he was getting the best of them in winning the favor of the people. When the day of election came, the popular bear-hunter beat both of his competitors by twenty-seven hundred and forty-seven votes. Thus David Crockett, unable to read and barely able to sign his name, became a member of Congress, to assist in framing laws for the grandest republic earth has ever known. He represented a constituency of about one hundred thousand souls.

An intelligent gentleman, travelling in West Tennessee, finding himself within eight miles of Colonel Crockett's cabin, decided to call upon the man whose name had now become quite renowned. This was just after Crockett's election to Congress, but before he had set out for Washington. There was no road leading to the lonely hut. He followed a rough and obstructed path or trail, which was indicated only by blazed trees, and which bore no marks of being often travelled.

At length he came to a small opening in the forest, very rude and uninviting in its appearance. It embraced eight or ten acres. One of the humblest and least tasteful of log huts stood in the centre. It was truly a cabin, a mere shelter from the weather. There was no yard; there were no fences. Not the slightest effort had been made toward ornamentation. It would be difficult to imagine a more lonely and cheerless abode.

Two men were seated on stools at the door, both in their shirt-sleeves, engaged in cleaning their rifles. As the stranger rode up, one of the men rose and came forward to meet him. He was dressed in very plain homespun attire, with a black fur cap upon his head. He was a finely proportioned man, about six feet high, apparently forty-five years of age, and of very frank, pleasing, open countenance. He held his rifle in his hand, and from his right shoulder hung a bag made of raccoon skin, to which there was a sheath attached containing a large butcher-knife.

"This is Colonel Crockett's residence, I presume," said the stranger.

"Yes," was the reply, with a smile as of welcome.

"Have I the pleasure of seeing that gentleman before me?" the stranger added.

"If it be a pleasure," was the courtly reply, "you have, sir."

"Well, Colonel," responded the stranger, "I have ridden much out of my way to spend a day or two with you, and take a hunt."

"Get down, sir," said the Colonel, cordially. "I am delighted to see you. I like to see strangers. And the only care I have is that I cannot accommodate them as well as I could wish. I have no corn, but my little boy will take your horse over to my son-in-law's. He is a good fellow, and will take care of him."

Leading the stranger into his cabin, Crockett very courteously introduced him to his brother, his wife, and his daughters. He then added:

"You see we are mighty rough here. I am afraid you will think it hard times. But we have to do the best we can. I started mighty poor, and have been rooting 'long ever since. But I hate apologies. What I live upon always, I think a friend can for a day or two. I have but little, but that little is as free as the water that runs. So make yourself at home."

Mrs. Crockett was an intelligent and capable woman for one in her station in life. The cabin was clean and orderly, and presented a general aspect of comfort. Many trophies of the chase were in the house, and spread around the yard. Several dogs, looking like war-worn veterans, were sunning themselves in various parts of the premises.

All the family were neatly dressed in home-made garments. Mrs. Crockett was a grave, dignified woman, very courteous to her guests. The daughters were remarkably pretty, but very diffident. Though entirely uneducated, they could converse very easily, seeming to inherit their father's fluency of utterance. They were active and efficient in aiding their mother in her household work. Colonel Crockett, with much apparent pleasure, conducted his guest over the small patch of ground he had grubbed and was cultivating. He exhibited his growing peas and pumpkins, and his little field of corn, with as much apparent pleasure as an Illinois farmer would now point out his hundreds of acres of waving grain. The hunter seemed surprisingly well informed. As we have mentioned, nature had endowed him with unusual strength of mind, and with a memory which was almost miraculous. He never forgot anything he had heard. His electioneering tours had been to him very valuable schools of education. Carefully he listened to all the speeches and the conversation of the intelligent men he met with.

John Quincy Adams was then in the Presidential chair. It was the year 1827. Nearly all Crockett's constituents were strong Jackson-men. Crockett, who afterward opposed Jackson, subsequently said, speaking of his views at that time:

"I can say on my conscience, that I was, without disguise, the friend and supporter of General Jackson upon his principles, as he had laid them down, and as I understood them, before his election as President."

Alluding to Crockett's political views at that time, his guest writes, "I held in high estimation the present Administration of our country. To this he was opposed. His views, however, delighted me. And were they more generally adopted we should be none the loser. He was opposed to the Administration, and yet conceded that many of its acts were wise and efficient, and would have received his cordial support. He admired Mr. Clay, but had objections to him. He was opposed to the Tariff, yet, I think, a supporter of the United States Bank. He seemed to have the most horrible objection to binding himself to any man or set of men. He said, 'I would as lieve be an old coon-dog as obliged to do what any man or set of men would tell me to do. I will support the present Administration as far as I would any other; that is, as far as I believe its views to be right. I will pledge myself to support no Administration. I had rather be politically damned than hypocritically immortalized.'"

In the winter of 1827, Crockett emerged from his cabin in the wilderness for a seat in Congress. He was so poor that he had not money enough to pay his expenses to Washington. His election had cost him one hundred and fifty dollars, which a friend had loaned him. The same friend advanced one hundred dollars more to help him on his journey.

"When I left home," he says, "I was happy, devilish, and full of fun. I bade adieu to my friends, dogs, and rifle, and took the stage, where I met with much variety of character, and amused myself when my humor prompted. Being fresh from the backwoods, my stories amused my companions, and I passed my time pleasantly.

"When I arrived at Raleigh the weather was cold and rainy, and we were all dull and tired. Upon going into the tavern, where I was an entire stranger, the room was crowded, and the crowd did not give way that I might come to the fire. I was rooting my way to the fire, not in a good humor, when some fellow staggered up towards me, and cried out, 'Hurrah for Adams.'

"Said I, 'Stranger, you had better hurrah for hell, and praise your own country.'

"'And who are you? said he. I replied:

"'I am that same David Crockett, fresh from the backwoods, half horse, half alligator, a little touched with the snapping-turtle. I can wade the Mississippi, leap the Ohio, ride upon a streak of lightning, and slip without a scratch down a honey-locust. I can whip my weight in wildcats, and, if any gentleman pleases, for a ten-dollar bill he can throw in a panther. I can hug a bear too close for comfort, and eat any man opposed to General Jackson.'"

All eyes were immediately turned toward this strange man, for all had heard of him. A place was promptly made for him at the fire. He was afterward asked if this wondrous outburst of slang was entirely unpremeditated. He said that it was; that it had all popped into his head at once; and that he should never have thought of it again, had not the story gone the round of the newspapers.

"I came on to Washington," he says, "and drawed two hundred and fifty dollars, and purchased with it a check on the bank in Nashville, and enclosed it to my friend. And I may say, in truth, I sent this money with a mighty good will, for I reckon nobody in this world loves a friend better than me, or remembers a kindness longer."

Soon after his arrival at Washington he was invited to dine with President Adams, a man of the highest culture, whose manners had been formed in the courts of Europe. Crockett, totally unacquainted with the usages of society, did not know what the note of invitation meant, and inquired of a friend, the Hon. Mr. Verplanck. He says:

"I was wild from the backwoods, and didn't know nothing about eating dinner with the big folks of our country. And how should I, having been a hunter all my life? I had eat most of my dinners on a log in the woods, and sometimes no dinner at all. I knew, whether I ate dinner with the President or not was a matter of no importance, for my constituents were not to be benefited by it. I did not go to court the President, for I was opposed to him in principle, and had no favors to ask at his hands. I was afraid, however, I should be awkward, as I was so entirely a stranger to fashion; and in going along, I resolved to observe the conduct of my friend Mr. Verplanck, and to do as he did. And I know that I did behave myself right well."

Some cruel wag wrote the following ludicrous account of this dinner-party, which went the round of all the papers as veritable history. The writer pretended to quote Crockett's own account of the dinner.

"The first thing I did," said Davy, "after I got to Washington, was to go to the President's. I stepped into the President's house. Thinks I, who's afeard. If I didn't, I wish I may be shot. Says I, 'Mr. Adams, I am Mr. Crockett, from Tennessee.' So, says he, 'How d'ye do, Mr. Crockett?' And he shook me by the hand, although he know'd I went the whole hog for Jackson. If he didn't, I wish I may be shot.

"Not only that, but he sent me a printed ticket to dine with him. I've got it in my pocket yet. I went to dinner, and I walked all around the long table, looking for something that I liked. At last I took my seat beside a fat goose, and I helped myself to as much of it as I wanted. But I hadn't took three bites, when I looked away up the table at a man they called Tash (attaché). He was talking French to a woman on t'other side of the table. He dodged his head and she dodged hers, and then they got to drinking wine across the table.

"But when I looked back again my plate was gone, goose and all. So I jist cast my eyes down to t'other end of the table, and sure enough I seed a white man walking off with my plate. I says, 'Hello, mister, bring back my plate.' He fetched it back in a hurry, as you may think. And when he set it down before me, how do you think it was? Licked as clean as my hand. If it wasn't, I wish I may be shot!

"Says he, 'What will you have, sir?' And says I, 'You may well say that, after stealing my goose.' And he began to laugh. Then says I, 'Mister, laugh if you please; but I don't half-like sich tricks upon travellers.' I then filled my plate with bacon and greens. And whenever I looked up or down the table, I held on to my plate with my left hand.

"When we were all done eating, they cleared everything off the table, and took away the table-cloth. And what do you think? There was another cloth under it. If there wasn't, I wish I may be shot! Then I saw a man coming along carrying a great glass thing, with a glass handle below, something like a candlestick. It was stuck full of little glass cups, with something in them that looked good to eat. Says I, 'Mister, bring that thing here.' Thinks I, let's taste them first. They were mighty sweet and good, so I took six of them. If I didn't, I wish I may be shot!"

This humorous fabrication was copied into almost every paper in the Union. The more respectable portion of Crockett's constituents were so annoyed that their representative should be thus held up to the contempt of the nation, that Crockett felt constrained to present a reliable refutation of the story. He therefore obtained and published certificates from three gentlemen, testifying to his good behavior at the table. Hon. Mr. Verplanck, of New York, testified as follows:

"I dined at the President's, at the time alluded to, in company with you, and I had, I recollect, a good deal of conversation with you. Your behavior there was, I thought, perfectly becoming and proper. And I do not recollect, or believe, that you said or did anything resembling the newspaper-account."

Two other members of Congress were equally explicit in their testimony.

During Crockett's first two sessions in Congress he got along very smoothly, cooperating generally with what was called the Jackson party. In 1829 he was again reelected by an overwhelming majority. On the 4th of March of this year, Andrew Jackson was inaugurated President of the United States. It may be doubted whether there ever was a more honest, conscientious man in Congress than David Crockett. His celebrated motto, "Be sure that you are right, and then go ahead," seemed ever to animate him. He could neither be menaced or bribed to support any measure which he thought to be wrong. Ere long he found it necessary to oppose some of Jackson's measures. We will let him tell the story in his own truthful words:

"Soon after the commencement of this second term, I saw, or thought I did, that it was expected of me that I would bow to the name of Andrew Jackson, and follow him in all his motions, and windings, and turnings, even at the expense of my conscience and judgment. Such a thing was new to me, and a total stranger to my principles. I know'd well enough, though, that if I didn't 'hurrah' for his name, the hue and cry was to be raised against me, and I was to be sacrificed, if possible. His famous, or rather I should say his infamous Indian bill was brought forward, and I opposed it from the purest motives in the world. Several of my colleagues got around me, and told me how well they loved me, and that I was ruining myself. They said this was a favorite measure of the President, and I ought to go for it. I told them I believed it was a wicked, unjust measure, and that I should go against it, let the cost to myself be what it might; that I was willing to go with General Jackson in everything that I believed was honest and right; but, further than this, I wouldn't go for him or any other man in the whole creation.

"I had been elected by a majority of three thousand five hundred and eighty-five votes, and I believed they were honest men, and wouldn't want me to vote for any unjust notion, to please Jackson or any one else; at any rate, I was of age, and determined to trust them. I voted against this Indian bill, and my conscience yet tells me that I gave a good, honest vote, and one that I believe will not make me ashamed in the day of judgment. I served out my term, and though many amusing, things happened, I am not disposed to swell my narrative by inserting them.

"When it closed, and I returned home, I found the storm had raised against me sure enough; and it was echoed from side to side, and from end to end of my district, that I had turned against Jackson. This was considered the unpardonable sin. I was hunted down like a wild varment, and in this hunt every little newspaper in the district, and every little pinhook lawyer was engaged. Indeed, they were ready to print anything and everything that the ingenuity of man could invent against me."

In consequence of this opposition, Crockett lost his next election, and yet by a majority of but seventy votes. For two years he remained at home hunting bears. But having once tasted the pleasures of political life, and the excitements of Washington, his silent rambles in the woods had lost much of their ancient charms. He was again a candidate at the ensuing election, and, after a very warm contest gained the day by a majority of two hundred and two votes.

CHAPTER X.

Crockett's Tour to the North and the East.

His Reelection to Congress.—The Northern Tour.—First Sight of a Railroad.—Reception in Philadelphia.—His First Speech.—Arrival in New York.—The Ovation there.—Visit to Boston.—Cambridge and Lowell.—Specimens of his Speeches.—Expansion of his Ideas.—Rapid Improvement.

Colonel Crockett, having been reelected again repaired to Washington. During the session, to complete his education, and the better to prepare himself as a legislator for the whole nation, he decided to take a short trip to the North and the East. His health had also begun to fail, and his physicians advised him to go. He was thoroughly acquainted with the Great West. With his rifle upon his shoulder, in the Creek War, he had made wide explorations through the South. But the North and the East were regions as yet unknown to him.

On the 25th of April, 1834, he left Washington for this Northern tour. He reached Baltimore that evening, where he was invited to a supper by some of the leading gentlemen. He writes:

"Early next morning. I started for Philadelphia, a place where I had never been. I sort of felt lonesome as I went down to the steamboat. The idea of going among a new people, where there are tens of thousands who would pass me by without knowing or caring who I was, who are all taken up with their own pleasures or their own business, made me feel small; and, indeed, if any one who reads this book has a grand idea of his own importance, let him go to a big city, and he will find that he is not higher valued than a coonskin.

"The steamboat was the Carroll of Carrollton, a fine craft, with the rum old Commodore Chaytor for head man. A good fellow he is—all sorts of a man—bowing and scraping to the ladies, nodding to the gentlemen, cursing the crew, and his right eye broad-cast upon the 'opposition line,' all at the same time. 'Let go!' said the old one, and off we walked in prime style.

"Our passage down Chesapeake Bay was very pleasant. In a very short run we came to a place where we were to get on board the rail-cars. This was a clean new sight to me. About a dozen big stages hung on to one machine. After a good deal of fuss we all got seated and moved slowly off; the engine wheezing as though she had the tizzic. By-and-by, she began to take short breaths, and away we went, with a blue streak after us. The whole distance is seventeen miles. It was run in fifty-five minutes.

"At Delaware City, I again embarked on board of a splendid steamboat. When dinner was ready, I set down with the rest of the passengers. Among them was Rev. O. B. Brown, of the Post-Office Department, who sat near me. During dinner he ordered a bottle of wine, and called upon me for a toast. Not knowing whether he intended to compliment me, or abash me among so many strangers, or have some fun at my expense, I concluded to go ahead, and give him and his like a blizzard. So our glasses being filled, the word went round, 'A toast from Colonel Crockett.' I give it as follows: 'Here's wishing the bones of tyrant kings may answer in hell, in place of gridirons, to roast the souls of Tories on.' At this the parson appeared as if he was stumpt. I said, 'Never heed; it was meant for where it belonged.' He did not repeat his invitation, and I eat my dinner quietly.

"After dinner I went up on the deck, and saw the captain hoisting three flags. Says I, 'What does that mean?' He replied, that he was under promise to the citizens of Philadelphia, if I was on board, to hoist his flags, as a friend of mine had said he expected I would be along soon.

"We went on till we came in sight of the city and as we advanced towards the wharf, I saw the whole face of the earth covered with people, all anxiously looking on towards the boat. The captain and myself were standing on the bow-deck; he pointed his finger at me, and people slung their hats, and huzzaed for Colonel Crockett. It struck me with astonishment to hear a strange people huzzaing for me, and made me feel sort of queer. It took me so uncommon unexpected, as I had no idea of attracting attention. But I had to meet it, and so I stepped on to the wharf, where the folks came crowding around me, saying, 'Give me the hand of an honest man.' I did not know what all this meant: but some gentleman took hold of me, and pressing through the crowd, put me into an elegant barouche, drawn by four fine horses; they then told me to bow to the people: I did so, and with much difficulty we moved off. The streets were crowded to a great distance, and the windows full of people, looking out, I suppose, to see the wild man. I thought I had rather be in the wilderness with my gun and dogs, than to be attracting all that fuss. I had never seen the like before, and did not know exactly what to say or do. After some time we reached the United States Hotel, in Chesnut Street."

"The crowd had followed me filling up the street, and pressing into the house to shake hands. I was conducted up stairs, and walked out on a platform, drew off my hat, and bowed round to the people. They cried out from all quarters, 'A speech, a speech, Colonel Crockett.'

"After the noise had quit, so I could be heard, I said to them the following words:

"'GENTLEMEN OF PHILADELPHIA:

"'My visit to your city is rather accidental. I had no expectation of attracting any uncommon attention. I am travelling for my health, without the least wish of exciting the people in such times of high political feeling. I do not wish to encourage it. I am unable at this time to find language suitable to return my gratitude to the citizens of Philadelphia. However, I am almost induced to believe it flattery—perhaps a burlesque. This is new to me, yet I see nothing but friendship in your faces; and if your curiosity is to hear the backwoodsman, I will assure you I am illy prepared to address this most enlightened people. However, gentlemen, if this is a curiosity to you, if you will meet me to-morrow, at one o'clock, I will endeavor to address you, in my plain manner.'

"So I made my obeisance to them, and retired into the house."

It is true that there was much of mere curiosity in the desire to see Colonel Crockett. He was a strange and an incomprehensible man. His manly, honest course in Congress had secured much respect. But such developments of character as were shown in his rude and vulgar toast, before a party of gentlemen and ladies, excited astonishment. His notoriety preceded him, wherever he went; and all were alike curious to see so strange a specimen of a man.

The next morning, several gentlemen called upon him, and took him in a carriage to see the various objects of interest in the city. The gentlemen made him a present of a rich seal, representing two horses at full speed, with the words, "Go Ahead." The young men also made him a present of a truly magnificent rifle. From Philadelphia he went to New York. The shipping astonished him. "They beat me all hollow," he says, "and looked for all the world like a big clearing in the West, with the dead trees all standing."

There was a great crowd upon the wharf to greet him. And when the captain of the boat led him conspicuously forward, and pointed him out to the multitude, the cheering was tremendous. A committee conducted him to the American Hotel, and treated him with the greatest distinction. Again he was feted, and loaded with the greatest attentions. He was invited to a very splendid supper, got up in his honor, at which there were a hundred guests. The Hon. Judge Clayton, of Georgia, was present, and make a speech which, as Crockett says, fairly made the tumblers hop.

Crockett was then called up, as the "undeviating supporter of the Constitution and the laws." In response to this toast, he says,

"I made a short speech, and concluded with the story of the red cow, which was, that as long as General Jackson went straight, I followed him; but when he began to go this way, and that way, and every way, I wouldn't go after him; like the boy whose master ordered him to plough across the field to the red cow. Well, he began to plough, and she began to walk; and he ploughed all forenoon after her. So when the master came, he swore at him for going so crooked. 'Why, sir,' said the boy, 'you told me to plough to the red cow, and I kept after her, but she always kept moving.'"

His trip to New York was concluded by his visiting Jersey City to witness a shooting-match with rifles. He was invited to try his hand. Standing, at the distance of one hundred and twenty feet, he fired twice, striking very near the centre of the mark. Some one then put up a quarter of a dollar in the midst of a black spot, and requested him to shoot at it. The bullet struck the coin, and as Crockett says made slight-of-hand work with it.

From New York he went to Boston. There, an the opponent of some of President Jackson's measures which were most offensive to the New England people, he was feted with extraordinary enthusiasm. He dined and supped, made speeches, which generally consisted of but one short anecdote, and visited nearly all the public institutions.

Just before this, Andrew Jackson had received from Harvard University the honorary title of LL.D. Jackson was no longer a favorite of Crockett. The new distinguished guest, the renowned bear-hunter, was in his turn invited to visit Harvard. He writes:

"There were some gentlemen that invited me to go to Cambridge, where the big college or university is, where they keep ready-made titles or nick-names to give people. I would not go, for I did not know but they might stick an LL.D. on me before they let me go; and I had no idea of changing 'Member of the House of Representatives of the United States,' for what stands for 'lazy, lounging dunce,' which I am sure my constituents would have translated my new title to be. Knowing that I had never taken any degree, and did not own to any—except a small degree of good sense not to pass for what I was not—I would not go it. There had been one doctor made from Tennessee already, and I had no wish to put on the cap and bells.

"I told them that I did not go to this branding school; I did not want to be tarred with the same stick; one dignitary was enough from Tennessee; that as far as my learning went, I would stand over it, and spell a strive or two with any of them, from a-b-ab to crucifix, which was where I left off at school."

A gentleman, at a dinner-party, very earnestly invited Crockett to visit him. He returned the compliment by saying:

"If you ever come to my part of the country, I hope you will call and see me."

"And how shall I find where you live?" the gentleman inquired.

"Why, sir," Crockett answered, "run down the Mississippi till you come to the Oberon River. Run a small streak up that; jump ashore anywhere, and inquire for me."

From Boston, he went to Lowell. The hospitality he had enjoyed in Boston won his warmest commendation. At Lowell, he was quite charmed by the aspect of wealth, industry, and comfort which met his eye. Upon his return to Boston, he spent the evening, with several gentlemen and ladies at the pleasant residence of Lieutenant-Governor Armstrong. In reference to this visit, he writes:

"This was my last night in Boston, and I am sure, if I never see the place again, I never can forget the kind and friendly manner in which I was treated by them. It appeared to me that everybody was anxious to serve me, and make my time agreeable. And as a proof that comes home—when I called for my bill next morning, I was told there was no charge to be paid by me, and that he was very much delighted that I had made his house my home. I forgot to mention that they treated me so in Lowell—but it is true. This was, to me, at all events, proof enough of Yankee liberality; and more than they generally get credit for. In fact, from the time I entered New England, I was treated with the greatest friendship; and, I hope, never shall forget it; and I wish all who read this book, and who never were there, would take a trip among them. If they don't learn how to make money, they will know how to use it; and if they don't learn industry, they will see how comfortable everybody can be that turns his hands to some employment."

Crockett was not a mere joker. He was an honest man, and an earnest man; and under the tuition of Congress had formed some very decided political principles, which he vigorously enforced with his rude eloquence.

When he first went to Congress he was merely a big boy, of very strong mind, but totally uninformed, and uncultivated. He very rapidly improved under the tuition of Congress; and in some degree awoke to the consciousness of his great intellectual imperfections. Still he was never diffident. He closed one of his off-hand after-dinner speeches in Boston, by saying:

"Gentlemen of Boston, I come here as a private citizen, to see you, and not to show myself. I had no idea of attracting attention. But I feel it my duty to thank you, with my gratitude to you, and with a gratitude to all who have given a plain man, like me, so kind a reception. I come from a great way off. But I shall never repent of having been persuaded to come here, and get a knowledge of your ways, which I can carry home with me. We only want to do away prejudice and give the people information.

"I hope, gentlemen, you will excuse my plain, unvarnished ways, which may seem strange to you here. I never had but six months' schooling in all my life. And I confess, I consider myself a poor tyke to be here addressing the most intelligent people in the world. But I think it the duty of every representative of the people, when he is called upon, to give his opinions. And I have tried to give you a little touch of mine."

Every reader will be interested in the perusal of the following serious speech, which he made in Boston. It is a fair specimen of his best efforts, and will give one a very correct idea of his trains of thought, and modes of expression. It also clearly shows the great questions which agitated the country at that time. It can easily be perceived that, as a stump orator in the far West, Crockett might have exercised very considerable power. This phase of his peculiar character is as worthy of consideration as any other.

"GENTLEMEN:

"By the entire friendship of the citizens of Boston, as well as the particular friendship with which you have received me this evening, I have been brought to reflect on times that have gone by, and review a prejudice that has grown up with me, as well as thousands of my Western and Southern friends. We have always been taught to look upon the people of New England as a selfish, cunning set of fellows, that was fed on fox-ears and thistle-tops; that cut their wisdom-teeth as soon as they were born; that made money by their wits, and held on to it by nature; that called cheatery mother-wit; that hung on to political power because they had numbers; that raised up manufactures to keep down the South and West; and, in fact, had so much of the devil in all their machinery, that they would neither lead nor drive, unless the load was going into their own cribs. But I assure you, gentlemen, I begin to think different of you, and I think I see a good many good reasons for so doing.

"I don't mean that because I eat your bread and drink your liquor, that I feel so. No; that don't make me see clearer than I did. It is your habits, and manners, and customs; your industry; your proud, independent spirits; your hanging on to the eternal principles of right and wrong; your liberality in prosperity, and your patience when you are ground down by legislation, which, instead of crushing you, whets your invention to strike a path without a blaze on a tree to guide you; and above all, your never-dying, deathless grip to our glorious Constitution. These are the things that make me think that you are a mighty good people."

Here the speaker was interrupted by great applause.

"Gentlemen, I believe I have spoke the truth, and not flattery; I ain't used to oily words; I am used to speak what I think, of men, and to men. I am, perhaps, more of a come-by-chance than any of you ever saw; I have made my way to the place I now fill, without wealth, and against education; I was raised from obscurity, and placed in the high councils of the nation, by the kindness and liberality of the good people of my district—a people whom I will never be unfaithful to, here or elsewhere; I love them, and they have honored me; and according as God has given me judgment, I'll use it for them, come of me what may.

"These people once passed sentence upon me of a two years' stay-at-home, for exercising that which I contend belongs to every freeman in this nation: that was, for differing in opinion with the chief magistrate of this nation. I was well acquainted with him. He was but a man; and, if I was not before, my constituents had made a man of me. I had marched and counter-marched with him: I had stood by him in the wars, and fought under his flag at the polls: I helped to heap the measure of glory that has crushed and smashed everything that has come in contact with it: I helped to give him the name of 'Hero,' which, like the lightning from heaven, has scorched and blasted everything that stood in its way—a name which, like the prairie fire, you have to burn against, or you are gone—a name which ought to be the first in war, and the last in peace—a name which, like 'Jack-o'-the lantern, blinds your eyes while you follow it through mud and mire.

"Gentlemen, I never opposed Andrew Jackson for the sake of popularity. I knew it was a hard row to hoe; but I stood up to the rack, considering it a duty I owed to the country that governed me. I had reviewed the course of other Presidents, and came to the conclusion that he did not of right possess any more power than those that had gone before him. When he transcended that power, I put down my foot. I knew his popularity; that he had come into place with the largest majority of any one that had gone before him, who had opposition: but still, I did not consider this as giving him the right to do as he pleased, and construe our Constitution to meet his own views.

"We had lived the happiest people under the sun for fifty years, governed by the Constitution and laws, on well-established constructions: and when I saw the Government administered on new principles, I objected, and was politically sacrificed: I persisted in my sins, having a clear conscience, that before God and my country, I had done my duty.

"My constituents began to look at both sides; and finally, at the end of two years, approving of my course, they sent me back to Congress—a circumstance which was truly gratifying to me.

"Gentlemen, I opposed Andrew Jackson in his famous Indian bill, where five hundred thousand dollars were voted for expenses, no part of which has yet been accounted for, as I have seen. I thought it extravagant as well as impolitic. I thought the rights reserved to the Indians were about to be frittered away; and events prove that I thought correct.

"I had considered a treaty as the sovereign law of the land; but now saw it considered as a matter of expedience, or not, as it pleased the powers that be. Georgia bid defiance to the treaty-making power, and set at nought the Intercourse Act of 1802; she trampled it under foot; she nullified it: and for this, she received the smiles and approbation of Andrew Jackson. And this induced South Carolina to nullify the Tariff. She had a right to expect that the President was favorable to the principle: but he took up the rod of correction, and shook it over South Carolina, and said at the same time to Georgia, 'You may nullify, but South Carolina shall not.'

"This was like his consistency in many other matters. When he was a Senator in Congress, he was a friend to internal improvements, and voted for them. Everything then that could cement the States together, by giving them access the one to the other, was right. When he got into power, some of his friends had hard work to dodge, and follow, and shout. I called off my dogs, and quit the hunt. Yes, gentlemen, Pennsylvania, and Ohio, and Tennessee, and other States, voted for him, as a supporter of internal improvements.

"Was he not a Tariff man? Who dare deny it! When did we first hear of his opposition? Certainly not in his expression that he was in favor of a judicious tariff. That was supposed to be a clincher, even in New England, until after power lifted him above the opposition of the supporters of a tariff.

"He was for putting down the monster 'party,' and being the President of the people. Well, in one sense, this he tried to do: he put down every one he could who was opposed to him, either by reward or punishment; and could all have come into his notions, and bowed the knee to his image, I suppose it might have done very well, so far as he was concerned. Whether it would have been a fair reading of his famous letter to Mr. Monroe, is rather questionable. He was to reform the Government. Now, if reformation consists in turning out and putting in, he did it with a vengeance.

"He was, last of all, to retrench the expenditures. Well, in time, I have no doubt, this must be done; but it will not consist in the abolishing useless expenditures of former Administrations. No, gentlemen; the spoils belonged to the victor; and it would never do to lessen the teats when the litter was doubled. The treasury trough had to be extended, and the pap thickened; kin were to be provided for; and if all things keep on as they are, his own extravagances will have to be retrenched, or you will get your tariff up again as high as you please.

"I recollect a boy once, who was told to turn the pigs out of the corn-field. Well, he made a great noise, hallooing and calling the dogs—and came back. By-and-by his master said, 'Jim, you rascal! you didn't turn out the pigs.' 'Sir,' said he, 'I called the dogs, and set them a-barking.'

"So it was with that big Retrenchment Report, in 1828. Major Hamilton got Chilton's place as chairman—and called the dogs. Ingham worked honestly, like a beaver; Wickliff was as keen as a cutworm: all of them worked hard; and they did really, I suppose, convince themselves that they had found out a great deal of iniquity; or, what was more desirable, convinced the people that Andrew Jackson and his boys were the only fellows to mend shoes for nothing, and find their own candles. Everett and Sargeant, who made the minority report, were scouted at. What has come of all this? Nothing—worse than nothing. Jackson used these very men like dogs: they knew too much, and must be got rid off, or they would stop his profligacy too. They were greased and swallowed: and he gave them up to the torments of an anti-Jackson conscience.

"Yes, gentlemen, as long as you think with him, very well; but if not—clear out; make way for some fellow who has saved his wind; and because he has just begun to huzza, has more wind to spare. General Jackson has turned out more men for opinion's sake, than all other Presidents put together, five times over: and the broom sweeps so low that it reaches the humblest officer who happens to have a mean neighbor to retail any little story which he may pick up.

"I voted for Andrew Jackson because I believed he possessed certain principles, and not because his name was Andrew Jackson, or the Hero, or Old Hickory. And when he left those principles which induced me to support him, I considered myself justified in opposing him. This thing of man-worship I am a stranger to; I don't like it; it taints every action of life; it is like a skunk getting into a house—long after he has cleared out, you smell him in every room and closet, from the cellar to the garret.

"I know nothing, by experience, of party discipline. I would rather be a raccoon-dog, and belong to a negro in the forest, than to belong to any party, further than to do justice to all, and to promote the interests of my country. The time will and must come, when honesty will receive its reward, and when the people of this nation will be brought to a sense of their duty, and will pause and reflect how much it cost us to redeem ourselves from the government of one man. It cost the lives and fortunes of thousands of the best patriots that ever lived. Yes, gentlemen, hundreds of them fell in sight of your own city.

"I this day walked over the great battle-ground of Bunker's Hill, and thought whether it was possible that it was moistened with the sacred blood of our heroes in vain, and that we should forget what they fought for.

"I hope to see our once happy country restored to its former peace and happiness, and once more redeemed from tyranny and despotism, which, I fear, we are on the very brink of. We see the whole country in commotion: and for what? Because, gentlemen, the true friends of liberty see the laws and Constitution blotted out from the heads and hearts of the people's leaders: and their requests for relief are

103

treated with scorn and contempt. They meet the same fate that they did before King George and his parliament. It has been decided by a majority of Congress, that Andrew Jackson shall be the Government, and that his will shall be the law of the land. He takes the responsibility, and vetoes any bill that does not meet his approbation. He takes the responsibility, and seizes the treasury, and removes it from where the laws had placed it; and now, holding purse and sword, has bid defiance to Congress and to the nation.

"Gentlemen, if it is for opposing those high-handed measures that you compliment me, I say I have done so, and will do so, now and forever. I will be no man's man, and no party's man, other than to be the people's faithful representative: and I am delighted to see the noble spirit of liberty retained so boldly here, where the first spark was kindled; and I hope to see it shine and spread over our whole country.

"Gentlemen, I have detained you much longer than I intended: allow me to conclude by thanking you for your attention and kindness to the stranger from the far West."

The following extract also shows the candor of his mind, his anxiety to learn, and the progress his mind was making in the science of political economy:

"I come to your country to get a knowledge of things, which I could get in no other way but by seeing with my own eyes, and hearing with my awful ears—information I can't get, and nobody else, from book knowledge. I come, fellow-citizens, to get a knowledge of the manufacturing interest of New England. I was over-persuaded to come by a gentleman who had been to Lowell and seen the manufactories of your State—by General Thomas, of Louisiana. He persuaded me to come and see.

"When I was first chose to Congress, I was opposed to the protecting system. They told me it would help the rich, and hurt the poor; and that we in the West was to be taxed by it for the benefit of New England. I supposed it was so; but when I come to hear it argued in the Congress of the nation, I begun to have a different opinion of it. I saw I was opposing the best interest of the country: especially for the industrious poor man. I told my people who sent me to Congress, that I should oppose it no longer: that without it, we should be obliged to pay a tax to the British Government, and support them, instead of our own labor. And I am satisfied of it the more since I have visited New England. Only let the Southern gentlemen come here and examine the manufactories, and see how it is, and it would make more peace than all the legislation in Congress can do. It would give different ideas to them who have been deluded, and spoke in strong terms of dissolving the Union."

Crockett returned to Washington just in time to be present at the closing scenes, and then set out for home. So much had been said of him in the public journals, of his speeches and his peculiarities, that his renown now filled the land.

CHAPTER XI.

The Disappointed Politician.—Off for Texas.

Triumphal Return.—Home Charms Vanish.—Loses His Election.—Bitter Disappointment.—Crockett's Poetry.—Sets out for Texas.—Incidents of the Journey.—Reception at Little Rock.—The Shooting Match.—Meeting a Clergyman.—The Juggler.—Crockett a Reformer.—The Bee Hunter.—The Rough Strangers.—Scene on the Prairie.

Crockett's return to his home was a signal triumph all the way. At Baltimore, Philadelphia, Pittsburgh, Cincinnati, Louisville, crowds gathered to greet him. He was feasted, received presents, was complimented, and was incessantly called upon for a speech. He was an earnest student as he journeyed along. A new world of wonders were opening before him. Thoughts which he never before had dreamed of were rushing into his mind. His eyes were ever watchful to see all that was worthy of note. His ear was ever listening for every new idea. He scarcely ever looked at the printed page, but perused with the utmost diligence the book of nature. His comments upon what he saw indicate much sagacity.

At Cincinnatti and Louisville, immense crowds assembled to hear him. In both places he spoke quite at length. And all who heard him were surprised at the power he displayed. Though his speech was rude and unpolished, the clearness of his views, and the intelligence he manifested, caused the journals generally to speak of him in quite a different strain from that which they had been accustomed to use. Probably never did a man make so much intellectual progress, in the course of a few months, as David Crockett had made in that time. His wonderful memory of names, dates, facts, all the intricacies of statistics, was such, that almost any statesman might be instructed by his addresses, and not many men could safely encounter him in argument. The views he presented upon the subject of the Constitution, finance, internal improvements, etc., were very surprising, when one considers the limited education he had enjoyed. At the close of these agitating scenes he touchingly writes:

"In a short time I set out for my own home; yes, my own home, my own soil, my humble dwelling, my own family, my own hearts, my ocean of love and affection, which neither circumstances nor time can dry up. Here, like the wearied bird, let me settle down for a while, and shut out the world."

But hunting bears had lost its charms for Crockett. He had been so flattered that it is probable that he fully expected to be chosen President of the United States. There were two great parties then dividing the country, the Democrats and the Whigs. The great object of each was to find an available candidate, no matter how unfit for the office. The leaders wished to elect a President who would be, like the Queen of England, merely the ornamental figure-head of the ship of state, while their energies should propel and guide the majestic fabric. For a time some few thought it possible that in the popularity of the great bear-hunter such a candidate might be found.

Crockett, upon his return home, resumed his deerskin leggins, his fringed hunting-shirt, his fox-skin cap, and shouldering his rifle, plunged, as he thought, with his original zest, into the cheerless, tangled, marshy forest which surrounded him. But the excitements of Washington, the splendid entertainments of Philadelphia, New York, and Boston, the flattery, the speech-making, which to him, with his marvellous memory and his wonderful fluency of speech, was as easy as breathing, the applause showered upon him, and the gorgeous vision of the Presidency looming up before him, engrossed his mind. He sauntered listlessly through the forest, his bear-hunting energies all paralyzed. He soon grew very weary of home and of all its employments, and was eager to return to the infinitely higher excitements of political life.

General Jackson was then almost idolized by his party. All through the South and West his name was a tower of strength. Crockett had originally been elected as a Jackson-man. He had abandoned the Administration, and was now one of the most inveterate opponents of Jackson. The majority in Crockett's district were in favor of Jackson. The time came for a new election of a representative. Crockett made every effort, in his old style, to secure the vote. He appeared at the gatherings in his garb as a bear-hunter, with his rifle on his shoulder. He brought 'coonskins to buy whiskey to treat his friends. A 'coonskin in the currency of that country was considered the equivalent for twenty-five cents. He made funny speeches. But it was all in vain.

Greatly to his surprise, and still more to his chagrin, he lost his election. He was beaten by two hundred and thirty votes. The whole powerful influence of the Government was exerted against Crockett and in favor of his competitor. It is said that large bribes were paid for votes. Crockett wrote, in a strain which reveals the bitterness of his disappointment:

"I am gratified that I have spoken the truth to the people of my district, regardless of the consequences. I would not be compelled to bow down to the idol for a seat in Congress during life. I have never known what it was to sacrifice my own judgment to gratify any party; and I have no doubt of the time being close at hand when I shall be rewarded for letting my tongue speak what my heart thinks. I have suffered myself to be politically sacrificed to save my country from ruin and disgrace; and if I am never again elected, I will have the gratification to know that I have done my duty. I may add, in the words of the man in the play, 'Crockett's occupation's gone.'"

Two weeks after this he writes, "I confess the thorn still rankles, not so much on my own account as the nation's. As my country no longer requires my services, I have made up my mind to go to Texas. My life has been one of danger, toil, and privation. But these difficulties I had to encounter at a time when I considered it nothing more than right good sport to surmount them. But now I start upon my own hook, and God only grant that it may be strong enough to support the weight that may be hung upon it. I have a new row to hoe, a long and rough one; but come what will, I will go ahead."

Just before leaving for Texas, he attended a political meeting of his constituents. The following extract from his autobiography will give the reader a very vivid idea of his feelings at the time, and of the very peculiar character which circumstances had developed in him:

"A few days ago I went to a meeting of my constituents. My appetite for politics was at one time just about as sharp set as a saw-mill, but late events have given me something of a surfeit, more than I could well digest; still, habit, they say, is second natur, and so I went, and gave them a piece of my mind touching 'the Government' and the succession, by way of a codicil to what I have often said before.

"I told them, moreover, of my services, pretty straight up and down, for a man may be allowed to speak on such subjects when others are about to forget them; and I also told them of the manner in which I had been knocked down and dragged out, and that I did not consider it a fair fight anyhow they could fix it. I put the ingredients in the cup pretty strong I tell you, and I concluded my speech by telling them that I was done with politics for the present, and that they might all go to hell, and I would go to Texas.

"When I returned home I felt a sort of cast down at the change that had taken place in my fortunes, and sorrow, it is said, will make even an oyster feel poetical. I never tried my hand at that sort of writing but on this particular occasion such was my state of feeling, that I began to fancy myself inspired; so I took pen in hand, and as usual I went ahead. When I had got fairly through, my poetry looked as zigzag as a worm-fence; the lines wouldn't tally no how; so I showed them to Peleg Longfellow, who has a first-rate reputation with us for that sort of writing, having some years ago made a carrier's address for the Nashville Banner; and Peleg lopped of some lines, and stretched out others; but I wish I may be shot if I don't rather think he has made it worse than it was when I placed it in his hands. It being my first, and, no doubt, last piece of poetry, I will print it in this place, as it will serve to express my feelings on leaving my home, my neighbors, and friends and country, for a strange land, as fully as I could in plain prose.

"Farewell to the mountains whose mazes to me

Were more beautiful far than Eden could be;

No fruit was forbidden, but Nature had spread

Her bountiful board, and her children were fed.

The hills were our garners—our herds wildly grew

And Nature was shepherd and husbandman too.

I felt like a monarch, yet thought like a man,

As I thanked the Great Giver, and worshipped his plan.

"The home I forsake where my offspring arose;

The graves I forsake where my children repose.

The home I redeemed from the savage and wild;

The home I have loved as a father his child;

The corn that I planted, the fields that I cleared,

The flocks that I raised, and the cabin I reared;

The wife of my bosom—Farewell to ye all!

In the land of the stranger I rise or I fall.

"Farewell to my country! I fought for thee well,

When the savage rushed forth like the demons from hell

In peace or in war I have stood by thy side—

My country, for thee I have lived, would have died!

But I am cast off, my career now is run,

And I wander abroad like the prodigal son—

Where the wild savage roves, and the broad prairies spread,

The fallen—despised—will again go ahead."

A party of American adventurers, then called filibusters, had gone into Texas, in the endeavor to wrest that immense and beautiful territory, larger than the whole Empire of France, from feeble, distracted, miserable Mexico, to which it belonged. These filibusters were generally the most worthless and desperate vagabonds to be found in all the Southern States. Many Southern gentlemen of wealth and ability, but strong advocates of slavery, were in cordial sympathy with this movement, and aided it with their purses, and in many other ways. It was thought that if Texas could be wrested from Mexico and annexed to the United States, it might be divided into several slaveholding States, and thus check the rapidly increasing preponderance of the free States of the North.

To join in this enterprise, Crockett now left his home, his wife, his children. There could be no doubt of the eventual success of the undertaking. And in that success Crockett saw visions of political glory opening before him. I determined, he said, "to quit the States until such time as honest and independent men should again work their way to the head of the heap. And as I should probably have some idle time on hand before that state of affairs would be brought about, I promised to give the Texans a helping hand on the high road to freedom."

He dressed himself in a new deerskin hunting-shirt, put on a foxskin cap with the tail hanging behind, shouldered his famous rifle, and cruelly leaving in the dreary cabin his wife and children whom he cherished with an "ocean of love and affection," set out on foot upon his perilous adventure. A days' journey through the forest brought him to the Mississippi River. Here he took a steamer down that majestic stream to the mouth of the Arkansas River, which rolls its vast flood from regions then quite unexplored in the far West. The stream was navigable fourteen hundred miles from its mouth.

Arkansas was then but a Territory, two hundred and forty miles long and two hundred and twenty-eight broad. The sparsely scattered population of the Territory amounted to but about thirty thousand. Following up the windings of the river three hundred miles, one came to a cluster of a few straggling huts, called Little Rock, which constitutes now the capital of the State.

Crockett ascended the river in the steamer, and, unencumbered with baggage, save his rifle, hastened to a tavern which he saw at a little distance from the shore, around which there was assembled quite a crowd of men. He had been so accustomed to public triumphs that he supposed that they had assembled in honor of his arrival. "Strange as it may seem," he says, "they took no more notice of me than if I had been Dick Johnson, the wool-grower. This took me somewhat aback;" and he inquired what was the meaning of the gathering.

He found that the people had been called together to witness the feats of a celebrated juggler and gambler. The name of Colonel Crockett had gone through the nation; and gradually it became noised abroad that Colonel Crockett was in the crowd. "I wish I may be shot," Crockett says, "if I wasn't looked upon as almost as great a sight as Punch and Judy."

He was invited to a public dinner that very day. As it took some time to cook the dinner, the whole company went to a little distance to shoot at a mark. All had heard of Crockett's skill. After several of the best sharpshooters had fired, with remarkable accuracy, it came to Crockett's turn. Assuming an air of great carelessness, he raised his beautiful rifle, which he called Betsey, to his shoulder, fired, and it so happened that the bullet struck exactly in the centre of the bull's-eye. All were astonished, and so was Crockett himself. But with an air of much indifference he turned upon his heel, saying, "There's no mistake in Betsey."

One of the best marksmen in those parts, chagrined at being so beaten, said, "Colonel, that must have been a chance shot."

"I can do it," Crockett replied, "five times out of six, any day in the week."

"I knew," he adds, in his autobiography, "it was not altogether as correct as it might be; but when a man sets about going the big figure, halfway measures won't answer no how."

It was now proposed that there should be a second trial. Crockett was very reluctant to consent to this, for he had nothing to gain, and everything to lose. But they insisted so vehemently that he had to yield. As what ensued does not redound much to his credit, we will let him tell the story in his own language.

"So to it again we went. They were now put upon their mettle, and they fired much better than the first time; and it was what might be called pretty sharp shooting. When it came to my turn, I squared myself, and turning to the prime shot, I gave him a knowing nod, by way of showing my confidence; and says I, 'Look out for the bull's-eye, stranger.' I blazed away, and I wish I may be shot if I didn't miss the target. They examined it all over, and could find neither hair nor hide of my bullet, and pronounced it a dead miss; when says I, 'Stand aside and let me look, and I warrant you I get on the right trail of the critter,' They stood aside, and I examined the bull's-eye pretty particular, and at length cried out, 'Here it is; there is no snakes if it ha'n't followed the very track of the other.' They said it was utterly impossible, but I insisted on their searching the hole, and I agreed to be stuck up as a mark myself, if they did not find two bullets there. They searched for my satisfaction, and sure enough it all come out just as I had told them; for I had picked up a bullet that had been fired, and stuck it deep into the hole, without any one perceiving it. They were all perfectly satisfied that fame had not made too great a flourish of trumpets when speaking of me as a marksman: and they all said they had enough of shooting for that day, and they moved that we adjourn to the tavern and liquor."

The dinner consisted of bear's meat, venison, and wild turkey. They had an "uproarious" time over their whiskey. Crockett made a coarse and vulgar speech, which was neither creditable to his head nor his heart. But it was received with great applause.

The next morning Crockett decided to set out to cross the country in a southwest direction, to Fulton, on the upper waters of the Red River. The gentlemen furnished Crockett with a fine horse, and five of them decided to accompany him, as a mark of respect, to the River Washita, fifty miles from Little Rock. Crockett endeavored to raise some recruits for Texas, but was unsuccessful. When they reached the Washita, they found a clergyman, one of those bold, hardy pioneers of the wilderness, who through the wildest adventures were distributing tracts and preaching the gospel in the remotest hamlets.

He was in a condition of great peril. He had attempted to ford the river in the wrong place, and had reached a spot where he could not advance any farther, and yet could not turn his horse round. With much difficulty they succeeded in extricating him, and in bringing him safe to the shore. Having bid adieu to his kind friends, who had escorted him thus far, Crockett crossed the river, and in company with the clergyman continued his journey, about twenty miles farther west toward a little settlement called Greenville. He found his new friend to be a very charming companion. In describing the ride, Crockett writes:

"We talked about politics, religion, and nature, farming, and bear-hunting, and the many blessings that an all-bountiful Providence has bestowed upon our happy country. He continued to talk upon this subject, travelling over the whole ground as it were, until his imagination glowed, and his soul became full to overflowing; and he checked his horse, and I stopped mine also, and a stream of eloquence burst forth from his aged lips, such as I have seldom listened to: it came from the overflowing fountain of a pure and grateful heart. We were alone in the wilderness, but as he proceeded, it seemed to me as if the tall trees bent their tops to listen; that the mountain stream laughed out joyfully as it bounded on like some living thing that the fading flowers of autumn smiled, and sent forth fresher fragrance, as if conscious that they would revive in spring; and even the sterile rocks seemed to be endued with some mysterious influence. We were alone in the wilderness, but all things told me that God was there. The thought renewed my strength and courage. I had left my country, felt somewhat like an outcast, believed that I had been neglected and lost sight of. But I was now conscious that there was still one watchful Eye over me; no matter whether I dwelt in the populous cities, or threaded the pathless forest alone; no matter whether I stood in the high places among men, or made my solitary lair in the untrodden wild, that Eye was still upon me. My very soul leaped joyfully at the thought. I never felt so grateful in all my life. I never loved my God so sincerely in all my life. I felt that I still had a friend.

"When the old man finished, I found that my eyes were wet with tears. I approached and pressed his hand, and thanked him, and says I, 'Now let us take a drink.' I set him the example, and he followed it, and in a style too that satisfied me, that if he had ever belonged to the temperance society, he had either renounced membership, or obtained a dispensation. Having liquored, we proceeded on our journey, keeping a sharp lookout for mill-seats and plantations as we rode along.

"I left the worthy old man at Greenville, and sorry enough I was to part with him, for he talked a great deal, and he seemed to know a little about everything. He knew all about the history of the country; was well acquainted with all the leading men; knew where all the good lands lay in most of Western States.

"He was very cheerful and happy, though to all appearances very poor. I thought that he would make a first-rate agent for taking up lands, and mentioned it to him. He smiled, and pointing above, said, 'My wealth lies not in this world.'"

From Greenville, Crockett pressed on about fifty or sixty miles through a country interspersed withe forests and treeless prairies, until he reached Fulton. He had a letter of introduction to one of the prominent gentlemen here, and was received with marked distinction. After a short visit he disposed of his horse; he took a steamer to descend the river several hundred miles to Natchitoches, pronounced Nakitosh, a small straggling village of eight hundred inhabitants, on the right bank of the Red River, about two hundred miles from its entrance into the Mississippi.

In descending the river there was a juggler on board, who performed many skilful juggling tricks, and by various feats of gambling won much money from his dupes. Crockett was opposed to gambling in all its forms. Becoming acquainted with the juggler and, finding him at heart a well-meaning, good-natured fellow, he endeavored to remonstrate with him upon his evil practices.

"I told him," says Crockett, "that it was a burlesque on human nature, that an able-bodied man, possessed of his full share of good sense, should voluntarily debase himself, and be indebted for subsistence to such a pitiful artifice.

"'But what's to be done, Colonel?' says he. 'I'm in the slough of despond, up to the very chin. A miry and slippery path to travel.'

"'Then hold your head up,' says I, 'before the slough reaches your lips.'

"'But what's the use?' says he: 'it's utterly impossible for me to wade through; and even if I could, I should be in such a dirty plight, that it would defy all the waters in the Mississippi to wash me clean again. No,' he added in a desponding tone, 'I should be like a live eel in a frying-pan, Colonel, sort of out of my element, if I attempted to live like an honest man at this time o' day.'

"'That I deny. It is never too late to become honest,' said I. 'But even admit what you say to be true—that you cannot live like an honest man—you have at least the next best thing in your power, and no one can say nay to it.'

"'And what is that?'

"'Die like a brave one. And I know not whether, in the eyes of the world, a brilliant death is not preferred to an obscure life of rectitude. Most men are remembered as they died, and not as they lived. We gaze with admiration upon the glories of the setting sun, yet scarcely bestow a passing glance upon its noonday splendor.'

"'You are right; but how is this to be done?'

"'Accompany me to Texas. Cut aloof from your degrading habits and associates here, and, in fighting for the freedom of the Texans, regain your own.'

"The man seemed much moved. He caught up his gambling instruments, thrust them into his pocket, with hasty strides traversed the floor two or three times, and then exclaimed:

"'By heaven, I will try to be a man again. I will live honestly, or die bravely. I will go with you to Texas.'"

To confirm him in his good resolution, Crockett "asked him to liquor." At Natchitoches, Crockett encountered another very singular character. He was a remarkably handsome young man, of poetic imagination, a sweet singer, and with innumerable scraps of poetry and of song ever at his tongue's end. Honey-trees, as they were called, were very abundant in Texas The prairies were almost boundless parterres of the richest flowers, from which the bees made large quantities of the most delicious honey. This they deposited in the hollows of trees. Not only was the honey valuable, but the wax constituted a very important article of commerce in Mexico, and brought a high price, being used for the immense candles which they burned in their churches. The bee-hunter, by practice, acquired much skill in coursing the bees to their hives.

This man decided to join Crockett and the juggler in their journey over the vast prairies of Texas. Small, but very strong and tough Mexican ponies, called mustangs, were very cheap. They were found wild, in droves of thousands, grazing on the prairies. The three adventurers mounted their ponies, and set out on their journey due west, a distance of one hundred and twenty miles, to Nacogdoches. Their route was along a mere trail, which was called the old Spanish road. It led over vast prairies, where there was no path, and where the bee-hunter was their guide, and through forests where their course was marked only by blazed trees.

The bee-hunter, speaking of the state of society in Texas, said that at San Felipe he had sat down with a small party at the breakfast-table, where eleven of the company had fled from the States charged with the crime of murder. So accustomed were the inhabitants to the appearance of fugitives from justice, that whenever a stranger came among them, they took it for granted that he had committed some crime which rendered it necessary for him to take refuge beyond the grasp of his country's laws.

They reached Nacogdoches without any special adventure. It was a flourishing little Mexican town of about one thousand inhabitants, situated in a romantic dell, about sixty miles west of the River Sabine. The Mexicans and the Indians were very nearly on an intellectual and social equality. Groups of Indians, harmless and friendly, were ever sauntering through the streets of the little town.

Colonel Crockett's horse had become lame on the journey. He obtained another, and, with his feet nearly touching the ground as he bestrode the little animal, the party resumed its long and weary journey, directing their course two or three hundred miles farther southwest through the very heart of Texas to San Antonio. They frequently encountered vast expanses of canebrakes; such canes as Northern boys use for fishing-poles. There is one on the banks of Caney Creek, seventy miles in length, with scarcely a tree to be seen for the whole distance. There was generally a trail cut through these, barely wide enough for a single mustang to pass. The reeds were twenty or thirty feet high, and so slender that, having no support over the path, they drooped a little inward and intermingled their tops. Thus a very singular and beautiful canopy was formed, beneath which the travellers moved along sheltered from the rays of a Texan sun.

As they were emerging from one of these arched avenues, they saw three black wolves jogging along very leisurely in front of them, but at too great a distance to be reached by a rifle-bullet. Wild turkeys were very abundant, and vast droves of wild horses were cropping the herbage of the most beautiful and richest pastures to be found on earth. Immense herds of buffaloes were also seen.

"These sights," says Crockett, "awakened the ruling passion strong within me, and I longed to have a hunt on a large scale. For though I had killed many bears and deer in my time, I had never brought down a buffalo, and so I told my friends. But they tried to dissuade me from it, telling me that I would certainly lose my way, and perhaps perish; for though it appeared a garden to the eye, it was still a wilderness. I said little more upon the subject until we crossed the Trinidad River. But every mile we travelled, I found the temptation grew stronger and stronger."

The night after crossing the Trinidad River they were so fortunate as to come across the hut of a poor woman, where they took shelter until the next morning. They were here joined by two other chance travellers, who must indeed have been rough specimens of humanity. Crockett says that though he had often seen men who had not advanced far over the line of civilization, these were the coarsest samples he had ever met.

One proved to be an old pirate, about fifty years of age. He was tall, bony, and in aspect seemed scarcely human. The shaggy hair of his whiskers and beard covered nearly his whole face. He had on a sailor's round jacket and tarpaulin hat. The deep scar, apparently of a sword cut, deformed his forehead, and another similar scar was on the back of one of his hands. His companion was a young Indian, wild as the wolves, bareheaded, and with scanty deerskin dress.

Early the next morning they all resumed their journey, the two strangers following on foot. Their path led over the smooth and treeless prairie, as beautiful in its verdure and its flowers as the most cultivated park could possibly be. About noon they stopped to refresh their horses and dine beneath a cluster of trees in the open prairie. They had built their fire, were cooking their game, and were all seated upon the grass, chatting very sociably, when the bee-hunter saw a bee, which indicated that a hive of honey might be found not far distant. He leaped upon his mustang, and without saying a word, "started off like mad," and scoured along the prairie. "We watched him," says Crockett, "until he seemed no larger than a rat, and finally disappeared in the distance."

CHAPTER XII.

Adventures on the Prairie.

Disappearance of the Bee Hunter.—The Herd of Buffalo Crockett lost.—The Fight with the Cougar.—Approach of Savages.—Their Friendliness.—Picnic on the Prairie.—Picturesque Scene.—The Lost Mustang recovered.—Unexpected Reunion.—Departure of the Savages.—Skirmish with the Mexicans.—Arrival at the Alamo.

Soon after the bee-hunter had disappeared, all were startled by a strange sound, as of distant thunder. It was one of the most beautiful of summer days. There was not a cloud to be seen. The undulating prairie, waving with flowers, lay spread out before them, more beautiful under nature's bountiful adornings than the most artistic parterre, park or lawn which the hand of man ever reared. A gentle, cool breeze swept through the grove, fragrant and refreshing as if from Araby the blest. It was just one of those scenes and one of those hours in which all vestiges of the Fall seemed to have been obliterated, and Eden itself again appeared blooming in its pristine beauty.

Still those sounds, growing more and more distinct, were not sounds of peace, were not eolian warblings; they were mutterings as of a rising tempest, and inspired awe and a sense of peril. Straining their eyes toward the far-distant west, whence the sounds came, they soon saw an immense black cloud just emerging from the horizon and apparently very low down, sweeping the very surface of the prairie. This strange, menacing cloud was approaching with manifestly great rapidity. It was coming directly toward the grove where the travellers were sheltered. A cloud of dust accompanied the phenomenon, ever growing thicker and rising higher in the air.

"What can that all mean?" exclaimed Crockett, in evident alarm.

The juggler sprang to his feet, saying, "Burn my old shoes if I know."

Even the mustangs, which were grazing near by, were frightened They stopped eating, pricked up their ears, and gazed in terror upon the approaching danger. It was then supposed that the black cloud, with its muttered thunderings, must be one of those terrible tornadoes which occasionally swept the region, bearing down everything before it. The men all rushed for the protection of the mustangs. In the greatest haste they struck off their hobbles and led them into the grove for shelter.

The noise grew louder and louder, and they had scarcely brought the horses beneath the protection of the trees, when they perceived that it was an immense herd of buffaloes, of countless hundreds, dishing along with the speed of the wind, and bellowing and roaring in tones as appalling as if a band of demons were flying and shrieking in terror before some avenging arm.

The herd seemed to fill the horizon. Their numbers could not be counted. They were all driven by some common impulse of terror. In their head-long plunge, those in front pressed on by the innumerable throng behind, it was manifest that no ordinary obstacle would in the slightest degree retard their rush. The spectacle was sublime and terrible. Had the travellers been upon the open plain, it seemed inevitable that they must have been trampled down and crushed out of every semblance of humanity by these thousands of hard hoofs.

But it so chanced that they were upon what is called a rolling prairie, with its graceful undulations and gentle eminences. It was one of these beautiful swells which the grove crowned with its luxuriance.

As the enormous herd came along with its rush and roar, like the bursting forth of a pent-up flood, the terrified mustangs were too much frightened to attempt to escape. They shivered in every nerve as if stricken by an ague.

An immense black bull led the band. He was a few feet in advance of all the rest. He came roaring along, his tail erect in the air as a javelin, his head near the ground, and his stout, bony horns projected as if he were just ready to plunge upon his foe. Crockett writes:

"I never felt such a desire to have a crack at anything in all my life. He drew nigh the place where I was standing. I raised my beautiful Betsey to my shoulder and blazed away. He roared, and suddenly stopped. Those that were near him did so likewise. The commotion occasioned by the impetus of those in the rear was such that it was a miracle that some of them did not break their heads or necks. The black bull stood for a few moments pawing the ground after he was shot, then darted off around the cluster of trees, and made for the uplands of the prairies. The whole herd followed, sweeping by like a tornado. And I do say I never witnessed a sight more beautiful to the eye of a hunter in all my life."

The temptation to pursue them was too strong for Crockett to resist. For a moment he was himself bewildered, and stood gazing with astonishment upon the wondrous spectacle. Speedily he reloaded his rifle, sprung upon his horse, and set out in pursuit over the green and boundless prairie. There was something now quite ludicrous in the scene. There was spread out an ocean expanse of verdure. A herd of countless hundreds of majestic buffaloes, every animal very ferocious in aspect, was clattering along, and a few rods behind them in eager pursuit was one man, mounted on a little, insignificant Mexican pony, not much larger than a donkey. It would seem that but a score of this innumerable army need but turn round and face their foe, and they could toss horse and rider into the air, and then contemptuously trample them into the dust.

Crockett was almost beside himself with excitement. Looking neither to the right nor the left, unconscious in what direction he was going, he urged forward, with whip and spur, the little mustang, to the utmost speed of the animal, and yet scarcely in the least diminished the distance between him and the swift-footed buffaloes. Ere long, it was evident that he was losing in the chase. But the hunter, thinking that the buffaloes could not long continue their flight at such a speed, and that they would soon, in weariness, loiter and stop to graze, vigorously pressed on, though his jaded beast was rapidly being distance by the herd.

At length the enormous moving mass appeared but as a cloud in the distant horizon. Still, Crockett, his mind entirely absorbed in the excitement of the chase, urged his weary steed on, until the buffalos entirely disappeared from view in the distance. Crockett writes:

"I now paused to allow my mustang to breathe, who did not altogether fancy the rapidity of my movements; and to consider which course I would have to take to regain the path I had abandoned. I might have retraced my steps by following the trail of the buffaloes, but it had always been my principle to go ahead, and so I turned to the west and pushed forward.

"I had not rode more than an hour before I found, I was completely bewildered. I looked around, and there was, as far as the eye could reach, spread before me a country apparently in the highest state of cultivation—extended fields, beautiful and productive, groves of trees cleared from the underwood, and whose margins were as regular as if the art and taste of man had been employed upon them. But there was no other evidence that the sound of the axe, or the voice of man, had ever here disturbed the solitude of nature. My eyes would have cheated my senses into the belief that I was in an earthly paradise, but my fears told me that I was in a wilderness.

"I pushed along, following the sun, for I had no compass to guide me, and there was no other path than that which my mustang made. Indeed, if I had found a beaten tract, I should have been almost afraid to have followed it; for my friend the bee-hunter had told me, that once, when he had been lost in the prairies, he had accidentally struck into his own path, and had travelled around and around for a whole day before he discovered his error. This I thought was a poor way of going ahead; so I determined to make for the first large stream, and follow its course."

For several hours Crockett rode through these vast and lonely solitudes, the Eden of nature, without meeting with the slightest trace of a human being. Evening was approaching, still, calm, and bright. The most singular and even oppressive silence prevailed, for neither voice of bird nor insect was to be heard. Crockett began to feel very uneasy. The fact that he was lost himself did not trouble him much, but he felt anxious for his simple-minded, good-natured friend, the juggler, who was left entirely alone and quite unable to take care of himself under such circumstances.

As he rode along, much disturbed by these unpleasant reflections, another novelty, characteristic of the Great West, arrested his attention and elicited his admiration. He was just emerging from a very lovely grove, carpeted with grass, which grew thick and green beneath the leafy canopy which overarched it. There was not a particle of underbrush to obstruct one's movement through this natural park. Just beyond the grove there was another expanse of treeless prairie, so rich, so beautiful, so brilliant with flowers, that even Colonel Crockett, all unaccustomed as he was to the devotional mood, reined in his horse, and gazing entranced upon the landscape, exclaimed:

"O God, what a world of beauty hast thou made for man! And yet how poorly does he requite thee for it! He does not even repay thee with gratitude."

The attractiveness of the scene was enhanced by a drove of more than a hundred wild horses, really beautiful animals, quietly pasturing. It seemed impossible but that the hand of man must have been employed in embellishing this fair creation. It was all God's work. "When I looked around and fully realized it all," writes Crockett, "I thought of the clergyman who had preached to me in the wilds of Arkansas."

Colonel Crockett rode out upon the prairie. The horses no sooner espied him than, excited, but not alarmed, the whole drove, with neighings, and tails uplifted like banners, commenced coursing around him in an extended circle, which gradually became smaller and smaller, until they came in close contact; and the Colonel, not a little alarmed, found himself completely surrounded, and apparently the prisoner of these powerful steeds.

The little mustang upon which the Colonel was mounted seemed very happy in its new companionship. It turned its head to one side, and then to the other, and pranced and neighed, playfully biting at the mane of one horse, rubbing his nose against that of another, and in joyous gambols kicking up its heels. The Colonel was anxious to get out of the mess. But his little mustang was not at all disposed to move in that direction; neither did the other horses seem disposed to acquiesce in such a plan.

Crockett's heels were armed with very formidable Spanish spurs, with prongs sharp and long. The hunter writes:

"To escape from the annoyance, I beat the devil's tattoo on his ribs, that he might have some music to dance to, and we went ahead right merrily, the whole drove following in our wake, head up, and tail and mane streaming. My little critter, who was both blood and bottom, seemed delighted at being at the head of the heap; and having once fairly got started, I wish I may be shot if I did not find it impossible to stop him. He kept along, tossing his head proudly, and occasionally neighing, as much as to say, "Come on, my hearties, you see I ha'n't forgot our old amusement yet." And they did come on with a vengeance, clatter, clatter, clatter, as if so many fiends had broke loose. The prairie lay extended before me as far as the eye could reach, and I began to think that there would be no end to the race.

"My little animal was full of fire and mettle, and as it was the first bit of genuine sport that he had had for some time, he appeared determined to make the most of it. He kept the lead for full half an hour, frequently neighing as if in triumph and derision. I thought of John Gilpin's celebrated ride, but that was child's play to this. The proverb says, 'The race is not always to the swift, nor the battle to the strong,' and so it proved in the present instance. My mustang was obliged to carry weight, while his competitors were as free as nature had made them. A beautiful bay, who had trod close upon my heels the whole way, now came side by side with my mustang, and we had it hip and thigh for about ten minutes, in such style as would have delighted the heart of a true lover of the turf. I now felt an interest in the race myself, and, for the credit of my bit of blood, determined to win it if it was at all in the nature of things. I plied the lash and spur, and the little critter took it quite kindly, and tossed his head, and neighed, as much as to say, 'Colonel, I know what you're after—go ahead!'—and he cut dirt in beautiful style, I tell you."

This could not last long. The wild steed of the prairie soon outstripped the heavily burdened mustang, and shooting ahead, kicked up his heels as in derision. The rest of the herd followed, in the same disrespectful manner. Crockett jogged quietly on in the rear, glad to be rid of such troublesome and dangerous companions. The horses soon reached a stream, which Crockett afterward learned was called the Navasola River. The whole herd, following an adventurous leader, rushed pell-mell into the stream and swam to the other side. It was a beautiful sight to behold these splendid animals, in such a dense throng, crossing the stream, and then, refreshed by their bath, sweeping like a whirlwind over the plain beyond.

Crockett's exhausted pony could go no further. He fairly threw himself upon the ground as if in despair. Crockett took from the exhausted animal the saddle, and left the poor creature to roll upon the grass and graze at pleasure. He thought it not possible that the mustang could wander to any considerable distance. Indeed, he fully expected to find the utterly exhausted beast, who could no longer stand upon his legs, dead before morning.

Night was fast closing around him. He began to look around for shelter. There was a large tree blown down by the side of the stream, its top branching out very thick and bushy. Crockett thought that with his knife, in the midst of that dense foliage with its interlacing branches, he could make himself a snug arbor, where, wrapped in his blanket, he could enjoy refreshing sleep. He approached the tree, and began to work among the almost impervious branches, when he heard a low growl, which he says he interpreted to mean, "Stranger, these apartments are already taken."

Looking about to see what kind of an animal he had disturbed, and whose displeasure he had manifestly encountered, he saw the brilliant eyes glaring through the leaves of a large Mexican cougar, sometimes called the panther or American lion. This animal, endowed with marvellous agility and strength, will pounce from his lair on a deer, and even a buffalo, and easily with tooth and claw tear him to pieces.

"He was not more than five or six paces from me," writes Crockett, "and was eying me as an epicure surveys the table before he selects his dish, I have no doubt the cougar looked upon me as the subject of a future supper. Rays of light darted from his large eyes, he showed his teeth like a negro in hysterics, and he was crouching on his haunches ready for a spring; all of which convinced me that unless I was pretty quick upon the trigger, posterity would know little of the termination of my eventful career, and it would be far less glorious and useful than I intend to make it."

The conflict which ensued cannot be more graphically described than in Crocket's own words:

"One glance satisfied me that there was no time to be lost. There was no retreat either for me or the cougar. So I levelled my Betsey and blazed away. The report was followed by a furious growl, and the next moment, when I expected to find the tarnal critter struggling with death, I beheld him shaking his head, as if nothing more than a bee had stung him. The ball had struck him on the forehead and glanced off, doing no other injury than stunning him for an instant, and tearing off the skin, which tended to infuriate him the more. The cougar wasn't long in making up his mind what to do, nor was I neither; but he would have it all his own way, and vetoed my motion to back out. I had not retreated three steps before he sprang at me like a steamboat; I stepped aside and as he lit upon the ground, I struck him violently with the barrel of my rifle, but he didn't mind that, but wheeled around and made at me again. The gun was now of no use, so I threw it away, and drew my hunting-knife, for I knew we should come to close quarters before the fight would be over. This time he succeeded in fastening on my left arm, and was just beginning to amuse himself by tearing the flesh off with his fangs, when I ripped my knife into his side, and he let go his hold, much to my satisfaction.

"He wheeled about and came at me with increased fury, occasioned by the smarting of his wounds. I now tried to blind him, knowing that if I succeeded he would become an easy prey; so as he approached me I watched my opportunity, and aimed a blow at his eyes with my knife; but unfortunately it struck him on the nose, and he paid no other attention to it than by a shake of the head and a low growl. He pressed me close, and as I was stepping backward my foot tripped in a vine, and I fell to the ground. He was down upon me like a night-hawk upon a June-bug. He seized hold of the outer part of my right thigh, which afforded him considerable amusement; the hinder part of his body was towards my face; I grasped his tail with my left hand, and tickled his ribs with my haunting-knife, which I held in my right. Still the critter wouldn't let go his hold; and as I found that he would lacerate my leg dreadfully unless he was speedily shaken off, I tried to hurl him down the bank into the river, for our scuffle had already brought us to the edge of the bank. I stuck my knife into his side, and summoned all my strength to throw him over. He resisted, was desperate heavy; but at last I got him so far down the declivity that he lost his balance, and he rolled over and over till he landed on the margin of the river; but in his fall he dragged me along with him. Fortunately, I fell uppermost, and his neck presented a fair mark for my hunting-knife. Without allowing myself time even to draw breath, I aimed one desperate blow at his neck, and the knife entered his gullet up to the handle, and reached his heart. He struggled for a few moments and died. I have had many fights with bears, but that was mere child's play. This was the first fight ever I had with a cougar, and I hope it may be the last."

Crockett, breathless and bleeding, but signally a victor, took quiet possession of the treetop, the conquest of which he had so valiantly achieved. He parted some of the branches, cut away others, and intertwining the softer twigs, something like a bird's nest, made for himself a very comfortable bed. There was an abundance of moss, dry, pliant, and crispy, hanging in festoons from the trees. This, spread in thick folds over his litter, made as luxuriant a mattress as one could desire. His horse-blanket being laid down upon this, the weary traveller, with serene skies above him and a gentle breeze breathing through his bower, had no cause to envy the occupant of the most luxurious chamber wealth can furnish.

He speedily prepared for himself a frugal supper, carried his saddle into the treetop, and, though oppressed with anxiety in view of the prospect before him, fell asleep, and in blissful unconsciousness the hours passed away until the sun was rising in the morning. Upon awaking, he felt very stiff and sore from the wounds he had received in his conflict with the cougar. Looking over the bank, he saw the dead body of the cougar lying there, and felt that he had much cause of gratitude that he had escaped so great a danger.

He then began to look around for his horse. But the animal was nowhere to be seen. He ascended one of the gentle swells of land, whence he could look far and wide over the unobstructed prairie. To his surprise, and not a little to his consternation, the animal had disappeared, "without leaving trace of hair or hide." At first he thought the mustang must have been devoured by wolves or some other beasts of prey. But then it was manifest they could not have eaten his bones, and something would have remained to indicate the fate of the poor creature. While thus perplexed, Crockett reflected sadly that he was lost, alone and on foot, on the boundless prairie. He was, however, too much accustomed to scenes of the wildest adventure to allow himself to be much cast down. His appetite was not disturbed, and he began to feel the cravings of hunger.

He took his rifle and stepped out in search of his breakfast. He had gone but a short distance ere he saw a large flock of wild geese, on the bank of the river. Selecting a large fat gander, he shot him, soon stripped him of his feathers, built a fire, ran a stick through the goose for a spit, and then, supporting it on two sticks with prongs, roasted his savory viand in the most approved style. He had a little tin cup with him, and a paper of ground coffee, with which he made a cup of that most refreshing beverage. Thus he breakfasted sumptuously.

He was just preparing to depart, with his saddle upon his shoulder, much perplexed as to the course he should pursue, when he was again alarmed by one of those wild scenes ever occurring in the West. First faintly, then louder and louder came the sound as of the trampling of many horses on the full gallop. His first thought was that another enormous herd of buffaloes was sweeping down upon him. But soon he saw, in the distance, a band of about fifty Comanche Indians, well mounted, painted, plumed, and bannered, the horse and rider apparently one animal, coming down upon him, their horses being urged to the utmost speed. It was a sublime and yet an appalling spectacle, as this band of half-naked savages, their spears glittering in the morning sun, and their long hair streaming behind, came rushing on.

Crockett was standing in full view upon the banks of the stream. The column swept on, and, with military precision, as it approached, divided into two semicircles, and in an instant the two ends of the circle reached the river, and Crockett was surrounded. Three of the savages performed the part of trumpeters, and with wonderful resemblance, from their lips, emitted the pealing notes of the bugle. Almost by instinct he grasped his rifle, but a flash of thought taught him that, under the circumstances, any attempt at resistance would be worse than unavailing.

The chief sprang from his horse, and advancing with proud strides toward Crockett, was struck with admiration at sight of his magnificent rifle. Such a weapon, with such rich ornamentation, had never before been seen on the prairies. The eagerness with which the savage regarded the gun led Crockett to apprehend that he intended to appropriate it to himself.

The Comanches, though a very warlike tribe, had held much intercourse with the Americans, and friendly relations then existed between them and our Government. Crockett, addressing the chief, said:

"Is your nation at war with the Americans?"

"No," was the reply; "they are our friends."

"And where," Crockett added, "do your get your spear-heads, your rifles, your blankets, and your knives?"

"We get them from our friends the Americans," the chief replied.

"Well," said Crockett, "do you think that if you were passing through their country, as I am passing through yours, they would attempt to rob you of your property?"

"No," answered the savage; "they would feed me and protect me. And the Comanche will do the same by his white brother."

Crockett then inquired of the chief what had guided him and his party to the spot where they had found him? The chief said that they were at a great distance, but had seen the smoke from his fire, and had come to ascertain the cause of it.

"He inquired," writes Crockett, "what had brought me there alone. I told him I had come to hunt, and that my mustang had become exhausted, and, though I thought he was about to die, that he had escaped from me. At this the chief gave a low chuckling laugh, and said that it was all a trick of the mustang, which is the most wily and cunning of all animals. But he said that as I was a brave hunter, he would furnish me with another. He gave orders, and a fine young horse was immediately brought forward."

The savages speedily discovered the dead body of the cougar, and commenced skinning him. They were greatly surprised on seeing the number of the stabs, and inquired into the cause. When Crockett explained to them the conflict, the proof of which was manifest in his own lacerated skin, and in the wounds inflicted upon the cougar, they were greatly impressed with the valor he had displayed. The chief exclaimed several times, in tones of commingled admiration and astonishment, "Brave hunter! brave man!" He also expressed the earnest wish that Crockett would consent to be adopted as a son of the tribe. But this offer was respectfully declined.

This friendly chief kindly consented to escort Crockett as far as the Colorado River. Crockett put his saddle on a fresh horse, and having mounted, the chief, with Crockett at his side, took the lead, and off the whole band went, scouring over the pathless prairie at a rapid speed. Several of the band were squaws. They were the trumpeters. They made the prairie echo with their bugle-blasts, or, as Crockett irreverently, but perhaps more correctly says, "The old squaws, at the head of the troop, were braying like young jackasses the whole way."

After thus riding over the green and treeless expanse for about three hours, they came upon a drove of wild horses, quietly pasturing on the rich herbage. One of the Indians immediately prepared his lasso, and darted out toward the herd to make a capture. The horses did not seem to be alarmed by his approach, but when he got pretty nigh them they began to circle around him, keeping at a cautious distance, with their heads elevated and with loud neighings. They then, following the leadership of a splendid stallion, set off on a brisk canter, and soon disappeared beyond the undulations of the prairie.

One of the mustangs remained quietly grazing. The Indian rode to within a few yards of him, and very skilfully threw his lasso. The mustang seemed to be upon the watch, for he adroitly dodged his head between his forefeet and thus escaped the fatal noose. The Indian rode up to him, and the horse patiently submitted to be bridled and thus secured.

"When I approached," writes Crockett, "I immediately recognized, in the captive, the pestilent little animal that had shammed sickness and escaped from me the day before. And when he caught my eye he cast down his head and looked rather sheepish, as if he were sensible and ashamed of the dirty trick he had played me. I expressed my astonishment, to the Indian chief, at the mustang's allowing himself to be captured without any effort to escape. He told me that they were generally hurled to the ground with such violence, when first taken with the lasso, that they remembered it ever after; and that the sight of the lasso will subdue them to submission, though they may have run wild for years."

All the day long, Crockett, with his convoy of friendly savages, travelled over the beautiful prairie. Toward evening they came across a drove of fat buffaloes grazing in the richest of earthly pastures. It was a beautiful sight to witness the skill with which the Indians pursued and hunted down the noble game. Crockett was quite charmed with the spectacle. It is said that the Comanche Indians are the finest horsemen in the world. Always wandering about over the boundless prairies, where wild horses are found in countless numbers, they are ever on horseback, men, women, and children. Even infants, almost in their earliest years, are taught to cling to the mane of the horse. Thus the Comanche obtains the absolute control of the animal; and when scouring over the plain, bareheaded and with scanty dress, the horse and rider seem veritably like one person.

The Comanches were armed only with bows and arrows. The herd early took fright, and fled with such speed that the somewhat exhausted horses of the Comanches could not get within arrow-shot of them. Crockett, however, being well mounted and unsurpassed by any Indian in the arts of hunting, selected a fat young heifer, which he knew would furnish tender steaks, and with his deadly bullet struck it down. This was the only beef that was killed. All the rest of the herd escaped.

The Indians gathered around the slain animal for their feast. With their sharp knives the heifer was soon skinned and cut up into savory steaks and roasting-pieces. Two or three fires were built. The horses were hobbled and turned loose to graze. Every one of the Indians selected his own portion, and all were soon merrily and even affectionately engaged in this picnic feast, beneath skies which Italy never rivalled, and surrounded with the loveliness of a park surpassing the highest creations of art in London, Paris, or New York.

The Indians were quite delighted with their guest. He told them stories of his wild hunting excursions, and of his encounters with panthers and bears. They were charmed by his narratives, and they sat eager listeners until late into the night, beneath the stars and around the glowing camp-fires. Then, wrapped in their blankets, they threw themselves down on the thick green grass and slept. Such are the joys of peace and friendship.

They resumed their journey in the morning, and pressed along, with nothing of special interest occurring until they reached the Colorado River. As they were following down this stream, to strike the road which leads to Bexar, they saw in the distance a single column of smoke ascending the clear sky. Hastening toward it, they found that it rose from the centre of a small grove near the river. When within a few hundred yards the warriors extended their line, so as nearly to encircle the grove, while the chief and Crockett advanced cautiously to reconnoitre. To their surprise they saw a solitary man seated upon the ground near the fire, so entirely absorbed in some occupation that he did not observe their approach.

In a moment, Crockett, much to his joy, perceived that it was his lost friend the juggler. He was all engaged in practising his game of thimbles on the crown of his hat. Crockett was now restored to his companion, and was near the plain road to Bexar. In describing this scene and the departure of his kind Indian friends, the hunter writes:

"The chief shouted the war-whoop, and suddenly the warriors came rushing in from all quarters, preceded by the old squaw trumpeters squalling like mad. The conjurer sprang to his feet, and was ready to sink into the earth when he beheld the ferocious-looking fellows that surrounded him. I stepped up, took him by the hand, and quieted his fears. I told the chief that he was a friend of mine, and I was very glad to have found him, for I was afraid that he had perished. I now thanked him for his kindness in guiding me over the prairies, and gave him a large bowie-knife, which he said he would keep for the sake of the brave hunter. The whole squadron then wheeled off and I saw them no more. I have met with many polite men in my time, but no one who possessed in a greater degree what may be called true spontaneous politeness than this Comanche chief, always excepting Philip Hone, Esq. of New York, whom I look upon as the politest man I ever did see; for when he asked me to take a drink at his own sideboard, he turned his back upon me, that I mightn't be ashamed to fill as much as I wanted. That was what I call doing the fair thing."

The poor juggler was quite overjoyed in meeting his friend again, whom he evidently regarded with much reverence. He said that he was very much alarmed when he found himself alone on the pathless prairie. After waiting two hours in much anxiety, he mounted his mustang, and was slowly retracing his steps, when he spied the bee-hunter returning. He was laden with honey. They had then journeyed on together to the present spot. The hunter had just gone out in search of game. He soon returned with a plump turkey upon his shoulders. They built their fire, and were joyously cooking their supper, when the neighing of a horse near by startled them. Looking up, they saw two men approaching on horseback. They proved to be the old pirate and the young Indian with whom they had lodged a few nights before. Upon being hailed they alighted, and politely requested permission to join their party. This was gladly assented to, as they were now entering a region desolated by the war between the Texans and the Mexicans, and where many small bands of robbers were wandering, ready to plunder any weaker party they might encounter.

The next morning they crossed the river and pushed on for the fortress of Alamo. When within about twenty miles of San Antonio, they beheld about fifteen mounted men, well armed, approaching them at full speed. Crockett's party numbered five. They immediately dismounted, made a rampart of their horses, and with the muzzles of their rifles pointed toward the approaching foe, were prepared for battle.

It was a party of Mexicans. When within a few hundred yards they reined in their horses, and the leader, advancing a little, called out to them in Spanish to surrender.

"We must have a brush with those blackguards," said the pirate. "Let each one single out his man for the first fire. They are greater fools than I take them for if they give us a chance for a second shot. Colonel, just settle the business with that talking fellow with the red feather. He's worth any three of the party."

"Surrender, or we fire!" shouted the fellow with the red feather. The pirate replied, with a piratic oath, "Fire away."

"And sure enough," writes Crockett, "they took his advice, for the next minute we were saluted with a discharge of musketry, the report of which was so loud that we were convinced they all had fired. Before the smoke had cleared away we had each selected our man, fired, and I never did see such a scattering among their ranks as followed. We beheld several mustangs running wild without their riders over the prairie, and the balance of the company were already retreating at a more rapid gait than they approached. We hastily mounted and commenced pursuit, which we kept up until we beheld the independent flag flying from the battlements of the fortress of Alamo, our place of destination. The fugitives succeeded in evading our pursuit, and we rode up to the gates of the fortress, announced to the sentinel who we were, and the gates were thrown open; and we entered amid shouts of welcome bestowed upon us by the patriots."

CHAPTER XIII.

Conclusion.

The Fortress of Alamo.—Colonel Bowie.—Bombardment of the Fort.—Crockett's Journal.—Sharpshooting.—Fight outside of the Fort.—Death of the Bee Hunter.—Kate of Nacogdoches.—Assault on the Citadel.—Crockett a Prisoner.—His Death.

The fortress of Alamo is just outside of the town of Bexar, on the San Antonio River. The town is about one hundred and forty miles from the coast, and contained, at that time, about twelve hundred inhabitants. Nearly all were Mexicans, though there were a few American families. In the year 1718, the Spanish Government had established a military outpost here; and in the year 1721, a few emigrants from Spain commenced a flourishing settlement at this spot. Its site is beautiful, the air salubrious, the soil highly fertile, and the water of crystal purity.

The town of Bexar subsequently received the name of San Antonio. On the tenth of December, 1835, the Texans captured the town and citadel from the Mexicans. These Texan Rangers were rude men, who had but little regard for the refinements or humanities of civilization. When Crockett with his companions arrived, Colonel Bowie, of Louisiana, one of the most desperate of Western adventurers, was in the fortress. The celebrated bowie-knife was named after this man. There was but a feeble garrison, and it was threatened with an attack by an overwhelming force of Mexicans under Santa Anna. Colonel Travis was in command. He was very glad to receive even so small a reinforcement. The fame of Colonel Crockett, as one of the bravest of men, had already reached his ears.

"While we were conversing," writes Crockett, "Colonel Bowie had occasion to draw his famous knife, and I wish I may be shot if the bare sight of it wasn't enough to give a man of a squeamish stomach the colic. He saw I was admiring it, and said he, 'Colonel, you might tickle a fellow's ribs a long time with this little instrument before you'd make make him laugh.'"

According to Crockett's account, many shameful orgies took place in the little garrison. They were evidently in considerable trepidation, for a large force was gathering against them, and they could not look for any considerable reinforcements from any quarter. Rumors were continually reaching them of the formidable preparations Santa Anna was making to attack the place. Scouts ere long brought in the tidings that Santa Anna, President of the Mexican Republic, at the head of sixteen hundred soldiers, and accompanied by several of his ablest generals, was within six miles of Bexar. It was said that he was doing everything in his power to enlist the warlike Comanches in his favor, but that they remained faithful in their friendship to the United States.

Early in the month of February, 1836, the army of Santa Anna appeared before the town, with infantry, artillery, and cavalry. With military precision they approached, their banners waving, and their bugle-notes bearing defiance to the feeble little garrison. The Texan invaders, seeing that they would soon be surrounded, abandoned the town to the enemy, and fled to the protection of the citadel. They were but one hundred and fifty in number. Almost without exception they were hardy adventurers, and the most fearless and desperate of men. They had previously stored away in the fortress all the provisions, arms, and ammunition, of which they could avail themselves. Over the battlements they unfurled an immense flag of thirteen stripes, and with a large white star of five points, surrounded by the letters "Texas." As they raised their flag, they gave three cheers, while with drums and trumpets they hurled back their challenge to the foe.

The Mexicans raised over the town a blood-red banner. It was their significant intimation to the garrison that no quarter was to be expected. Santa Anna, having advantageously posted his troops, in the afternoon sent a summons to Colonel Travis, demanding an unconditional surrender, threatening, in case of refusal, to put every man to the sword. The only reply Colonel Travis made was to throw a cannon-shot into the town. The Mexicans then opened fire from their batteries, but without doing much harm.

In the night, Colonel Travis sent the old pirate on an express to Colonel Fanning, who, with a small military force, was at Goliad, to entreat him to come to his aid. Goliad was about four days' march from Bexar. The next morning the Mexicans renewed their fire from a battery about three hundred and fifty yards from the fort. A three-ounce ball struck the juggler on the breast, inflicting a painful but not a dangerous wound.

Day after day this storm of war continued. The walls of the citadel were strong, and the bombardment inflicted but little injury. The sharpshooters within the fortress struck down many of the assailants at great distances.

"The bee-hunter," writes Crockett, "is about the quickest on the trigger, and the best rifle-shot we have in the fort. I have already seen him bring down eleven of the enemy, and at such a distance that we all thought that it would be a waste of ammunition to attempt it." Provisions were beginning to become scarce, and the citadel was so surrounded that it was impossible for the garrison to cut its way through the lines and escape.

Under date of February 28th, Crockett writes in his Journal:

"Last night our hunters brought in some corn, and had a brush with a scout from the enemy beyond gunshot of the fort. They put the scout to flight, and got in without injury. They bring accounts that the settlers are flying in all quarters, in dismay, leaving their possessions to the mercy of the ruthless invader, who is literally engaged in a war of extermination more brutal than the untutored savage of the desert could be guilty of. Slaughter is indiscriminate, sparing neither sex, age, nor condition. Buildings have been burnt down, farms laid waste, and Santa Anna appears determined to verify his threat, and convert the blooming paradise into a howling wilderness. For just one fair crack at that rascal, even at a hundred yards' distance, I would bargain to break my Betsey, and never pull trigger again. My name's not Crockett if I wouldn't get glory enough to appease my stomach for the remainder of my life.

"The scouts report that a settler by the name of Johnson, flying with his wife and three little children, when they reached the Colorado, left his family on the shore, and waded into the river to see whether it would be safe to ford with his wagon. When about the middle of the river he was seized by an alligator, and after a struggle was dragged under the water, and perished. The helpless woman and her babes were discovered, gazing in agony on the spot, by other fugitives, who happily passed that way, and relieved them. Those who fight the battles experience but a small part of the privation, suffering, and anguish that follow in the train of ruthless war. The cannonading continued at intervals throughout the day, and all hands were kept up to their work."

The next day he writes: "I had a little sport this morning before breakfast. The enemy had planted a piece of ordnance within gunshot of the fort during the night, and the first thing in the morning they commenced a brisk cannonade, point blank against the spot where I was snoring. I turned out pretty smart and mounted the rampart. The gun was charged again; a fellow stepped forth to touch her off, but before he could apply the match, I let him have it, and he keeled over. A second stepped up, snatched the match from the hand of the dying man, but the juggler, who had followed me, handed me his rifle, and the next instant the Mexican was stretched on the earth beside the first. A third came up to the cannon. My companion handed me another gun, and I fixed him off in like manner. A fourth, then a fifth seized the match, who both met with the same fate. Then the whole party gave it up as a bad job, and hurried off to the camp, leaving the cannon ready charged where they had planted it. I came down, took my bitters, and went to breakfast."

In the course of a week the Mexicans lost three hundred men. But still reinforcements were continually arriving, so that their numbers were on the rapid increase. The garrison no longer cherished any hope of receiving aid from abroad.

Under date of March 4th and 5th, 1836, we have the last lines which Crockett ever penned.

"March 4th. Shells have been falling into the fort like hail during the day, but without effect. About dusk, in the evening, we observed a man running toward the fort, pursued by about half a dozen of the Mexican cavalry. The bee-hunter immediately knew him to be the old pirate, who had gone to Goliad, and, calling to the two hunters, he sallied out of the fort to the relief of the old man, who was hard pressed. I followed close after. Before we reached the spot the Mexicans were close on the heels of the old man, who stopped suddenly, turned short upon his pursuers, discharged his rifle, and one of the enemy fell from his horse. The chase was renewed, but finding that he would be overtaken and cut to pieces, he now turned again, and, to the amazement of the enemy, became the assailant in his turn. He clubbed his gun, and dashed among them like a wounded tiger, and they fled like sparrows. By this time we reached the spot, and, in the ardor of the moment, followed some distance before we saw that our retreat to the fort was cut off by another detachment of cavalry. Nothing was to be done but fight our way through. We were all of the same mind. 'Go ahead!' cried I; and they shouted, 'Go ahead, Colonel!' We dashed among them, and a bloody conflict ensued. They were about twenty in number, and they stood their ground. After the fight had continued about five minutes, a detachment was seen issuing from the fort to our relief, and the Mexicans scampered of, leaving eight of their comrades dead upon the field. But we did not escape unscathed, for both the pirate and the bee-hunter were mortally wounded, and I received a sabre-cut across the forehead. The old man died without speaking, as soon as we entered the fort. We bore my young friend to his bed, dressed his wounds, and I watched beside him. He lay, without complaint or manifesting pain, until about midnight, when he spoke, and I asked him if he wanted anything. 'Nothing,' he replied, but drew a sigh that seemed to rend his heart, as he added, 'Poor Kate of Nacogdoches.' His eyes were filled with tears, as he continued, 'Her words were prophetic, Colonel," and then he sang in a low voice, that resembled the sweet notes of his own devoted Kate:

'But toom cam' the saddle, all bluidy to see, And hame came the steed, but hame never came he.'

He spoke no more, and a few minutes after died. Poor Kate, who will tell this to thee?

The romantic bee-hunter had a sweetheart by the name of Kate in Nacogdoches. She seems to have been a very affectionate and religious girl. In parting, she had presented her lover with a Bible, and in anguish of spirit had expressed her fears that he would never return from his perilous enterprise.

The next day, Crockett simply writes, "March 5th. Pop, pop, pop! Bom, bom, bom! throughout the day. No time for memorandums now. Go ahead! Liberty and Independence forever."

Before daybreak on the 6th of March, the citadel of the Alamo was assaulted by the whole Mexican army, then numbering about three thousand men. Santa Anna in person commanded. The assailants swarmed over the works and into the fortress. The battle was fought with the utmost desperation until daylight. Six only of the Garrison then remained alive. They were surrounded, and they surrendered. Colonel Crockett was one. He at the time stood alone in an angle of the fort, like a lion at bay. His eyes flashed fire, his shattered rifle in his right hand, and in his left a gleaming bowie-knife streaming with blood. His face was covered with blood flowing from a deep gash across his forehead. About twenty Mexicans, dead and dying, were lying at his feet. The juggler was also there dead. With one hand he was clenching the hair of a dead Mexican, while with the other he had driven his knife to the haft in the bosom of his foe.

The Mexican General Castrillon, to whom the prisoners had surrendered, wished to spare their lives. He led them to that part of the fort where Santa Anna stood surrounded by his staff. As Castrillon marched his prisoners into the presence of the President, he said:

"Sir, here are six prisoners I have taken alive. How shall I dispose of them?"

Santa Anna seemed much annoyed, and said, "Have I not told you before how to dispose of them? Why do you bring them to me?"

Immediately several Mexicans commenced plunging their swords into the bosoms of the captives. Crockett, entirely unarmed, sprang, like a tiger, at the throat of Santa Anna. But before he could reach him, a dozen swords were sheathed in his heart, and he fell without a word or a groan. But there still remained upon his brow the frown of indignation, and his lip was curled with a smile of defiance and scorn.

And thus was terminated the earthly life of this extraordinary man. In this narrative it has been the object of the writer faithfully to record the influences under which Colonel Crockett was reared, and the incidents of his wild and wondrous life, leaving it with the reader to form his own estimate of the character which these exploits indicate. David Crockett has gone to the tribunal of his God, there to be judged for all the deeds done in the body. Beautifully and consolingly the Psalmist has written:

"Like as a father pitieth his children, so the Lord pitieth them that fear him. For he knoweth our frame; he remembereth that we are dust."

Made in the USA
San Bernardino, CA
24 May 2014